peacekeeper

Montgomery Brothers ~ Book 2

laura pavlov

dedication

Caroline & Brock,

I dedicate this book to you both as you get ready to walk down the aisle in just a few days. You are everything a great love story should be...two amazing, kind souls that found one another. You have a history together, you survived the distance during your college years, and your love for one another never wavered. I am honored to have been a part of your journey and am so excited for your big day!! Cheers to you and many, many happy years together!

10.24.2020

Love you,

Laura xo

one

. . .

Laney

I TOSSED a few T-shirts in the suitcase and slipped two dresses in my garment bag.

"This is why moving in with me would have been a good idea," Charlie said, sprawled out on my white duvet.

"Yeah. Had I known this was going to happen, I probably would have taken you up on that."

"We could always pack this place up and store your stuff at my apartment." He pushed up to sit and reached for my hand. This man knew how to calm me when I was in a manic state.

And I was definitely in a manic state.

"I have a few months left on my lease. I had it all planned around the wedding, you know?"

"Yep. Four months and counting. All right, don't worry about anything. If you need help covering the rent, I've got you."

I dropped to sit on his lap, needing his warmth more than ever. More than I liked to admit. "Thanks. I have some money in savings, and hopefully, I can find something temporary in Napa. Dad and I will take shifts with Mom, and I can work a few hours a day."

"Just go and do what you need to do. Don't stress about money. I can help too." Charlie wrapped his arms around me, and his chin rested on my shoulder.

"Okay. And you're fine meeting with Sabrina on Saturday to handle the tasting on your own?" I asked.

Sabrina was the event coordinator at Hopper Hotel in Chicago where we were having our reception. We had so many things that required our attention these next few weeks. A lot I could do remotely, but Charlie would have to cover the rest on his own. Everything had happened so fast.

I was going home to help care for my mother. She'd been diagnosed with Stage 3 breast cancer and she would start chemotherapy tomorrow. Hopefully, it would shrink the tumor and make it easier to remove in a couple of weeks. I needed to be there, and if that meant postponing my life—then so be it.

"Yes, baby. Don't worry about a thing. I've got it covered. You just go and take care of your mom. I wish I could go with you, but work is crazy. I'll come out when I can, and hopefully, you'll be back soon. What did Margo say?"

I turned to face him. "She understood. She said she can't promise me anything when I get back, but she'll try to hold my position. You know, *the show must go on*, I guess. There are parties to plan and she'll most likely need to fill my position."

I understood it. I'd waited a long while to become an event coordinator at the W Hotel. I'd started as the assistant to the assistant and finally earned my rank as one of three head event planners. We did a slew of weddings, bat mitzvahs, bar mitzvahs, quinceañeras and other celebratory events, and had waitlists of up to one year. My job meant everything to me up until a few days ago, but today, I didn't really care whether it would be waiting for me when I returned. I was focused on my mother. The woman who had always been my pulse, my North Star, my biggest supporter. Hearing that she was sick, well, it was like a punch to the gut. I just wanted to get home.

It had been years since I'd had any desire to return to Napa. I normally flew in and out quickly for the holidays and encouraged my family to come visit me in Chicago as often as possible. Home held too many painful memories that I normally dreaded. But right now, I didn't care about any of that. I just needed to be with my mom.

"We'll figure it out. Hopefully, the surgery happens soon, and she'll be good to go in a few weeks," Charlie said.

He was hopeful. I was a bit more realistic. I'd read a lot about what my mom was about to go through. This wasn't going to be a sprint. It would be more like a marathon. I'd know more once I got there. I'd spent the last forty-eight hours taking care of everything here because I didn't know how long I'd be gone.

"Yep. And I'll FaceTime you tonight when I get there."

"Sounds good. You ready?" He reached for my bags and we trekked out to the car.

I'd have a few hours on the flight to think about everything, as I hadn't had much time to process this. I couldn't wrap my head around it. My mom was one of the healthiest people I knew. This came out of left field.

And I'd be back home.

The place I'd been raised.

Where my heart had crumbled into a million little pieces.

I'd most likely have to see Harrison Montgomery. Charlie knew I had an ex-boyfriend back home. But that didn't begin to describe what Harrison had been to me. How do you tell your fiancé that your ex-boyfriend was also your best friend, your soulmate—your first and last *everything*? Sure, I'd moved on, and I'd found my own happily ever after with Charlie. My feelings for Harrison Montgomery were in the past. And that's exactly where they needed to stay.

———

"I ran into Monica Montgomery at the market," Mom said, pausing to pass me the salad as we all sat around the farmhouse table we'd had for as long as I could remember.

"How is she? I haven't seen her in a while." Dad refilled my wine glass and winked.

"She's well. I told her what was going on and that you'd insisted on coming home to help me through this."

"What did she say?" I asked quietly.

Monica, Harrison's mother, had been like a second mom to me growing up, but I'd cut ties with all the Montgomerys when Harrison and I broke up. Hell, I'd cut ties with this whole town. The Montgomerys were everywhere. Three brothers that oozed charm and charisma, and everyone wanted to know them. It had always been Harrison and me from as early as I could remember. We were the best of friends, and then we fell madly in love. I'd never existed in Napa without him by my side. But grief could be a cruel mistress —and people changed. I'd received a front row seat to that life lesson.

"Well, I told her you were taking a leave from work but that you were hoping to find something temporary here." Mom paused to sip her water. "She said they were overwhelmed right now with all the events at the winery and she could use the help if you're open to it."

I took my time chewing my food. Seriously? Of course, I loved Monica, and I'd practically grown up at the Montgomery vineyard. Hell, I lost my virginity out in the barn on their property. But I assumed Harrison spent a lot of time at the winery, at least that had always been his plan—to take over at some point. And seeing him again daily would be difficult. Impossible. My family didn't know just how bad things had ended between us. We'd never spoken much again outside of an awkward run-in during one of the short stints when I was home.

No.

Harrison turned his back on me. He was a wound I had no desire to reopen.

"Well, I was planning to stop by a few places for possible jobs tomorrow when we get home, but I'll keep it in mind."

"Honey, this is as good as it gets. It's temporary, and she'll work around your schedule and my treatments. That's going to be hard to beat. Her face lit up when I told her you were coming home. She looked like I'd stabbed her in the heart when I broke the news that you and Charlie were engaged a few weeks ago, so maybe seeing you will be a good thing. Give everyone a little closure." Mom shrugged.

"I agree with Mom. You should jump at this," Dad said.

My older brother's gaze landed on me. Sam knew how difficult it was for me to be home. Submerged in all these old memories.

"Give the girl a day to get settled and put out her feelers. They're all going to line up for the famed Laney Mae Landers, party planner extraordinaire, to work for them."

I laughed. Sam lived in San Francisco but was just a car ride away from home. He was busy since becoming a partner at an accounting firm. My brother and numbers—well, they were one. He and his long-time girlfriend, Gia, had an apartment in the city, but they visited my parents often.

"Thanks for the vote of confidence. Tell Gia she needs to come visit a lot while I'm home."

"I will. She had the late shift tonight," Sam said. Gia was a pediatric nurse at the hospital.

"So, are you ever going to propose to the poor woman?" I raised a brow in challenge as he passed me the basket of rolls.

"Well, that's something I wanted to discuss with all of you. I actually bought a ring. I was thinking of waiting to pop the question until after your wedding, Laney. But with everything going on right now," he paused to smile at Mom and her eyes glossed over with emotion, "I thought it might be nice to have even more to look forward to."

I fist bumped the ceiling. "Freaking *finally*. You took long enough. And don't be silly. I think having two weddings to look forward to is great."

"I can't think of anything better. Both of my babies finding the people they want to spend the rest of their lives with is more than I can ask for." Mom pushed to her feet and hurried over to hug us.

"Her parents will have to pay for this one, right?" Dad said with a wink.

He was teasing, but it sent a pang to my chest. My parents were both teachers. They taught at the private school my brother and I attended from kindergarten through twelfth grade. That's the only way we could have ever afforded the hefty tuition. And with Mom's current medical situation, I knew they were tight on money. Thankfully, their house was paid off, as this was the home where my father had grown up. My parents rented it from my grandparents for many years until they signed it over to Mom and Dad officially a few years ago. But I worried about how they were going to cover the cost of my wedding. I'd insisted on having it at a less expensive venue than the place I worked, which was ridiculously priced. Even with the employee discount, it was more than I wanted them to spend. Truth be told, I was starting to wonder if Charlie and I should just elope. We hadn't sent out invites nor put down much of a deposit as of yet, so there was still plenty of time to make a change.

Charlie would understand. He was probably the most understanding man I'd ever known. He'd picked me up and put me back together over the past three years. There wasn't much he wouldn't do for me. But I knew he wanted to have a big wedding back in Chicago where he'd grown up, and I didn't want to take that away from him unless I absolutely had to. I'd get a better feel for Mom and Dad's situation now that I was home for a while. They'd insisted it was fine and gave me a budget to work with, but I worried they'd be stretching themselves thin to pull it off, especially now with Mom's current situation.

"Yes, Gia's mom tells me every time we have dinner with them that they're biting at the bit to plan a wedding." Sam rolled his eyes.

Gia's father was a prominent attorney in the city, and her parents would want to throw the gala of the year. She was their only daughter and I'm sure they would spare no expense. Gia was the opposite of her parents—down-to-earth and sweet. Most importantly, she was perfect for my brother.

"Phew." Dad wiped at his brow and we all chuckled.

When I looked up, Mom's gaze locked with mine. Her blue eyes were sparkling, and she nearly took my breath away when she smiled. I'd been trying to hold it together since I'd heard the news, but now that I was here, in this safe space, with my family—I lost it. Tears sprang from eyes and I covered my mouth to try to muffle the sobs.

Mom gasped and jumped back to her feet, coming to my side of the table and wrapping her arms around me. "My little Laney Mae, don't you do that. Everything is fine. I'm just so happy to have you home."

"Honey, you know I was teasing about paying for the wedding, right?" Dad asked nervously.

I laughed through my tears. "Yes. I'm not upset, I promise. Just happy to be home."

And terrified that Mom won't be okay.

That nothing will ever be the same.

Mom kissed the top of my head. "How about we let the boys clean up this mess and we head upstairs and get you unpacked and talk about the wedding?"

Mom was starting chemo tomorrow. The wedding was the last thing I wanted to talk about. It was odd that I was an actual wedding planner, and I'd prefer to elope. But I wouldn't deprive Charlie of the wedding he wanted after all he'd done for me. I put a lot into the planning of other people's big day, but it just wasn't something I really cared all that much about for myself. But if this was what she wanted to talk about tonight, then so be it.

I plopped down on my bed. My room smelled like watermelon bubblegum. The walls were a pale pink and decorated with posters and photos from my childhood. It was like stepping into a time machine—nothing had changed. I'd never taken down the pictures of Harrison and me, for whatever reason, but I'd definitely be making some changes to my room now that I'd be home for a while. I glanced on the nightstand and saw my senior prom photo. I swear I put that one away the last time I visited.

"Did you take this picture out of my nightstand?" I asked my mother who'd stretched out beside me on the bed.

She stroked my hair when I settled back down and faced her. "Yes. I found it in the drawer. I love that photo."

"Mom, you do realize at some point my future husband is going to visit, and I think he might be offended by the shrine to Harrison Montgomery." I laughed, reaching for the photo again and studying it. We were so young. Seniors in high school. Ready for our next adventure. We'd chosen the same college because we couldn't stand to be apart back then. Or as my mom once reminded me, he'd picked the school he wanted to attend, and I followed. But he'd begged me to, and I'd obliged all too eagerly.

"Harrison is a part of your past, Laney. You can't just pretend it never happened."

"That's not what I'm doing."

"Isn't he the reason you never want to come home?"

"I come home at Christmas." I chewed the inside of my cheek.

"Oh yes. The forty-eight hours you spend at home each year. You've never even brought Charlie here to see where you grew up."

"You like coming to Chicago. And that's where my life is now," I said, closing my eyes as her fingers stroked my hair.

"Well, I'm glad you're home now, baby girl. I'm sorry you had to leave your job and Charlie, but I'm sure glad you're going to be here with me through this."

I opened my eyes and studied her. Under all that bravado, I saw the fear. The worry.

"It's okay to be scared, you know. But you're going to kick cancer's ass. And I'm going to be right beside you cheering you on."

"I know you will, my love. Thank you."

Fuck you, cancer.

You don't get to have my mom.

Not now and not ever.

two

. . .

Harrison

I'D BEEN in a funk since hearing about Lyla Landers. I couldn't wrap my head around the fact that she had breast cancer. It didn't surprise me that Laney was coming home to help her mother through this. That was Laney. She was loyal as hell and always there for everyone. She'd stayed far away from Napa since our breakup, which had surprised the hell out of me because she was so close to her family. I heard her parents and her brother flew out to visit her often. I'd only seen her twice in the five years since we'd ended things. And both times had been uncomfortable. Icy. Distant. Laney hated me now. I'd thought I was doing the right thing by ending it with her. Forcing her to go back to school and move forward with her life while I stayed home to help my family pick up the pieces. Her mom had been right—Laney had done everything for me. She didn't need to stay behind while I wallowed in grief. So, I'd set her free.

I'd do it again if it meant she'd be happy.

And now she was getting married to some dude in Chicago and she barely acknowledged my existence. It sucked, but life wasn't always fair. Some things were out of our control.

"Brother, you have got to pull yourself out of this funk. You're bringing me down, and we can't have that. You're a fucking sad sack,"

Jack, my younger brother said, as we stepped off the helicopter when we landed back in Napa.

We commuted back and forth from Montgomery Media, in the city, to the vineyard here. I spent most of my time at the winery these days. Mom was overwhelmed. Jack went back and forth helping Ford, our oldest brother, who ran the family-owned media company started by my grandfather, which specialized in television broadcasting, news and sports. But today, Jack wanted to wrap up a few projects he had going on in Napa.

"I'm not a sad sack, you asshole. But yes, hearing that Lyla has cancer is upsetting. Have some fucking feelings, man."

"I'm all about the feelings, you know that. But I don't bottle shit up. I express it. You've been moping around ever since you heard that Laney Mae was engaged."

I rolled my eyes. "Not true. I'm happy for her. I'm upset about her mother."

"Then fucking *do something*. You've known the woman your entire life. Quit being a pussy. Drive over there. Check on her. Man up, Har-bear." Jack chuckled as I climbed into the driver's seat and my brother slid in beside me. I hated the stupid nickname Jack had been calling me since we were kids.

"Mom said Laney was home to be with Lyla. She won't want to see me." I pulled out on the road heading for the winery.

"Dude. This is your problem. You're so afraid of rumpling anyone's feathers, you're not doing what you want."

"What the hell does that mean? I don't want to make anyone uncomfortable when they're going through a hard time," I said, shaking my head. He was clueless. He had the social grace of a Rottweiler puppy. He just did what he wanted all the fucking time. I didn't operate that way.

"Here's the deal. Lyla has cancer. It's bad or Laney Mae wouldn't be here. The woman was like a second mother to you. Stop being a pussy and drive your ass over there and tell her you're thinking of her. Offer to help. Whatever she needs. People are rarely offended by kindness."

That just might be the wisest thing Jack had ever said. But I wouldn't tell him that.

I pulled in the driveway and put the car in park, scrubbing a hand over my face. "Yeah. Maybe I'll go over there later."

Jack groaned. "Not later. Do it now. I've got things covered here. You're of no help right now anyway. Just go rip off the Band-Aid. See Laney Mae, tell her mother you're here for her, and you're sorry for all she's going through—you'll feel like a new man, which will benefit all of us."

"You're an asshole," I said as he jumped out of the car.

"I've been called worse. You can thank me later."

I pulled out on the road and drove the short distance down to the Landers' house. It was the smallest home in our neighborhood, but it had always been my favorite. They were such a warm family. And they loved their daughter just like I always had. Hell, I still do. She would forever be a part of me. If I thought back on my childhood, there wasn't one moment that I could recall that didn't involve Laney Landers. She was every good memory I ever had.

I sucked in a breath and gathered myself. It had been a long while since I'd seen Laney. Almost two years. I heard she was home last Christmas, but I swear she didn't leave the house for fear of running into me. I saw Lyla, Dave, and Sam a couple times a year, and they were always kind. Jack was right. I needed to do this.

I walked up the paved drive to the front porch and knocked. The door swung open and Sam stood on the other side. "Harrison, hey. Good to see you, man."

"Hi, I, uh, I thought I'd stop by and see how your mom was doing. I just heard about what was going on, and I wanted to see if there was anything I could do to help."

"She'd love to see you. You know you've always been her favorite. I think she likes you more than she likes me," he said, waving me inside.

"Is Laney here?" I asked under my breath, needing to know what I was walking into.

He chuckled. "Yeah, she's home, but she and Dad ran to the store to pick up a few things for Mom. She had her first chemo treatment today, and Laney was with her, holding her hand, of course. She and Dad are taking shifts. I took a half day at work today so I could come out and check on everyone."

I followed him into the living room where Lyla Landers sat on the tan oversized couch. The same couch where I'd made out with her daughter more times than I could count.

"Look who stopped by, Mom," Sam said. "I'll let you two catch up. I need to call Gia back."

I nodded and moved toward Lyla. She looked better than I'd expected, but I wasn't surprised. She was a strong woman. Just like her daughter.

"Harrison. It's so good to see you. Come, sit," she said, patting the seat beside her on the sofa.

I dropped down on the sofa and turned to face her. "You look well. I'm so sorry that you're going through this. I just wanted to offer to help in any way that I can."

She smiled. "That's sweet of you. I appreciate it. I wasn't sure if your mom told you, but Laney is home."

Yes. I knew Laney was home. Knew she was engaged. The news still stung. Hell, she was the only girl I'd ever loved. And that was just something I had to live with.

I pushed the thought away.

"Yes. I heard that. I hope she won't mind that I'm here."

She reached for my hand. "She'll be fine. You two have been through so much together. It makes me sad that you have this rift between you."

I'd never discussed what happened between Laney and me with her family—I'd barely told my own family. I just didn't talk about it. It served no purpose. It is what it is. I can't change what happened. And Laney's happy, so that's all that really mattered.

"Yeah. Well, I'm pretty sure she hates me."

She chuckled. "I'm sure you've heard the saying, 'There's a fine line between love and hate.' It's always bothered me—the role I played in what happened."

I kept my face blank. Lyla didn't know that I'd walked in on the conversation between her and Laney all those years ago. At least I didn't think she did. I doubted Sam ever put the pieces together and told them that I'd stopped by. He'd have no reason to, it wasn't out of the norm for me to have been there.

"What do you mean?"

She sucked in a long breath and squeezed my hand. "You know I love you, Harrison. I couldn't have picked a better person to have grown up with my little girl. To have been her best friend and her first love."

"Thank you." I nodded awkwardly because I had no idea where this was going.

"After your father passed away, and you and Laney returned home that summer, I, well—I didn't support her decision to stay here with you and leave school. I don't know if you ever knew that, because I think you ended things and urged her to return to school as well, shortly after the argument I'd had with her."

I ran a hand over my face, unsure why we were dredging all of this up now. Sure, I'd walked in on the conversation and it had stung like hell. But the truth was—Lyla was right. Her daughter needed to do what was best for her. They didn't know I'd heard them and it didn't really matter. It had been a wake-up call. I was drowning in grief. I was no good to Laney at the time and she deserved better.

"Yeah, she did the right thing going back."

"It was never that I didn't want you two to be together. I just thought she should spread her wings. Go out in the world and experience life a little. I always hoped you'd find your way back to one another."

"Lyla, I don't blame you for what happened. It was the right thing to do. And everything worked out. Laney finished school and I'm sure she graduated at the top of her class. She's engaged and she's found the person she wants to spend the rest of her life with." I covered her hand with mine.

Her eyes were wet with emotion. "Yes. And Charlie is a wonderful man. He really is. But, Harrison, you should know that Laney has never been the same since you two broke up. She lost that—light she used to have. And sometimes I feel like she's just going through the motions."

I sucked in a long, slow breath. I didn't know how to respond. I'd never been the same either. Maybe that was just part of life. Things didn't always work out, and you needed to move forward and do the best you could with what you had.

"We're home," Dave Landers called out as he entered the kitchen.

Lyla swiped at the single tear that ran down her face and forced a smile. "Look who stopped by."

Laney came to a stop when her father set the bags on the counter. Her gaze locked with mine, the darkest ocean blues only rivaled by the deep sea. I used to tease her that I'd drown in those eyes. Her long blonde hair fell around her shoulders in loose waves, and she didn't look away. She wore skinny jeans and a white T-shirt, and she looked fucking gorgeous.

Fucking perfect.

I fisted my hands at my sides, fighting the urge to move toward her. It had always been there—this invisible pull between us. And it was stronger than ever at the moment.

Laney had always been the most beautiful girl I'd ever laid eyes on, and that certainly hadn't changed. She shifted on her feet and moved toward me.

"Hey, Harrison." She swallowed and I studied the movement as it traveled down her lean neck.

I pushed to my feet. "Nice to see you, Laney. I hope you don't mind me stopping by to see your mom."

"No, of course not." She stopped a few feet from me, keeping her distance, and pulled her gaze from mine as if she couldn't stand the sight of me any longer.

Jesus. Maybe we'd never get past this. The pain of losing Laney was indescribable. I'd grieved for my father after he'd been killed in a car accident, but Laney was a different kind of grief because she was alive and well. But she'd never forgiven me for ending things. I'd honestly thought we'd find our way back to one another, just as her mother did. Obviously, Laney didn't see it that way. She only called me once, the day after she returned to school, and I hadn't taken the call because I thought it was too soon. I reached out a few months later, hoping we could repair things, once she was settled back at school and had accepted the distance. But she never spoke to me again. She fiddled with the ring on her finger, and I wanted to punch the fucking wall. Laney was engaged. She was marrying another man.

How the fuck did that happen?

"I hear congratulations are in order. When's the wedding?" I asked, and my tone came out harsher than I'd intended.

"Thanks. We're getting married in four months. Still working out the details." Her face hardened as her gaze locked with mine again.

I nodded. "All right, well, I'll get out of your hair."

"Please stop by again, Harrison. It really made my day to see you."

"Of course. Where do you get your treatments done? Here in Napa?"

"No, we drive into the city to the hospital," Lyla said, wrapping the blanket around her shoulders.

"You're driving back and forth to the city every day?" I asked with surprise.

"Yes, that's how common folks do it," Laney hissed, raising a brow at me in challenge.

"Laney Mae," her mother and father both said in unison.

"What? I'm just stating the facts," she said, turning to reach for the bags on the counter and unloading the items.

"What's going on in here?" Sam asked, as he strode back into the room.

"Nothing." Laney rolled her eyes.

"Why don't you use the helicopter? I can have it ready for you every morning, and it will at least alleviate the commute for you. I can have a car available to drive you to and from the hospital once you land. It will cut a few hours off your day at least."

"That's a very generous offer, son. I do think the commute is going to be a lot, Lyla," Dave said, looking to his wife.

"Thank you. That would be really helpful, Harrison." Sam nodded at me.

"I don't mind driving her," Laney said, crossing her arms in front of her chest and glaring at me.

"Are you sure that wouldn't be too much trouble?" Lyla turned her attention to me, ignoring her daughter. "That would actually make things a lot easier."

"Mom, I don't mind driving you."

"Laney, you're being terribly rude. It would help a lot. Don't look a gift horse in the mouth."

Laney shot me one final cutting look. If looks could kill, I'd be a dead man. She stormed out of the room and I heard the door slam in the distance.

"Well, that was awkward," Sam said with a laugh. "Guess she hasn't outgrown those tantrums."

"Emotions are high. She's upset about what Mom is going through," Dave said, clearing his throat. "But we are very grateful for the offer, Harrison."

"You got it. Text me the schedule for your treatments, and I'll get everything set up for you this afternoon and send you the information."

"Thank you so much," Lyla said, swiping at her cheeks again as a few more tears ran down her face.

"Of course. I'm happy to help in any way I can." I hugged her goodbye and Sam walked me to the door.

"Don't worry about Laney. She'll come around. You always did have a way of getting her to throw a fit. I don't think I've seen her unravel like that in years." He laughed.

I didn't laugh.

The girl hated me, and that stung.

Seeing her again stirred up all sorts of feelings in me that I hadn't felt in a long time.

I missed her. Missed everything about her. Laney Landers was the reason I hadn't had a decent relationship since the day we broke up. No one compared to her.

And no one ever would.

"All right, I'll text you the info in a little bit." I leaned in and gave him one of those half dude hugs.

"Thanks, Harrison. It means a lot."

I waved and walked to my car. I glanced up at Laney's bedroom window. I'd climbed onto her roof dozens of times when we were young and snuck into that room. She stood in the window watching me leave. I waved and smiled, and she glared one last time before yanking the curtains closed.

This was her way of telling me she was shutting me out.

She didn't want my help.

She didn't want to see me.

But what Laney didn't know…I wasn't going away.

Not this time.

three

. . .

Laney

WE PULLED up to the hanger where the Montgomerys kept their helicopter. Scratch that. Helicopters. They owned an endless slew of toys. Cars and planes and helicopters. I'd never been impressed by Harrison's money. It never mattered to me. It was him that I loved, not his stuff. But, sure, we'd taken many trips together over the years, and it did make life easier to have access to quicker travel. I'd behaved like a spoiled brat yesterday, because seeing him again—was painful. It hurt my heart to be around him. To be reminded of what we had. What we lost.

Mom came upstairs to talk to me after I stormed off last night, and she made some valid points. I'd sent Harrison a text per her insistence and apologized for being rude. He sent me all the info for the commute this week. He and Jack would be traveling with us to the city this morning. I knew they went back and forth often, and this really did make things easier for Mom. Why couldn't I just appreciate the gesture and be okay with seeing him? Why did it have to hurt so much? Even all these years later. A sharp pain settled in my chest as he approached.

"Laney Mae Landers," Jack sang out my name like he always had when we were growing up. He and Ford called me Laney Mae and refused to drop the middle name because that's how they'd met me. I loved both of Harrison's brothers, as I'd known them my entire life. And unfortunately, I'd cut them all off after the breakup. I couldn't have them in my life if I wanted to move on from their brother.

"Jack-ass Montgomery." I laughed, as he scooped me off my feet and spun me around.

"The one and only. You're looking good, girl." He set me back down and turned to my mom. "Mrs. Landers, it's so good to see you. I'm sorry for all you're going through. I hope you don't mind me tagging along. I was in Napa last night and need to get to work in the city this morning."

"Don't be silly, sweetheart. It's so good to see you." Mom hugged Jack as I looked up to find Harrison staring at me.

"Hey." He nodded.

"Hi. Thanks for doing this," I said, avoiding his gaze.

"Damn, are these two still acting weird?" Jack asked. "Come on. You've known each other your entire life. You're the dynamic duo, remember? Get over it already."

My mom's head fell back with a chuckle, and she nodded. "I agree."

Jack held the door open, and we all climbed inside the helicopter and buckled up. I sat next to my mother and across from Harrison and Jack.

"How's Ford?" I asked, suddenly very curious about all the Montgomery boys. I'd known everything about them up until a few years ago. Who they dated, what trouble they'd gotten into—and now I knew nothing.

"Oh man, he's doing really well. He met a girl." Jack shrugged. "Harley's been really good for him. She owns the bakery downstairs in the Montgomery Media building. You would love her. They're getting married next month at the winery. That's part of the reason Mom needs help. She's got too many events planned, and Melanie, one of our event planners, is on maternity leave. You'd really be helping her out by coming on board a few hours a day."

"I'm happy for him," I said.

I was glad Ford didn't end up with his ex-girlfriend, Madison. He'd found her in bed with his best friend right before their father was killed in a car accident. That's when everything changed.

For everyone.

"My mom offered you a job at the winery? She didn't mention it to me," Harrison mumbled.

I studied his features as he looked down at his phone. Damn. He was so handsome. Always had been. Tall and lean with dark hair. Dark scruff peppered his chin now, which was new. It looked sexy as hell and I wiped my sweaty palms on my jeans. I hated how good he looked. How it made me feel to be around him. Our knees were practically touching, and butterflies swarmed my belly. I twisted my engagement ring around my finger and thought of Charlie. Did he give me butterflies? Not really. But he made me feel safe. He loved me. And he was always there for me.

Harrison was not. He had been my entire life, until the one time I needed him most. And I couldn't forgive that. *No.* I shifted my knees away from him before I spoke.

"Well, I'm still looking. I have my feelers out." I shrugged.

"Why are you still looking? You need a temporary job and my mother offered you one. What's the problem?" Harrison asked, an edge in his tone. He didn't like being left out of the loop and he sure as hell didn't like that he had no say over my decision. I'd always gone to him for advice and help when we were together. The man loved to solve problems for others. But he had no say in what I did anymore.

"It's not up to you to decide what I do," I hissed.

Mom leaned her head back and closed her eyes and Jack chuckled, before covering his mouth with his hand.

"I wasn't telling you what to do, I was asking why you wouldn't jump at this opportunity. You need something and she's offering it to you. What's the fucking problem?"

Now it was my turn to laugh. Harrison Montgomery never lost his shit in front of others. But I knew a different side of him, and he was showing it right now. He hadn't shown it five years ago when he dumped me and had zero emotion about it. He hadn't shown it when I called him crying in desperate need of his help, and he'd ignored my calls. All three calls, in fact. But right here, right now, he was losing his shit. And I enjoyed it. Maybe too much.

"The *fucking problem* is that maybe I don't want to work with *you*. Has that every crossed your big, stupid brain, genius?" I shouted, and my mother reached for my hand and squeezed, her eyes still closed, as the ridiculous conversation was obviously too much for her.

This wasn't her first rodeo with me. I had a temper. And the only person that usually brought it out was Harrison Montgomery. Because he was a stubborn, arrogant asshole sometimes, and he needed to be put in his place.

Jack leaned forward and clasped his hands together. "It feels like the good ole days. I wish I had some popcorn right now."

"Shut up, Jack," Harrison snarled. "Laney, take the stupid job. I'll stay out of your way."

"Take the stupid job, Laney Mae. It's temporary, and I know it would help Mom out. Plus, I'd get to see you more. That's a good thing, right?" Jack wriggled his brows and I couldn't help but laugh.

"I think you should take the stupid job, too, sweetie," Mom said, her eyes still closed.

Damn me, for losing my temper in front of my mother. Especially right now, with all she was going through. I squeezed her hand. "Sorry, Mom. I shouldn't be arguing with *him* when you are about to go in for a treatment. It was very selfish."

I looked up to see Harrison roll his eyes. "*Him*? I have a name."

"It's fine," Mom whispered. "Just take the job and put us all out of our misery, dear."

"Fine. I'll do it. But you stay in your lane, Montgomery," I said, raising a brow in challenge.

"I think she's talking to you, brother. I'm allowed in her lane." A wide grin spread across Jack's handsome face.

"Whatever. I have actual work to do. I won't be bothering you," Harrison said, and his dark, broody gaze locked with mine.

"We're here," the pilot called out as we settled on the ground.

"That was quick." My mother opened her eyes and looked out the windows.

"Quick, but painful," Jack said, looking between his brother and me with one brow raised.

We stepped outside, and Harrison turned to speak to me. "Text me when you're done. I'm flying back with you."

"So much for staying in your lane." I smirked.

"Trust me. I heard you loud and clear, Laney. I'll keep my distance as much as possible. But unfortunately, I need to get back to the winery and I can't ask the pilot to fly us separately just because you hate me."

Something in my chest squeezed. He sounded wounded and vulnerable. I felt bad for being difficult when he was doing us a favor. But I had my reasons, and I needed to remember them. It would be all too easy to fall back into old habits.

"Don't be ridiculous. I don't hate you. And I appreciate you helping my mom out. I'm sorry if I seem ungrateful. I really am thankful you're doing this for her. I just think it's best that we keep our distance for the most part."

Jack was talking to my mother off to the side and she had a big grin on her face.

"All right. Well, let me know when you're done and we'll head back," Harrison said, studying me like he was trying to figure me out. I knew him too well. He didn't understand my anger. Maybe mine was the first and last heart he ever broke. "So, Henry will drive you over and pick you up. I just sent you his number. Let him know when you're ready to leave the hospital."

"Okay. Thank you."

Jack walked toward me and picked me up off the ground again. "Glad you're back, Laney Mae. I missed you."

A lump formed in the back of my throat and I tried to swallow and push it away.

"Jesus. Put her down already," Harrison hissed, his voice laced with anger. Jack set me down, and I didn't miss the way his brother's jaw clenched nor that his hands were fisted at his side. I couldn't help but chuckle.

"Good luck, Lyla." Jack hugged my mom before gripping Harrison's shoulder. "Let's go, brother."

I stepped into the car with Mom and we headed to the hospital.

"Well, that was interesting," Mom said.

"Yeah. Not sure the hour and a half drive wouldn't have been easier."

"Don't be silly. We're saving hours of time this way. It's very generous of him to do this and you're being really tough on him, Laney. What is this about? I know he broke your heart, sweetie, but it's been years and you're marrying Charlie. You've known Harrison your entire life, you need to forgive him."

I leaned back against the seat and let out a long breath. "This is not about a broken heart, Mom. It's so much more than that."

"Well, what, then? You've barely come home since you and Harrison broke up. You know, he told me he tried to call you many times and you never responded."

"What? When did he tell you that?" I huffed.

"A few years ago. I ran into him at the grocery store. He was very upset about it. I honestly think he thought you two would find your way back to one another. He just wanted you to go back to school while he grieved his father. And if you remember, I wanted the same thing," she said as we pulled to a stop in front of the hospital.

"It's complicated. And that's not the whole story. I called him when I first got back to school. I was heartbroken and I needed him. I *really* needed him, Mom. And he just wasn't there for me. Sure, months later he reached out, but the wound was too deep. You can't just cut people out of your life and then think you can have them back when you feel like it."

Mom squeezed my hand. "Honey, he was grieving his father."

I pinched the bridge of my nose. This was why I didn't like coming home. I didn't want to discuss this. Not with my mom, not with Harrison, not with anyone. I'd gotten through everything on my own. And I wanted to move forward.

"I know. And I spent that whole summer after his father's death trying to be there for him. I loved him so much, Mom. *He dumped me*, if you remember. But this is all water under the bridge. I promise I'll try to be nicer to him. I don't want to talk about the past anymore. I want to focus on you. That's why I'm here. I didn't come home to patch my friendship up with Harrison. So, let's get our heads in the game and get ready for day two of chemo. Okay?"

"Yes. Thanks for being here, sweetheart."

"There's nowhere else I want to be." I reached for her hand and helped her out of the car.

We checked in and settled in the same chemotherapy suite as we were in yesterday. The nurse came in and started a PICC line in a vein just above the elbow in Mom's arm so she could get started. I wrapped her favorite blanket around her and put on a movie, and she dozed off.

My phone vibrated with an incoming text.

Charlie ~ How are you doing? You at the hospital now?

Me ~ Yes. She's a trouper. Almost finished. How are you?

Charlie ~ Good. Work is crazy, per usual. I miss you and our Taco Tuesdays.

Me ~ Me too. Go get tacos with Jared and Nat.

Charlie ~ Not any fun without you. And they always eat all the chips. Love you. Call me when you get home.

I laughed. Charlie and I did Taco Tuesday with my best friend, Natalie, and her boyfriend, Jared, every week.

Me ~ I will. Love you.

When we finished up Mom's treatment, she was tired from the anti-nausea medication and leaned on my shoulder during the car ride back to the helicopter. It was the first time I was genuinely thankful for Harrison providing the transportation. Mom hadn't been this out of it yesterday and getting her home sooner would be helpful.

I sent a text to Harrison when we left the hospital to let him know we were on our way. He was waiting for us when we arrived.

Harrison opened the car door. "How's she doing?"

"A little more tired today, but otherwise okay."

He helped me get her out of the car and into the helicopter. A lump settled in my throat as she leaned against me and dozed once we were buckled. This was going to be tough. Watching her suffer. Watching her fight for her life. I was embarrassed that I'd behaved like a child this morning. None of that seemed important now.

"I'm sorry about earlier," I whispered, once we were up in the air.

"You don't need to be sorry, Laney. I get it. You don't want to be around me. You've moved on with your life just like I asked you to do. I'm happy you're happy. I really am. That's the one good thing that came out of all of this." His dark gaze drilled into mine as he waited for a response.

"Thank you."

"Yep." He turned his head and looked out the window.

"Are you happy?" I kept my tone low. I couldn't help it. I needed to know.

He ran a hand over the back of his neck and shook his head. "I honestly don't know."

"I'm guessing that means you're not. Why is that? A guy who has everything?" I asked, suddenly wanting to know everything about him.

He chuckled, but it wasn't genuine. It was laced with sarcasm. "I'm far from a guy who has everything. Maybe I was that guy once. Not anymore."

"But that's by design, right? I mean, you can have whatever you want. For whatever reason, you just changed what you wanted."

What? What in the hell was I even saying? Why was I going there? Why did everything have to feel so familiar with him?

"I didn't change my mind about what I wanted, Laney. *Never*. I just did what I thought was right," he said, looking up to meet my gaze. And what I saw crushed me.

Harrison Montgomery appeared broken.

There was a time in my life when I would have done anything I could to fix him. Put him back together. Because loving him was a part of me. He'd been the center of my universe for most of my life. But not anymore. I didn't know this man sitting beside me, did I?

"Maybe you just need to decide what makes you happy."

"Is that what you did?" he asked.

My heart raced and I bit down hard on the inside of my cheek. We were having this conversation without *really* having it—because we weren't acknowledging anything. Not really. Harrison and I had always been able to communicate with just a simple look. A smile. A nod. A raised brow. But I didn't know what he was asking me anymore. And bringing up the past meant dredging up things I didn't want to remember. Memories I'd buried a long time ago.

"I guess so. I mean, sometimes you just need to survive, right? I found a way to do that, and you should do the same."

My words were harsh, but truthful. What I'd once had with him, what I'd thought was my future—it didn't exist anymore. So, I'd found a different future. Was it the fairy tale? Not really. Did it need to be? No. I realized that fairy tales were sort of like the magic of first loves. They didn't last. The real world was a bit more jaded. Darker. I learned to accept that and move forward.

"Yeah, I know. Can I ask you something?"

I shifted a bit as Mom adjusted herself against me. "Yes."

"Do you ever think about the past, Laney? About how things would have been if my father hadn't been in that accident?"

I sucked in a long, slow breath and fought back the tears that threatened to escape. I'd shed my last tear over this boy years ago when he broke my heart. I wasn't looking back. I was looking forward.

"No. Not anymore," I said. The words had more of a bite than I meant them to, but they needed to be said. Looking back would take me to a place I didn't want to go.

He nodded and his gaze locked with mine. "Okay."

"I'm getting married in a few months, Harrison. There's no sense dwelling on the past."

"Yeah. I get that. I'm happy for you. I really am. I just wish we didn't have this." He motioned with his hand between us. "I don't even know what this is. But I wish we could get past it. You're the best friend I've ever had. I miss that."

I swiped at the single tear that ran down my cheek and cursed myself internally for letting my emotions show this way.

"We grew up together, I think it's normal to miss that. I'd be lying if I said I didn't miss our friendship. But I don't know how to be friends with you, Harrison. Not anymore."

He shrugged. "How about we just start with you not hating me? We can be cordial, right?"

"I did throw sand in your face the first time we met, so I don't know if cordial is really our thing," I said with a laugh, and a wide grin spread across his handsome face.

God, he was beautiful.

"Yeah. I remember being temporarily blind for a few minutes after the assault. And I do recall that I was actually helping you."

I covered my face with my hands and shook my head. "I thought you were the enemy. *Mustard Face Mason* started a war with me that day. You were in the wrong place at the wrong time."

"I always thought I was in the right place at the right time. That was the day we met. And why do you insist on calling him that?" He smiled, and my belly did little flips. Harrison took me back to a place that I remembered fondly. Before everything changed.

Before everyone changed.

Including me.

"If you choose to eat a sandwich smothered in mustard and literally never wipe your face once—be prepared to carry the title *Mustard Face Mason* for life."

Harrison barked out a full-bodied, soulful laugh. It was a sound that reminded me of my childhood. Of sunshine and running through the fields at his vineyard. Of toilet papering Bobby Jones' house after he scored the winning touchdown at the state meet. Of late night make-out sessions with this boy. Of moving across the country to attend college together. Harrison Montgomery held all the memories of my past. Of both happy times and sad times. I always thought he was my forever.

But things weren't always as they seemed.

four

. . .

Harrison

"ARE you hiding back here because you know Laney is working today?" my mother asked as she strolled in my office.

I rolled my eyes. "No. I'm just busy."

But yes, I was giving Laney the space she'd asked for. I knew she needed this job and I didn't want to get in the way of that. I'd avoided joining them on the helicopter the past few days when they went to the city for her mother's treatments because our conversation the last time we spoke brought up all sorts of memories, and I didn't want to dwell on them. We were history. She was getting married and I needed to respect that.

"All right. Well, I asked her to bring you all the invoices for the events this month once she gets everything organized. How about dinner tonight?"

"Sure." I glanced up to meet her gaze.

"Okay, I'll see you later. Love you."

"Love you," I called out.

I submerged myself in work and tried to block out the fact that Laney was working just a few feet away. I hadn't realized how much I'd missed her until she came back home. Okay, that was bullshit. I'd missed Laney every single day since the day she left for school. The day everything changed. I'd tried to move past it, and I wondered if I ever really would. Sure, I'd slept with several women since we ended things. But no one ever meant anything to me. She was all I ever saw, no matter how hard I tried to move forward. I was embarrassed to admit that to myself. Ashamed even. That I'd used other women to fill a physical need, but I'd had no real feelings for any of them. I'd been in two relationships over the years, but they never went anywhere. I'd been labeled *emotionally unavailable* by several women. There couldn't be truer words spoken. I wondered if this was my punishment for what I'd done. The decision I'd made when I was drowning in grief and not thinking straight.

I spent the next few hours placing orders at the winery and rushing from one meeting to the next, avoiding the girl who haunted my thoughts. I settled behind my desk to check emails when someone knocked on the door.

"It's open," I called out, my eyes remaining on my monitor.

"Hey. I have those invoices for you. Your mom said to get them to you today." Laney strode through the door wearing a white dress that ended just above her knees. Her hair tumbled down her chest in blonde, beautiful waves. Her blue eyes sparkled, and the light coming through my office window shined around her like a goddamned halo.

She was an angel.

My angel.

I thought about what her mother said about Laney not being the same since our breakup. I understood it. Because I wasn't the same. Hadn't been since the day she left.

"Yeah, thanks," I said, reaching for the papers, and purposely grazing my fingers along her hand. Craving that closeness. A zip of electricity coursed through my veins at the mere contact, scorching and blazing. My need for this woman was unexplainable.

She yanked her hand away as if she'd been burned. Laney didn't want to be around me, obviously touching her was out of the question. Her cheeks pinked, and she let out a long, labored breath.

"Okay, then. Do you need anything else?" she asked.

I motioned for her to sit in the chair in front of my desk. "How did your mom do these past few days?"

"She did well. I mean, she's tired. A little nauseous even with the anti-nausea meds, but you know her—she's a trouper."

"Yeah. She is. I'm glad to hear it's going well. And they'll do surgery once they shrink the tumor?" I asked.

"Yes. She'll do the chemo for a couple weeks and then have surgery. Thanks again for letting us take the helicopter. It helps a lot. We get there and back so much quicker. You haven't joined us. You don't have any work in the city you need to do?"

"Nah. Ford and Jack have it covered for now, and babysitting those two gets exhausting," I said, rolling my eyes.

"Still breaking up all their squabbles, huh?" She laughed.

"Yes. I don't think that'll ever change. But they're grown men, they can figure it out. And there's a lot going on here. How'd your first few days go?"

"Really well. It's busy, and I like the distraction."

"You were working for a hotel back in Chicago, right?" I inquired. I wanted to know more about who Laney was now. Hell, I wanted to know everything.

"Yes. I worked my way up to event planner. It's pretty much my dream job," she said, tucking her hair behind her ear. I wanted to run my fingers through her silky waves. Taste her sweet mouth. Touch her soft skin.

Jesus. Get a grip, man.

"So, you graduated from Columbia," I said, clearing my throat. "And then what took you to Chicago?"

She fidgeted in the chair and clasped her hands together. "Well, I wanted to get out of New York, and I knew I didn't want to come home. I always loved Chicago. You know that. And Natalie was moving there with Jared—you remember them, right?"

Natalie was Laney's best friend, and Jared had started dating her right before I left Columbia. I didn't know him well, but I'd always liked Natalie. So, Laney moved to a city where she only knew two people, all to avoid coming back home? All to avoid me? There was more to this, but she certainly wasn't going to be forthcoming with me.

"Yes, of course I remember them. So, they stayed together, huh?" I asked.

"Yeah. They're really great together."

"And I know how much you like Chicago. You almost went to Northwestern."

She nodded. "Almost."

I shook off the feeling that she resented me for choosing to go to Columbia. I'd wanted to attend there ever since my family took a trip to New York. Their business school was one of the best in the country. It was a no-brainer. But Laney and I didn't want to do the long-distance thing, so she'd gone with me to Columbia. And for what? I left. We didn't end up together anyway. Her mom was right. She'd given up her own dreams to follow mine.

"So, where'd you meet your fiancé? Is it Charles?" I didn't look at her when I said his name. I never knew it was possible to hate a person that I didn't even know, but I did.

She cocked her head to the side. "You really want to do this?"

"Yes. I wouldn't have asked if I didn't."

"Okay. His name is Charlie. He's from Chicago. He's a great guy. I think you'd like him." Her tongue swiped out to wet her bottom lip and I nearly came out of my seat. I forced myself to stay put. My hands gripped the edge of my desk and I looked down to see the whites of my knuckles.

"You didn't meet him at school?"

"No. I met him after I moved to Chicago. Why?"

"I just assumed you dated him when you went back to school and then moved together to Chicago."

"You know what happens when you assume. And why does it matter when I met him anyway? We weren't together. We weren't even speaking," she said, her tone harsh. Laced with anger.

"Well, you blocked me from all social media when you got back to school, and you never took my calls when I reached out, so I figured you had a boyfriend."

She leaned forward in her seat. Face hard. Eyes steel. "*Wrong, Harrison.* You didn't take *my* call."

"Hell, Laney. You called me the day after you left. I figured it would complicate things if we spoke too soon. I thought we should wait a couple months. Let things settle."

She pushed to her feet. "I'm done with this conversation. I need to get home. Do you need anything else from me?"

I studied her. Her face was flushed, her hands fisted at her sides.

"No. That'll be it for today."

She turned on her heels and walked out the door.

What the hell was that? Every time I thought I was taking a few steps forward, it seemed like I got bitch-slapped back to square one.

To that day that changed everything.

I still remembered it as if it were yesterday and not five years ago. Every detail engrained in my head. Laney and I had been hanging out in my room that day after a few hours of playing tennis. I hadn't been myself since Dad's accident and I was struggling with how to tell her about my plans.

"You sure you're okay?" Laney asked, rolling on her side in my bed to face me.

"Sure."

"Harrison, I know you. What's going on?"

I didn't want her to be disappointed. But I'd made up my mind and I'd been putting it off for a few days.

"I, um, I'm not going back to school," I blurted.

"What? We're leaving in a few days. You're not going back? Why? How? What does this mean?" Laney pushed to sit up and tugged her hand away from me.

I'd expected the reaction. We'd had a plan. We always did. And I'd changed course. It wasn't fair to her, but I needed to do it for my family.

"Listen, Laney. The closer we get, the more I know that I can't leave. Not now. I can't do that to my mom. I can't. And Ford, Jesus Christ, he's a mess. He blames himself. How do I fly across the country and leave them?"

Tears streamed down her beautiful face. "Okay. Then I won't go either. We'll just go to school here."

I vividly remember being relieved. I couldn't leave my family and I didn't want to be apart from Laney. My father's death rocked our world, and everyone was a mess. When it was time to return to school, it had been almost three months since his accident, but the wounds were still fresh. Still raw. I wasn't myself. None of us were. And Laney was my lifeline. She kept me above water. And I wanted my girl with me.

"Are you sure?" I asked, pulling her back down on the bed and kissing her hard.

"Yes. I'm positive. I don't want to be away from you."

So fucking sweet. I was completely okay with her staying back with me. It was selfish, but I was drowning, and I couldn't see straight. My mom struggled to get out of bed most days back then, and Ford was a shell of himself. Jack had completely jumped ship on his plans for the future, and my family was struggling to keep it together.

"I'm sorry, baby. I just can't leave them right now."

"I get it. I wouldn't want to leave either."

"Jack told us this morning that he doesn't want to try to go pro in the future anymore. He wants to finish playing for SC and then come work for the family business."

My baby brother had talked about playing for the NFL since the first time he spiraled a football at my head. Back then, there'd been talk about him leaving after his sophomore year at the University of Southern California to go pro. He'd been all about it. That's all he and Dad talked about. But after the accident, he said he wanted to stay close. Going to school in LA would allow him to come home often, and he'd decided after graduation he wouldn't pursue football. So much had changed in such a short time.

"Wow. That's all he's ever talked about doing."

"Yep. But it's a grind. He wouldn't have a say in where he lived, and he couldn't just come home when he wanted. He doesn't want to do that to Mom. I get why he's doing it; I just hope he doesn't regret it later. And we're all worried about Ford."

"Do you think you'll regret giving up Columbia later?" she asked, chewing the inside of her cheek.

"No. My family needs me. I have to do this. But you don't, Laney." I pushed the hair away from her face.

"You need me. I want to be with you."

My chest squeezed as I thought back to that conversation. I'd been a selfish bastard. At that point, I was just trying to get through life one day at a time. I'd never faced any sort of adversity before my father's death. I hadn't realized how uncomplicated and easy my life had been up until then. Hell, I'd never wanted for anything. I worked hard, sure. But opportunities always came my way. Always had. I had an amazing family. Loving and caring. I had the perfect girlfriend, who I'd known my entire life. I couldn't have asked for more.

But after Dad's accident—everything changed. In the blink of an eye. My life shattered into a million little pieces. My father's death affected me profoundly. He'd been my constant throughout my life, my voice of reason, and now I was lost. And the pain it caused my mother, my brothers—at times it was more than I could bear. But there were responsibilities waiting. Shoes to fill. We were all struggling to make it through the day back then. We'd been forced to grow up fast. The absence of one man had caused the earth to crumble beneath our feet. I didn't know how to repair that. How to keep it together.

"Okay. Well, take some time to think about it."

"I don't need to. I'm staying. I'm going home to talk to my parents. I need to withdraw from Columbia and sign up for classes here. We can just go to community college and then transfer into UCSF or USF."

I nodded. It was wrong to ask this of her. But Laney was stubborn and when she set her mind to something, there was no talking her out of it.

"Okay."

She kissed me hard and pushed to her feet. "Love you. Call me later."

I can still remember watching her walk toward the door, her white tennis skirt swooshing back and forth as she turned to leave. That was the last moment we shared before I rocked both of our worlds.

I was lying on my bed with my eyes closed wondering if I'd ever feel normal again. Grief was vicious that way. It swallowed you whole and wrapped you up tight, not allowing you to see light at the end of the tunnel.

A constant sadness set up permanent residence in my chest. An overwhelming feeling of loss.

And a knock on my door was the beginning of the wheels coming off the cart.

"Come in," I called out.

"Hi, sweetheart," Mom said. Dark circles framed her gaze, and her sunken cheeks made it obvious she wasn't eating much.

"Hey." I pushed to sit up and she came in and dropped down at the foot of my bed.

"So, we haven't even talked about you leaving for school. I can't believe it's already August."

"Yeah. I was going to speak to you tonight. I'm not going back, Mom. I can't. I'm going to community college until I can transfer into a university in the city. I need to be close to home."

She studied me for a few seconds before speaking. "Okay."

I recall being completely stunned by her reaction. I'd been prepared for a fight. Mom had never been big on not seeing something through. She always insisted we finish what we started. But that day, she'd appeared—relieved.

"Good. I'm glad you understand."

"I do. I just think we all need one another right now. Jack has to go back tomorrow. This going back and forth with football practice and trying to be in two places at once is too much for him. We will go to as many games as we can, and he'll come home often. Even if just for one night," Mom said, her voice cracking as she spoke. She swiped at her cheek with the sleeve of her shirt.

I pulled her close and wrapped my arms around her. "It'll be okay. I promise."

She looked up at me and nodded. "What about Laney?"

"She's going to stay home too."

Mom turned to look at me with surprise. "Her parents are okay with that? I don't see them just letting her leave school to support you. She's got two years left. Do you think that's the best plan for her?"

I sat back and took in a long breath. "I don't know. I want to be with her, but I can't leave right now."

"I understand that, honey. I think that's what you need to do under the circumstances. But Laney needs to do what's best for her. Not what's best for us."

I shrugged. I didn't know what to do. I pushed to my feet. "I'm going to go talk to her, make sure this is what she wants."

"You may need to help her through this, Harrison. She tends to put you first most of the time." Mom gave me a knowing look and I turned to leave.

I'd walked to the Landers' house, as it wasn't far up the road and I needed time to clear my head. When I made my way up the paved path, Sam was just coming out of the house.

"How are you doing, bud?" he asked, as he walked toward his car. His gaze filled with empathy, the way everyone looked at us now. I wondered if that would ever change.

"I'm all right. Where are you off to?"

"Going to meet some friends for dinner. Go on in, they're upstairs. Good luck. Laney just dropped a bomb and they aren't happy."

I nodded. *"Yeah. That's what I came to talk to her about."*

"I don't think she'll change her mind unless you force the issue. You know how she gets."

I ran a hand through my hair and leaned back in my chair, gazing out the window at the grape fields. I hated thinking back to that day. I'd watched Sam drive off and made my way up the front porch and into the Landers' house. It had always been a second home to me.

A door slammed upstairs, and I froze in place. Maybe I should come back later.

"Laney Mae, you're acting ridiculous," Lyla shouted, her voice carrying down the stairs.

"Come on, sweetie. We just need you to hear us out," her father said.

"I'm staying," Laney said, and I heard the door creak open.

"Listen to me. You have two years invested at Columbia. You've taken out student loans, and you've invested a lot into this education to just throw it away," her mother said.

"I'm not throwing it away. I'll transfer somewhere after I do a semester at community college. It's not a big deal. Harrison needs me."

"Honey, that doesn't mean you need to leave school. You can still be there for him from New York. You can talk every day," Dave Landers said.

"I'm not doing the long-distance thing, Dad. That never works."

"Sweetheart, have you ever stopped to think about what you want? You wanted to go to Northwestern, but you chose Columbia because it's what Harrison wanted. And right now, his family needs him, and I respect that he's going to stay home to help his mother through this. But that doesn't mean you need to leave school and throw it all away. You've already registered. Who knows how much this will cost you to withdraw? We aren't the Montgomerys, sweetheart. We aren't made of money. You know how much we love

Harrison, but he's all you've ever known. Maybe the time apart will be good for both of you. He's been your best friend, your only boyfriend, and maybe it's time to spread your wings. There's a big world out there, honey. You need to experience some things on your own. If it's meant to be, you'll find your way back to one another." Lyla's words cut me deep. But there was truth in what she said, and I hated it. She was right.

"How dare you say that," Laney shouted through her hysterics. *"I'll run away. I'll move in with the Montgomerys. I swear I will."*

Jesus. It was a lot to process at the time. The thought of what I was doing to their family? I loved the Landers. I realized in that moment how selfish I'd been, letting Laney go along with what I wanted all this time. I couldn't think straight as the reality of it all set in.

My mother needed me. My brothers needed me.

And Laney Landers needed me to set her free.

And that's exactly what I did.

I slipped out the front door and walked back home and prepared what I'd say when I ripped both our hearts out.

My heart was already broken after the loss of my father, by the devastation I saw on my mother's face every day, the grief consuming Ford, and the broken spirit I saw Jack trying to hide.

Losing Laney Mae Landers was par for the course at that point.

five

. . .

Laney

TWO WEEKS PASSED IN A BLUR. I'd been going with Mom to treatments every day, and after a few scans, we received the good news that her tumors were shrinking. She would continue with chemo treatments for another two weeks and her surgery was scheduled for a few days after that. I spent my afternoons at the winery, and I was actually enjoying myself. Watching my mother's energy get zapped day after day was difficult, but I was happy to be beside her. Having a job to go to provided me a reprieve, and Dad stayed with her in the afternoons.

Theresa, the main event coordinator at the winery, planned the majority of the events. I was filling in for Melanie who was on maternity leave, and we were pretty inundated at the moment. Ford and Harley's wedding was only two weeks away and we were getting together later in the week to go over final details. I couldn't wait to meet the woman who'd finally stolen Ford's heart. He'd always been the toughest Montgomery brother to read, but I knew there was a teddy bear under that stoic exterior. We'd been close before—well, before everything went to hell in a handbag.

"Hey. You're coming with us." Harrison stepped in my doorway with his arms crossed over his chest. Jack stood beside him shoveling a donut in his mouth.

They were both tall and lean, dark and gorgeous—and there wasn't a woman whose head wouldn't turn at the sight of them.

"Laney Mae, have you tried these treats yet? Harley makes the best fucking pastries," Jack said over a mouthful of cake.

I laughed. "Not yet, but I'm looking forward to it. Where exactly am I going?"

I'd been spending more time with Harrison than I should. It was a dangerous game...letting him in little by little, while trying hard to keep him at a distance. I talked to Charlie every night and guilt consumed me as I hadn't shared the depth of my relationship with Harrison with him.

The history.

The love.

The hurt.

All the secrets I'd kept for far too long.

"Dude, you really need to learn to finish chewing before you speak. How in the hell are you ever going to get a woman with those manners?" Harrison said, reaching for my elbow and assisting me out of my chair.

Impatient much?

"Don't you worry your pretty little head about me getting a woman. I had a fine lady in my bed just last night. Third one this week, and it's only Thursday." Jack wriggled his brows as we all walked out the door toward the Montgomery house. I hadn't been there in five years. My pulse raced at the thought of walking back inside the place I once considered my second home.

"Thanks for that visual," I said, swatting Jack in the arm. "Where are you taking me? I have work to do."

Harrison pushed the front door open and I followed him inside. A lump formed in the back of my throat when we entered, because apparently, I was a glutton for nostalgia.

"Mom wants us to get a bunch of pictures together and make a slideshow for the rehearsal dinner. She's hoping you'll help her with it, because you know the woman is clueless when it comes to technology." Harrison led the way into the living room where a few boxes labeled *photos* were stacked. "I also have a bunch of pictures of Ford and Harley together on my phone that I compiled with Harley's best friend, Molly. But we want to add in a few from their childhoods as well."

"That's sweet. I love when people add personal touches to their weddings," I said, as Harrison and I dropped down on the floor in front of the boxes. Jack wandered off somewhere.

"Are you doing a slideshow for your wedding?" Harrison asked, taking the top off the first box and avoiding my gaze when I looked up.

"Um, no. Oddly enough, I'm not super into planning my own wedding. I think I like planning other people's weddings more." I laughed.

"That's odd for a wedding planner."

I rolled my eyes. "Not really. I mean, I do it all day, every day. I wouldn't mind just eloping, to be honest. And I'm really starting to consider that option with all that's going on with Mom. I just don't have the energy to put into planning a big event."

"What does your fiancé have to say about it?" Harrison's tone had a bite, and he kept his focus on the pictures as he tossed a pile of photos on the floor.

"His name is Charlie." I glared in his direction, but he ignored me.

"Oh, are we talking about *Cock*?" Jack barked out a laugh as he joined us in the living room.

I whipped around and gasped. "What?"

"The dude you're marrying. Come on, Laney Mae. You're the wittiest girl I know. You didn't realize his initials spell out cock?"

Charles Oliver Cunningham.

Jesus. I hadn't thought about it.

"Of course, you put that together, Jack-ass." I chuckled. "How do you even know his name?"

"Your engagement was announced in the paper. In *our* paper," Harrison said. His dark brown gaze turned stone cold when it locked with mine.

"Oh my god. What? That's how you found out?" I whispered. I sure as hell hadn't announced my engagement in the Montgomerys' newspaper. Not that it was a secret, but I wasn't cruel.

"Yep. That was a great day," Jack said, sarcasm oozing as he cocked his head toward his brother.

"I would never do that. I don't know who did? I don't even live here."

"It doesn't matter. You're getting married. No point keeping it a secret. It's not like we've spoken in years," Harrison said, raising a brow in challenge.

"And whose fault is that?" I hissed.

"I never said we couldn't remain friends. That we couldn't be in one another's life. That was your stubborn ass who decided that, Laney. Don't put that on me." Harrison pushed to his feet and ran a hand through his dark hair. My gaze landed on his full lips. I could still feel them on mine. I'd kissed this boy enough times to remember everything. The way he felt. The way he tasted. The way he took charge every time his mouth covered mine.

Commanding.

Claiming.

Owning.

"How in the hell could we stay friends after everything that happened?"

"It was a break. A break so you could go back to school and live your life. And I—I could help repair my family. It wasn't supposed to be forever," he said, scrubbing a hand over his face.

"Well, thanks for the news flash. That's not what you said when you ripped my heart out. Nor is it what you did when I called you and you sent me to voicemail. The friends I have are there for one another. They don't pick and choose when it's convenient for them." My voice boomed through the living room, echoing off the high ceilings.

I was on my feet now and in his face. How dare he blame what happened on me.

"Whoa, whoa, whoa. That's a lot of anger there, kids. You know what we need?" Jack said, moving between us. "We need some fun. And you both know what I'm talking about."

Jack took off around the corner and returned with a white rectangular laundry basket, and my head fell back in laughter.

"No freaking way, Jack-ass," I said, stepping away from his brother and letting go of some of that anger.

"Yes, freaking way, Laney Mae. *This is so on.* I need it. And you both definitely need it. Let's do this. Mom isn't home. Lorena is in the library. She'll be none the wiser."

Lorena had worked for the Montgomerys for as long as I'd known them.

"I don't have time for games." Harrison didn't hide his lack of amusement as he crossed his arms over his chest.

"Brother, you've got plenty of time. I can't think of anyone that needs some fun more than you."

"Thanks, Jack." He glared at his brother.

Things were getting heated, and this was exactly what I didn't want to happen. We needed to stop arguing and move on. "All right. Come on. One ride isn't going to kill anyone."

"You're kidding me. You're actually doing this?" Harrison mumbled, as he walked toward the stairs behind his brother and me.

I followed Jack to the top of the staircase while Harrison waited at the bottom. Just like we'd always done. On rainy days. On summer days that were too hot to go outside. And every time their parents went on date night. Even Ford joined in a few times, though he told us it was a ridiculous game.

"He needs this as much as you do," Jack whispered when he dropped the laundry basket down for me to get in.

"I don't need it. I'm just fine."

"Sure, you are." He tilted his head to the side and studied me.

"I didn't post my engagement in the paper. You know I wouldn't do that. Not that it really matters. I'm getting married. So what?" I said, keeping my voice low. Why did I feel guilty about Harrison finding out I was marrying Charlie? It wasn't like he cared anymore. We hadn't spoken in years.

"It matters, Laney Mae. It'll always matter." He motioned for me to step into the laundry basket.

The lump that lodged in my throat when we arrived at the Montgomery house was growing with every passing minute. It was too much. I needed space. I needed to leave their house. Leave this town. And stay away.

Fuck you, cancer, for forcing me to come home. For making Mom suffer and making me deal with the ghosts of my past. And right now, there was a big ole annoying brother ghost shaking me in this stupid laundry basket.

"What speed do you want, girl?" he asked, his voice loud and full of humor.

I laughed. I couldn't help it. I was tucked in this plastic contraption getting ready to be rocketed down the grand curving staircase. I was a grown woman. This wasn't normal. Life had never been normal with these boys, and obviously, nothing had changed.

With the exception of me.

I'd changed.

"There's only one speed, Jack-ass." I paused and waited for him to sing it out with me, as we'd done dozens of times in the past.

"Full speed," we shouted at the same time, and my head fell back in laughter as he pulled back and launched me forward.

I screamed out. I hadn't been chucked down a flight of stairs in a flimsy laundry basket in a long time. My stomach dipped, and I tucked my head in my knees as I flew down toward Harrison. He always waited at the bottom to stop me from crashing into the entry table. My arms were wrapped around my legs and adrenaline pumped.

I looked up just as I slammed into Harrison and he gripped the basket, falling forward on top of me. I barked out a laugh and couldn't stop. He did the same and stayed planted there for longer than necessary, gripping the sides of the basket to keep his weight from crushing me. I pressed a hand against his hard chest. A harmless touch. I couldn't help myself. He pulled back and looked down at me. His cheeks were flushed, and his dark gaze danced with mischief. I wanted to reach up and run my fingers along the scruff peppering his chin. My hands fisted beside me to stop myself from doing so. The smell of mint and cedar surrounded me, and I bit down hard on my cheek to keep from pressing my mouth to his.

"Oh my god. That was kind of awesome," I said, still trying to catch my breath. It was the most fun I'd had in a while. In a long while, in fact. The most I'd laughed. The most I'd smiled in as long as I could remember.

Harrison stepped back and reached for my hand to help me out. Goose bumps covered my arms at the contact. Maybe it was the familiarity. The warmth. The comfort I'd always had with him. It felt good and I didn't want to let go.

"Is she in one piece?" Jack called out from the top of the staircase.

"She is." Harrison's gaze locked with mine, his thumb stroking the inside of my palm. Chill bumps spread across my skin.

"Let's do it one more time," I said, before reluctantly pulling my hand away. I held his gaze for a moment before turning to run back up the stairs.

What was I doing here? Playing with fire by stirring up old feelings. I was with Charlie now, and spending time with Harrison was a bad idea. The truth was—I didn't know if I could ever just be friends with Harrison Montgomery. We had too much history. Too strong a connection.

But I couldn't stop. Even if it meant getting burned.

Again.

Because maybe having him back in my life to some capacity was better than not having him in my life at all. Maybe this was our new normal.

I jumped back in the laundry basket one more time and Jack and I did our same routine before he launched me forward again.

And again.

Five times total.

Lorena finally came out and put an end to our shenanigans.

This was enough of a blast from the past for one day.

———

"Laney, do you have time to sit down and meet with Ford and Harley?" Monica asked. She stepped in my office beside a beautiful woman with long, dark hair and a flowy white dress.

I pushed to my feet. "Yes, of course. You must be the infamous Harley."

"I could say the same about you. I've heard endless tales." She raised a brow before leaning forward to hug me. She was gorgeous. I looked down to see her pink tennis shoes which made me smile, because Ford was formal by nature. I loved it. He'd found his match. They were a striking couple. He wore a navy suit and held a phone to his ear, tossing me a wink before announcing that he had to step outside to take the call. Monica said she'd be back to check on us shortly.

"Don't believe anything they say," I teased.

"It's all good, trust me. They all sing your praises. And I understand you're getting married as well?" Harley asked, and I motioned for her to take a seat.

"Yeah. Not for a couple months. Still in the planning stages. I'm actually thinking about canceling the whole thing and eloping," I admitted before dropping down in my chair. I was working out in the lobby at the front desk, but Harrison insisted I take the back office to work on the slideshow and to have my own space.

"Oh, man, do I ever get that. I would have done the same thing. But, you know, Ford's a bit *bougie*, and I just can't do it to him." She laughed. "So, I've embraced it. And honestly, I haven't done much. Theresa and Monica have handled most of the planning for me, so it's been painless. And I hear you're really doing a lot of the last-minute details now."

"It's been fun. I'm glad I get to help with this one. I've known Ford for a long time, and it's really nice to see him get his happily ever after." My chest squeezed as the words left my mouth. They both looked so happy.

I wondered if people said the same about Charlie and me. He'd pushed so hard for this wedding. I'd fought it for a year and a half and finally agreed a few months ago. He was a good man. A great man, actually. I was lucky that I'd found him and that he loved me so fiercely. I just didn't know if I loved him enough. Or as much as I should. Maybe I'd never feel that again. Comparing every man to Harrison was a dead end. What we shared was once in a lifetime. I'd never have that history, that connection with someone else again, which was okay, because it came with a shit ton of pain, and I wasn't looking for that. Charlie and I had a good thing. Something we could build on.

"Yeah. He said you all grew up together. I hope you're planning on coming to the wedding?"

"Um, I think I'll probably be working the event, so I'll be there," I said.

"No way. The Montgomery boys consider you family. You're coming as a guest. I insist."

I chewed the inside of my cheek. Lines were getting blurred and it made me uncomfortable. I was falling into old habits now that I was home, and I needed to tread with caution.

"Hey," Harrison said, strolling into my office like he owned the place. I guess he did, so I couldn't really fault him that. "Ford asked me to step in. He's on a call with the guys from Japan, and he's putting out a fire."

Harley chuckled. "There's really not anything to do. I think he just wanted me to meet Laney Mae and walk the grounds with your mom, which we already did. So, do you go by Laney or Laney Mae?"

"It's just Laney now. But for whatever reason, Jack and Ford have always called me Laney Mae."

Harrison laughed. "You used to threaten me that I had to drop the Mae. But my brothers never listened."

"Stubborn asses," I said.

Harley's eyes ping-ponged between us, and she cocked her head to the side. "Well, we all know which brother listens best."

"Damn straight. I'm glad you two got to meet before the big day," he said.

"Me too. I'd really like Laney to attend the wedding as a guest, not work the event." Harley crossed her arms in front of her chest. I liked her. She was confident and cool and everything I'd hoped Ford would find in a partner.

"Yeah, I think that would be great. Does that work for you?" he asked, raising a brow in challenge.

"Um, sure. Yes. Thank you," I stumbled on my words. "Mom is scheduled for surgery the Monday after, so that will be the last bit of fun for a while."

"Your fiancé is welcome to come as your date," Harley offered.

"He lives far away and I'm sure he wouldn't want to attend the wedding of a stranger," Harrison hissed, before pushing to his feet and heading to the door. "I need to get back to work."

"Well, that was interesting. Looks like someone isn't too happy about your upcoming nuptials," she teased once Harrison left my office.

"I think he's fine with it. It's just been a long time since we've seen one another. I guess it's a little weird for both of us."

She studied me. "Yeah, Ford said you and Harrison were insepa-rable since kindergarten. He said he never knew why you broke up after their father's death, but that it was very final. That had to be tough, huh?"

I let out a long breath. I never talked about my relationship with Harrison with anyone. It was off-limits. I left it where it belonged—in the past. But Harley wasn't prying. She appeared to genuinely care. And it wasn't a secret, it just wasn't my favorite topic.

"Yep. We met in kindergarten. He tried to stick up for me in the sandbox and I thanked him by chucking a fistful of sand in his face." I laughed at the memory and reached for my water bottle before contin-uing. "After their dad passed away, they all went through a really tough time. I tried to be there for all of them, especially Harrison. He didn't want to return to school so I decided to stay back with him. To support him. But in the end, he told me he needed space. He didn't want to be tied to a relationship anymore. He pretty much begged me to go back to school without him. And that was it."

The pain from that day still clung to me like a second skin. The shock. The devastation that followed his words. He was cold and distant. Not himself at all. A complete stranger. I'd pleaded with him to change his mind, like some lovesick, pathetic puppy. And when he didn't, I grew angry and told him I hated him.

Hey, I never claimed to be the most mature person on the planet. I think flying down a staircase in a laundry basket is an acceptable sport.

"Wow. And you never spoke again. You never talked it out? After the history you shared?" Her puzzled gaze searched mine.

47

"Nope. It's in the past. No sense dredging it up. He was done. He made it loud and clear. And we both moved on."

She chuckled. "Right. Because his response just now about your fiancé is clearly that of a man who has moved on."

"No. Really. This is the first time we've even spoken in all these years. I mean, I ran into him twice in the short stints I came home, which wasn't much, but we barely acknowledged one another. It's easier that way. And now I'm just here to help my mom, so I guess this is closure for both of us." I shrugged.

"You didn't come home much after you returned to school? Because of Harrison?" she asked, looking at me with so much empathy I wanted to tell her everything. All the hurt. All the anger. I chewed the inside of my cheek and pushed that vulnerability away. The people that say *sharing is caring* are full of shit. Sharing is dangerous.

"I guess. I don't know."

"Listen, Laney, I know you don't know me well. But Ford, Jack, and Harrison consider you family, so I consider you family as well. And if you ever need to talk, please know that I'm here. And trust me when I tell you—I've been through my fair share of shit. So, nothing shocks me. I'm a good listener. And a good secret keeper. Even with my nosy ass fiancé always lurking around." She winked and looked over her shoulder at Ford who'd just leaned in the doorframe.

"Did I hear my name, beautiful?" Ford stepped in and moved toward me, leaning over to give me a warm hug. "Hey there, Laney Mae. It's good to see you. Sorry to hear about your mom."

"Thank you. It's good to see you too."

"You weren't eavesdropping, were you?" Harley laughed.

"No, I wasn't. Just happened to walk in and catch something about me lurking." He helped her to her feet, dropping to sit in the chair and pulling her onto his lap. And my heart exploded. They were so light and easy with one another. I envied it.

"Well, I've just been getting to know Laney. You know, nobody calls her Laney Mae except for you and Jack."

He wrapped his arms around her and kissed her neck. "Hey, when I met her that very first day, she was Laney Mae. It stuck. Don't know what to tell you."

"You are one stubborn ass man, Ford Montgomery, but I sure love you."

"Love you too, baby. I need to get back to the office, things are blowing up." He chuckled.

"I'm so glad I got to visit with you," Harley said, pushing off Ford's lap and moving to her feet.

I walked them to the door, and Ford hugged me tight before Harley wrapped her arms around me. "I have a hunch you and I are going to be good friends, Laney. See you soon."

I waved goodbye and moved back to my seat.

My phone vibrated and it was a FaceTime call from Charlie.

Just what I needed. A dose of reality.

Get out of the past and focus on the future.

And Charlie is my future.

six

. . .

Harrison

I STOOD beside Ford and glanced out at the crowd all here to attend my brother and Harley's wedding. My gaze locked with Laney's. She'd fought hard to make herself busy and act like she was working the event, but Harley had asked her here as a guest and I would damn well make sure that happened. They even had her seated at our table, beside me. Exactly where she belonged.

Having Laney Landers back home had been exactly what I needed. I swear it was the first time in five years I actually felt like myself. She was everything good in my life. Always had been. And I missed her. I missed everything about her.

She wore a long pale pink dress that hugged her curves in all the right places and I'd found it difficult not to stare. Damn, she was gorgeous. Her hair was curled and pulled back in a long ponytail at the nape of her neck. The dress showed off her slender shoulders and tanned skin. Laney didn't have to try...she was always the prettiest girl in the room to me. Always had been.

We'd made some progress over the past few weeks. She didn't seem to hate me anymore. I wouldn't say she cared for me per se, but her words were no longer laced with venom.

The doors swung open at the back of the church, and Harley

DeLuca stepped inside with her hand wrapped around her grandfather's arm. She was a vision. Her dark hair was up in a bun, piled on top of her head, surrounded by a crown making her look like some kind of royalty. Her lacy dress was fitted to her waist, and then a full skirt swirled all around her. When she made her way up to my brother, she lifted the skirt just enough to show off her sparkly tennis shoes. Everyone chuckled, with the exception of Ford. He just stared at her with complete awe. Something in my chest squeezed and a lump formed in my throat, making it hard to breathe. We'd been through some serious shit these past few years, losing Dad being the worst of it. And Ford had the toughest time out of all of us, carrying a lot of unnecessary guilt on his shoulders. I let out a long breath, and Jack's hand landed on my shoulder. We were all feeling it. Like we were coming out of the other side of grief. Experiencing real happiness for the first time in a long time. I was fucking happy for my brother. My gaze locked with Laney's and she smiled. Her deep blue eyes showed me all the empathy in the world.

Ford and Harley said their vows, and her best friend, Molly, and her sister, Chanel, took turns fixing her train. Chanel had been a family friend since we were kids, and we'd learned that she and Harley shared the same father, Hanky. *Our Hanky.* My father's best friend and Ford's godfather. The news had come as a blow and rocked all of our worlds. But here we were. Celebrating together. Sans Hanky. I didn't know if that wound would ever heal for Ford or Harley.

I listened as they spoke their truths to one another. Shared how they'd each saved the other and let all that love flow between them. We followed them out and met for photos afterward, finally making it back to the winery and into the tent for the reception. I found Laney sitting at our table talking to Jack's date, Willow. We'd all grown up together, and I was glad to see that Laney hadn't tried to slip away.

I dropped down to sit beside her, and Jack and Willow made their way to the bar.

Laney pushed to her feet. "Come on."

I laughed. "Where are we going?"

"You've got some explaining to do," she said, chuckling as we snuck out through the back of the tent and walked toward the barn.

The barn where we'd learned to ride horses together.

Shared our first kiss.

Lost our virginity.

Damn, when Laney picked a place to chat, she sure did choose one full of visuals.

She kicked off her heels and hopped up on a hay bale.

"What's going on?" I asked, shoving my hands in my pockets so I didn't do something stupid. Something that would push her even further away.

"Um, *Chanel and Harley*? Sisters? How is that possible?"

I laughed and dropped down to sit beside her. My knee knocked into hers as I turned to face her. "Yep. Trust me, it came as a shock to all of us. Hanky is Harley's father. He never told anyone, including Harley. She grew up with a monster for a mother and no father. Thankfully, her grandparents stepped in and raised her."

She shook her head and gasped. "Hanky is her father? He had an affair? Did Marie forgive him?"

We'd all grown up in Napa and attended the same school, and Laney knew them all well.

"He claims he was drugged by Harley's mother, but regardless, he knew he had a daughter. He took a paternity test all those years ago and kept her a secret. Turns out he lied about his and Dad's car accident as well."

Her face paled. "What? What do you mean? How?"

"He was the driver that night. It was the same night Harley confronted him about being her father. She heard him and Dad arguing when they got in the car. Dad insisted he tell Marie and the kids, and Hanky didn't want to."

Laney pushed to her feet and paced in circles in front of me. "You're serious?"

"Dead serious."

"Holy shit. I sure missed a lot."

I laughed. "Yeah, you did. Stick with me, kid, I'll fill you in on all that's going on."

She nodded. Moved closer to me before placing a hand on my cheek. Her palm was warm. Comforting. And every inch of me hardened at her touch. I adjusted myself as inconspicuously as I could, so she wouldn't notice the raging boner beneath my tuxedo pants.

"How are you doing with all this? Finding out your dad wasn't driving that car. Learning that Hanky isn't who you thought he was. I know how close the two of you were."

I placed my hand over hers. Needed her to keep it there. "Ford took it the hardest. Hanky let him carry that guilt for five years, Laney. Made him think he'd caused the accident. That Dad had driven off the road in a rage over his argument with Ford."

"Jesus, Harrison. And that's part of the reason you chose not to return to school. You were so worried about Ford. I know you were worried about your mom too, but Ford was drowning in grief. We didn't know if he'd come out of it."

"Yeah. The decision Hanky made sure affected a lot of people in the big picture, huh?" I wrapped my arms around her, needing her to know how sorry I was for what I'd done to her. "I'm sorry for hurting you. If I could go back and do it over again, I swear I'd do things differently. Talk to you about what I was going through. I didn't just lose my girlfriend, Laney. I lost my best friend."

Her body trembled as she leaned against me. "What would you have done differently?"

"I wouldn't have let you go back without me. I would have told you that I was just trying to do the right thing by you, because I loved you *that* much."

She pushed back and shook her head. "No. You wanted us to experience things on our own. You weren't doing it for me. If we're going to have it out, let's be honest. That's one thing we've always been."

"That's what I'm trying to do. I'm telling you the truth."

"So, why wouldn't you have told me that then?" Her puffy ocean blues searched mine. I saw the hurt. The disbelief.

"I was at your house that day, Laney. I heard your parents trying to convince you to go back to school. They were right. You'd only gone to Columbia because it's where I wanted to go. You'd always done everything for me. It wasn't fair. And I wasn't in a good place. My whole world was crumbling beneath me. I wasn't any good for you. I thought I was doing the right thing. The unselfish thing. I thought we'd just wait a few months and get back on track. I never thought it would turn into this—years of us not speaking. But I guess you realized you were happier without me."

"No. That's not right. I don't even know what to say." She covered her mouth as her words broke on a sob.

"Hey," a voice called out, and we both turned to see Jack standing there, "thought I might find you here."

"Give us a minute, Jack," I said, unable to hide my frustration.

"I would, trust me. But Laney Mae's got a visitor. Your fiancé, *Cock* is here. I left him with your brother and Gia and told him I'd get you. Apparently, he wanted to surprise you. Flew in for your mom's surgery and figured you wouldn't mind sneaking out of the wedding early."

"Charlie's here?" she whispered. "Oh my god. I need to go. I shouldn't be here. I shouldn't." She slipped her heels back on and hurried toward Jack.

"Laney, we need to finish this conversation," I said, not moving from the hay bale.

"No. We don't, Harrison. The past is in the past. Exactly where it belongs."

She was wrong.

We weren't done talking this shit through.

Not even close.

———

I knocked on the Landers' front door, as Jack stood beside me.

"You nervous, brother?" he asked.

"No."

"You think we're going to see Cock?" he whispered before his head fell back in laughter.

"Don't make this awkward. Let's just check on Lyla, drop off the flowers, and call it done."

I hadn't seen Laney since the wedding, and she'd been very short in her responses to me when I texted. She'd let my mom know she needed a few days off work to care for her mother post-surgery. I'd offered to bring a nurse in, but she'd shot me down. They'd just returned home from the hospital today and apparently Lyla was doing really well. They'd removed the tumor and now it was a waiting game to see how they'd proceed.

"Harrison, Jack, so nice of you to stop by. Lyla will be thrilled to see you," Dave said, looking a bit sleep-deprived and slightly disheveled.

Sam came around the corner and gave me a half dude hug, thanking us for stopping by before leading us to the living room where Lyla sat on the couch. With her daughter beside her and who I could only assume was Laney's fiancé sitting on the other side of her.

I hate him.

There was no logic behind my disdain for a man I didn't know. But it was there, and I fought to keep it at bay.

"Oh my. It's so nice to see you both," Lyla said.

I leaned down and hugged her before handing her the large floral arrangement Mom had ordered for us to pick up on our way over. "Of course. So happy to see you're doing well."

"I am, sweetheart. I'm feeling better than expected. We were just discussing that this one is fine to go back to work tomorrow because between her and Dave, I have more attention than necessary." She thrusted her thumb at Laney. "Oh, I'm so sorry. Have you both met Charlie yet?"

"Yep, I met *Charlie Brown* the other day at the wedding. I'm Jack, in case you forgot, and this is my badass brother, Harrison. The *Har-Bear*."

Jesus. What the hell is wrong with him?

Everyone laughed at my brother's insanity, as Charlie pushed to his feet. My gaze locked with Laney's.

"Nice to meet you," Charlie said. He was a bit shorter than me, but he seemed nice enough. Didn't matter. I was never going to like the man who was marrying Laney. She was mine. Always had been. Anything else just felt—wrong.

He extended his hand and I gripped it hard and nodded. "Good to meet you."

It wasn't. But I wouldn't make this more awkward than it already was.

He dropped back down and wrapped an arm around Laney's shoulder, and my hands fisted at my sides. I looked up to find Lyla studying me.

"So, Charlie, how long are you here?" Jack asked.

"I fly out tomorrow. I wish I'd come under better circumstances, but I'm glad I got to be here for Lyla's surgery. And it's been nice to get to see where Laney grew up," he said.

I wanted to shove my fist down his throat. I stared at his hand as he caressed Laney's shoulder, and before I could stop myself, a growl escaped me.

Jack laughed. Lyla laughed. Sam and Dave laughed.

Laney glared at me.

And stupid Charlie looked between us with confusion.

Laney pushed to her feet. "Excuse me for a minute. I need to speak to Harrison about my work schedule. We'll be right back."

She led me out of the living area and down the hall. She opened the door and used her hand to wave me into the garage.

"What the hell are you doing?" she hissed.

"Meaning?"

"Meaning, you can't growl when my boyfriend wraps an arm around me. You're acting like a child." She crossed her arms over her chest.

I leaned forward, crowding her. Her cheeks flushed pink and I didn't miss her labored breaths in response to my nearness.

"I don't like him."

She took a step back. "You don't say. Well, too bad. It's not up to you."

"We need to finish our conversation from the other night, Laney."

"It's done. There's nothing more to discuss."

"I disagree." I stepped forward, needing to be close to her. I put my hand under her chin and tilted her face up to meet my gaze. "Why won't you talk to me?"

She sucked in a long breath, eyes wet with emotion. She moved closer, resting a hand on my chest. "I'm getting married, Harrison. There's nothing to talk about."

"Do you really want to marry him?" I asked, my lips grazing

her ear.

She fisted my T-shirt in her hands and sighed. "I'm engaged."

I tangled my fingers in her hair, skimming the soft skin on her neck. "That's not what I asked you."

She pushed me back and tucked her hair behind her ears. "Stop complicating this. It's been five years."

"My point exactly. Time to move past this shit."

"I already have."

"Bullshit, Laney. You feel this pull between us as much as I do. It's always been there. Always will be."

"So, what? It doesn't mean anything. Once I leave, we'll go another five years without seeing one another."

"And why is that?"

"Because my life is elsewhere now," she said, squaring her shoulders and holding her chin high.

"Your home is here, and you know it. I think you're scared of how much you feel when you're here. But you can't run from it."

"That's rich coming from you. You're the one who told me to leave."

"And I've explained to you why I did that," I said.

"It doesn't matter anymore. We're both in different places. I'm glad we can put it behind us and be friends."

A friendship was better than her hating me.

"I'm good with that. So, we can finish our conversation over lunch this week. Friends eat lunch together, right?" I smirked.

"You're exhausting. I'll be back at work on Wednesday." She rolled her eyes.

The door flew open and Jack stood there with a wide grin spread across his face. "Hey, Cock's getting antsy and wondering where you are."

Laney huffed and stormed past my brother. "His name is Charlie, Jack-ass."

Jack's laughter boomed and I couldn't help but join in. Laney wanted to be friends—no problem. I'd already held that title most of her life.

I'd found a way in, and I wasn't backing down this time.

seven

. . .

Laney

I BROUGHT Mom a tray with toast and tea and set it on the bed
before fluffing the pillows and helping her lie back.

"Honey, will you stop fussing? I'm fine."

"Are you sure you're okay with me going to the winery? I'll just
work for a few hours."

"I'm positive. Dad's downstairs, too. And, if I'm being honest, I
want to read a book and just relax. All this attention is a bit much."

"Okay, well, I'm just up the road if you need me." I turned toward
the door. "Hey, there's something I wanted to ask you."

She reached for the teacup and took a sip. "Sure. What is it?"

"Did you announce my engagement in the paper?"

She set her mug down and dabbed her mouth with the napkin. "I
did."

"Did you announce it in the local paper here in Napa? Or just the
one owned by the Montgomerys?" I placed my hands on my hips and
studied her.

"Nope. Just the one paper."

I moved to sit on the edge of the bed. "Why would you do that?"

"Because you weren't going to tell him. And, well, I thought he
should know."

"Why? What would possess you to think that was a good idea?" I was annoyed. Not that Harrison knew—of course he was bound to find out. But I didn't like that he found out that way. It was cold. I'd assumed he'd just heard from someone in town. Although, I didn't know why it mattered how he found out.

"I'd just found out I had cancer. I hadn't told you yet, so I didn't know all of this would bring you home." She paused and reached for my hand, wrapping hers around mine. "You haven't wanted to come home since you and Harrison broke up. I know that you both have a lot of hurt over what happened. I guess I just decided that life is short —and I wanted to make sure you were marrying Charlie for the right reasons. I knew if Harrison saw the announcement, it would allow him the time to do something about it before it was too late, I guess."

"It *is* too late, Mom. Where is this coming from?"

"I don't know, sweetheart. Call it mother's intuition. Something changed in you after you left and went back to school on your own."

"Yeah. He dumped me and I was heartbroken. But I moved on," I said, fidgeting with my engagement ring.

Charlie had asked what the story was with Harrison after my ridiculous ex-boyfriend basically growled at him in front of everyone. I told him more about our history, which wasn't that hard to figure out after he saw the shrine in my bedroom. If I'd known he was coming, I would have put everything away, but maybe it was good that I was forced to tell him more about what we'd shared. I couldn't tell him everything, because then he'd know that I never really got the other half of my heart back after I gave it away the first time. Charlie was marrying a woman with half of a heart, and he seemed okay with it. He listened, and he nodded, and he asked a slew of questions—and then we just moved on. He trusted me. A part of me wondered if it was normal. Charlie didn't have a jealous bone in his body, and neither did I when it came to him. Was something missing? The passion? The emotion? I was wrestling with all that I was feeling. Being here, back at home—it was proving more challenging than I could have ever imagined. I thought I'd moved on from Harrison Montgomery, but in truth, I'd just moved away. And the sooner I got out of here—the better.

"That wasn't it, sweetheart. Now, I own my part in this. Dad and I encouraged you to return to school because we thought it was best for you. We never thought you needed to end things with Harrison. We just wanted you to finish school and spread your wings a bit. But you changed after that. You lost your light. It was more than a broken heart; it was like a part of you—I don't know—like a part of you died. And I feel partly responsible for that. Dad and I adore Charlie, and if he makes you happy then you have our blessing to marry him. But if there are any doubts, or if he isn't the one—I encourage you to find that out now. I've seen a change in you in these few weeks since you've been home, and it makes my heart explode to see you happy."

Tears streamed down my face and I pushed to my feet. She was right. I had lost my light. I'd been trying for a long time to get it back. So many secrets. So many words that I couldn't bring myself to say. Not to anyone.

I nodded. "I am happy, Mom. I promise. And I understand why you posted my engagement now. But there's too much water under the bridge with Harrison. I'm glad we're friends again. I did miss having him in my life. But too much has happened. Too much has changed. I've changed. Charlie knows me, and he loves me."

"And you love him?" she whispered.

"Of course. Yes. I do. I love him. I do love Charlie. What's not to love?"

"Who are you trying to convince, honey? Me or you?"

I rolled my eyes. "I love you, Mom. I need to get to work." I reached for a tissue on the nightstand and swiped at my tear-streaked cheeks.

"Laney Mae," she called out. She only used my full name when I was in trouble, but this time, her tone was soft.

I stopped in the doorway, but I didn't turn around to face her. This conversation had already dredged up more than I could handle at the moment. "Yeah?"

"It's okay to not know what you want, to say you need more time, to question and explore things. This is the time to do that, sweetheart. You only get one shot at this life, and you deserve to be happy."

I nodded and walked away. I didn't know which way was up anymore. But I'd agreed to marry Charlie, and he was a good man.

There was no question about it. He understood me. He allowed me to take space when I needed it. He didn't make me talk about every single thing on my mind, and I appreciated that. Charlie didn't push me. He let me be. And maybe that's what I needed in my life. Maybe everyone was different, and we didn't all want the fireworks and the passion.

But sure, watching Ford and Harley say their vows did leave me wondering if something was missing between Charlie and me. That feeling like you couldn't live without the other. All-consuming. There was so much love between Ford and Harley as they spoke to one another, you could feel that deep love that lived there. I didn't feel that same connection to my fiancé. So yes, I had some reservations.

And then I reminded myself that he'd flown here to support my mother through her surgery. He didn't question me or sulk when I said I wasn't comfortable having sex under my parents' roof—after we'd been apart for weeks. I'm the only one who knew that I'd had sex in this house quite a few times in the past. Well, I suppose Harrison knew that as well, since it had been with him. We couldn't keep our hands off one another at that time in our lives. We'd sneak off just about anywhere we could to be together. But that's what kids do. That's puppy love.

I didn't need that intensity in my life. Marrying Charlie would be like marrying my best friend. He'd never hurt me. And there was something to be said about that.

I arrived at the winery and pushed the thought out of my head as I made my way to my office, settling behind the desk and turning on my laptop. I left the door open, and Monica popped her head inside.

"Good morning, sweetheart. I saw your light on. How's your mom doing?"

"She's doing well, better than expected. The doctors think they got everything, but we'll wait and see. She's still got a long road ahead of her with reconstructive surgery, but I think she's just taking it one day at a time."

Monica dropped down in the chair across from me. "She's lucky to have you here with her."

"Thank you, that's sweet of you to say."

"I mean it. And I wanted to thank you for all the work you put into Ford and Harley's wedding. It went off without a hitch. It was such a great day," she said.

"I was just the wingman. Theresa did all the hard stuff." I chuckled. "Thank you for making this position for me—giving me an office and making me feel like part of the team."

"We're lucky to have you. You know, if you ever decide to move back home, there will always be a spot for you here."

I smiled and fought back the tears that threatened again. What was wrong with me today? It just all felt like too much. I shook my head, but no words came, and I covered my face with my hands and tried to pull myself together. Monica came around the desk and bent down in front of me.

"Are you okay, Laney?"

I nodded as the dam I'd tried to keep at bay opened, and tears streamed down my face.

"I don't know what's wrong with me. It's just been a lot lately. Being home. And remembering all that I left behind."

She rubbed my back with one hand and placed the other on my cheek. "You didn't leave anything behind, sweetheart. You just took a different path for a while. I understand that, sometimes it's necessary. We don't always choose our journey, Laney. Life has a way of doing that for us."

I swiped at my face with the sleeve of my cardigan, trying to swallow over the enormous lump lodged in my throat. "I feel like I've lost myself somewhere along the way."

"You didn't lose yourself, honey. Do you know that when I met you and you were just five years old, I told Ford Senior that I thought you were an old soul? I'd never met a child that was more empathetic and caring than you in my life. I believe that's why Harrison was so drawn to you. Your warmth and your goodness—it's contagious. And I think you had your life mapped out early on, and your world got flipped on its side. You did what you needed to do to survive. It doesn't mean you're lost. It means you're finding your way. And we've all had to do that over the past few years."

"I never thought about it that way. It's just hard to be back when so much has happened. Having Charlie here made me realize that he doesn't know much about my life before him. Not because he doesn't want to, but because I haven't shared it with him. I just don't want to for some reason." My words broke on a sob. "And Harrison, he doesn't know anything about my life after I left. No one does. I feel like my two worlds are colliding now and I don't know how to handle that."

"Talk to them. Keeping things bottled up isn't good for anyone. You're not hurting them by telling them these things—you're hurting yourself by keeping it bottled up, sweetheart. You don't need to carry the world on your shoulders. You have a lot of people who love you."

Monica wrapped her arms around me, and I fell into her. Needing all that warmth and comfort. I'd been so focused on Mom and Charlie and Harrison—and it felt good to just let it all out. We sat like that for a few minutes before I finally calmed my breathing and looked up at her, sitting back in my seat.

"Thank you. I appreciate it."

"Always. I love you, Laney," she said, pushing to stand and reaching for the tissue on my desk. She handed me a few and I cleaned my face up.

"I love you, too."

Someone cleared their throat in the doorway and we both turned to see Harrison standing there.

"Everything okay?" The look of concern on his face nearly brought me to my knees. No one in the world knew me better than Harrison Montgomery. I didn't like admitting that, but it was the truth. Hell, there were times I thought he knew me better than I knew myself.

"Yes. We were just having a nice chat about Ford and Harley's wedding. You come see me later, okay?" Monica said, and a warm smile spread across her face as she winked at me before walking out the door.

"I will. Thank you."

"Hey." Harrison raised a brow in question. "Is everything okay with your mom?"

"Yeah. Come in. She's doing well."

He dropped down to sit in the chair across from me. "You sure?"

"Yep. I asked her about the engagement announcement, and she is the one who posted it. *Just in your newspaper.* Nowhere else."

"Is that right?" He smoothed out his fitted dress pants as he stretched his long legs out and crossed them at the ankle.

"It is. She wanted you to know before I got hitched, I guess. In case we had anything to work out between us." I chewed the inside of my cheek after the words left my mouth.

"That was nice of her. Do we?"

"Do we what?" I asked just above a whisper.

"Do we have something to work out?"

"I guess we never got closure. Maybe this is our time to do that." I dabbed at my eyes one last time with the tissue and tossed it in the trash.

"All right. There's no harm in us being friends, right? That's how we started out. We can finish the conversation we started that night at the barn, answer a few questions, and hang out like old times."

"Okay." I let out a long breath. Maybe I owed this to myself and to Harrison. To really put this behind us both once and for all.

"Come on. Things are slow today. I want to take you somewhere."

I didn't question him. Monica's words repeated in my head, *it's all part of the journey.* I pushed to my feet and followed him to the door. I didn't ask where we were going because it didn't really matter. I couldn't move forward with my life until I closed this chapter, and that's what I intended to do.

"Where are we going?" I finally whined after our third turn down a side street. I swear we'd walked close to a mile already and I yanked off my cardigan as the sun shined down from above.

"You want a piggyback ride, for old times' sake?" he asked, glancing over his shoulder to look at me. Butterflies swarmed my belly, as his dark gazed locked with mine. Damn. Harrison Montgomery had managed to get better looking with age, and he'd already been the best-looking boy I'd ever seen when we were together.

"No," I huffed, tying my cardigan around my waist. "But it's hot as hell out here."

"Not sure why you're wearing a sweater in the summer." He smirked.

Wiseass.

"The winery is freezing," I huffed.

"We're here."

"Why in the world would we come to St. Vincent's?" I rolled my eyes. I'd gone to school here most of my life. My parents worked here, well, when it wasn't summer break like it was now. Although my dad still taught a few summer classes at the high school.

"For once in your life, can you just not question the *why?* Just follow me. Have a little faith."

He opened the gate to the elementary side of the school. I hadn't been on this side of the campus in years. "I have faith in lots of things. But that doesn't mean I won't question where I'm going."

He laughed and stayed a few steps ahead of me before coming to a stop on the playground. He dropped down on one of the swings. The ground beneath the playground equipment used to be filled with sand, but for hygiene purposes, it was now covered in black mats.

"Take a seat, Laney."

"Why are we here?" I moaned, dropping to sit in the swing beside him.

He reached in his pocket and pulled out a sandwich-sized baggy filled with white sand and handed it to me. "You can throw sand in my face if you need to. But we're going to talk."

My head fell back in laughter. "You brought sand?"

"I sure did."

I took the bag from his hand and unzipped the top, running my fingers through the soft granules. "And if I don't like what you say, I can throw handfuls in your face?"

"It wouldn't be the first time, so yes." He leaned back in the swing and looked at me.

"I'll keep it close by," I teased. "So, what did you want to talk about?"

"The conversation we started at Ford's wedding."

My head fell back in frustration. "Yes, the one my *fiancé* interrupted. I mean, what's the point, Harrison? The past is in the past. Let's just leave it alone."

"What are you so afraid of?" he asked, his feet keeping his swing moving at a steady motion.

"I'm not afraid of anything."

His swing came to an abrupt stop and he studied me. "I don't believe that, Laney. I owned up to why I pushed you away. Now you tell me what happened when you went back to school and then decided you hated me and never came back home much again."

I halted my swing as well. "What, breaking my heart wasn't enough of a reason to hate you for five years?"

He didn't laugh when I did. I tried to make light of it, but he wasn't having it.

"Not considering the circumstances, no, I don't think so."

Why does this boy have to know me so well?

"I don't know what to tell you. You hurt me really bad. I moved on with my life. There's not much more to discuss."

"Does that bullshit work on your fiancé? Because it sure as shit doesn't work on me. If you aren't ready to tell me why you're so angry with me, that's fine. *But own it.* Don't try to pacify me, I'm not that easily fooled."

I reached in the bag of sand and grasped a handful before chucking it at his chest. "You're an asshole, Harrison. That's reason enough."

I stormed off the swing and charged across the playground. He caught my arm and spun me around. My chest slammed into his. "Stop running, Laney."

My breaths came hard and fast, as his dark gaze drilled into me. His lips were full and pouty, and I ached to push up and kiss him. My hands moved to his chest of their own volition and they lingered there.

"I'm not running," I said, just above a whisper.

"Yeah, you are. But this time I'm coming after you."

"Why?" My voice startled me, breathy and laced with need.

"Because I care about you. I always will." He leaned down, his lips close enough that it wouldn't take much to press mine to his. His chest pounded beneath my fingertips, and my legs threatened to give out. My entire body heated, and I squeezed a fistful of his dress shirt in my hands before pushing him away.

"Trust me. You shouldn't, Harrison. I'm not the same person I used to be." I took a step back, putting space between us. "And I'm *engaged*."

"I know you. I've always known you. That doesn't change because we haven't spoken or because you're marrying someone else. We both deserve to have closure."

"We got closure when you broke up with me five years ago." I turned on my heels and started walking.

"My father died, Laney. My world turned upside down. I thought I was doing the right thing."

His words cut deep. I stopped moving and turned around. "So, then let's just call it done. Why dredge up the past?"

"Okay, then," he said, moving toward me. "Let's not dwell on the past. We can move forward—as friends, if that's what you want. I miss you, and you're going to be leaving soon, so the least you could do is hang out with me. For old times' sake."

I rolled my eyes and bit the inside of my cheek hard to keep from smiling. "What is it that you want to do?"

"I just want to spend time with you—as friends. You're the best friend I've ever had. You can even tell me all about your wedding plans if it makes you feel better. Let's go to Renaldo's for pizza after work. I'll even let you put pineapple on the whole thing."

Renaldo's was only the best pizza in town—and he knew I'd be hard pressed to turn him down. We'd been best friends our entire life. There was no harm in hanging out with an old friend, right?

"Fine. I'll do it. But only because you agreed to put pineapple on the whole pizza."

"Deal."

We started walking back toward the winery.

Maybe I'd just made a deal with the devil.

But I didn't care.

Because for the first time in a long time…I couldn't wipe the smile off my face.

eight

. . .

Harrison

"DO you remember when you snuck out of your house junior year, because we wanted to sleep out here under the stars?" I asked her, laughing at the memory.

"Um, *yes*. Because I got grounded for two whole weeks and couldn't see you," Laney said, lying on her side as she stretched out on the plaid blanket. We'd grabbed sandwiches at the winery and come out here to eat. It had been our favorite spot when we were growing up, and we'd both worked late, which meant we needed dinner.

We'd spent a lot of time together since we'd agreed to be friends again. We picked up where we left off all those years ago—minus the fabulous sex we used to have. And the kissing. *The fucking kissing.* I used to kiss this girl till my lips were chapped and swollen, and it still wasn't enough. Now I had to keep my hands to myself. But the crazy thing about it…I didn't even care. Yeah, I wanted Laney more than I'd ever wanted anything or anyone. But I was happy just to have her in my life again, in whatever capacity she was willing to offer.

I laughed. "Yeah, I remember bringing a lawn chair and plopping it outside your bedroom window just so I could see you."

She rolled onto her stomach, pushing the other half of her sandwich out of the way, and a big grin spread across her pretty face. "Well, they did take my phone from me. What did they expect us to do?"

"Your parents brought bottled water out to me so I wouldn't dehydrate in the heat." I pushed to sit up, yanking my tie off and unbuttoning my dress shirt before pulling it off and setting it beside me. I had a white T-shirt beneath, and it was too hot for long sleeves out here.

"They were always crazy about you."

"Yeah. I felt the same about them," I said.

Laney sat up and pulled her long blonde hair over one shoulder.

"I'm glad we gave this friendship thing a try." She smiled, and I swear to Christ, my chest squeezed.

"Me too. It's been too long. So, what did you decide about the wedding? Did you talk to Charlie about eloping?" I asked, trying to keep my voice even. It was difficult to talk to her about marrying someone else. But right now, I was a starved man begging for scraps. I'd take Laney Landers any way I could have her. Being around her had awakened something in me. And yeah, physically, I was in a chronic state of discomfort.

Blue balls are real, my friends.

But it was all worth it. Just to have this time with her.

"Yeah. He wasn't thrilled, but he agrees it's just not the right time with everything that's going on with Mom. We canceled our venue and thankfully, we hadn't done much more as far as planning goes, so we're going to postpone things until I get back home and we can figure out what we want to do."

She didn't look at me as she spoke about her wedding, but it was impossible to miss the lack of disappointment there. She appeared— relieved. Maybe I was reading into things, or just being hopeful, but Laney postponing her wedding gave me a sliver of hope. If she was happy, I'd never do anything to get in the way of that. But instinct told me something was missing there.

"And how do you feel about that?"

"I feel fine. I told you I wasn't really all that into having a big wedding." Her ocean blues locked with mine.

"I just remember you always talking about wanting a big wedding when we were young," I said, pressing the issue.

She gazed out at the vineyard, the sun setting just behind her—it looked like a goddamned portrait. Her blonde hair shining in the last bit of sunlight and the pinks and oranges in the sky making the perfect background against her tanned skin. She wore a fitted white T-shirt that outlined her perky tits and her pink floral skirt flowed around her legs that were tucked beneath her. My hands fisted beside me to keep from reaching out to touch her.

"Yeah, maybe once upon a time. People change. *I changed.*" She picked at the grass beside her and continued to look off in the distance as she spoke.

"You don't seem like you changed to me. And I think I know you pretty damn well."

Her head turned slowly to face me. "I did."

"How so?"

"Well, I don't trust people so easily anymore. Remember you used to get annoyed with me because I trusted everyone."

I laughed. "You just see the good in people. I wasn't annoyed by it —I was probably envious. And I think you still see the good in every-one, Laney."

"I want to," she whispered and swiped at the single tear rolling down her cheek.

I was taken aback at the sight of it. I moved close to her and put an arm over her shoulder. "Hey, what's going on?"

She covered her face with her hands. "Nothing. Do you ever feel like you're just lost? That's how I've felt these past few years."

"I get that. The first year after my father's accident I sort of felt like I was swimming against a current. Not sure where I was going most of the time. I think it's normal to feel that way when you're going through big life changes. You're getting married…you're home taking care of your mom as she battles breast cancer. Of course, you feel lost."

She sighed and leaned her head against my shoulder, and damn, if she didn't fit perfectly there. Always had.

"Yeah. That's true. Mom's doing so well though. I think we're actu-ally driving her crazy fawning all over her."

"Nah. It's good she has you here. You aren't thinking of leaving sooner, are you?" I tried to hide the panic from my voice. I wasn't ready to see Laney go again. Having her back just felt so...right.

"No, I'm going to stay for a few more weeks. I want to help her through the reconstructive surgery, and emotionally, I think it's been helpful to have me back in the house. I lie in bed with her every night and we talk and laugh like old times. I think it helps to keep her moving forward."

"Good," I said, rubbing her arm as she leaned against me. "I like having you here."

"Yeah. I'd be lying if I didn't say being home has been nice. A lot better than I expected. And working at the winery is a godsend." She paused to take a sip of water. "I heard from my boss back in Chicago this morning. She had to replace me. She said they were too busy and being down one event planner had been difficult. So, I don't have a job to rush back to anymore."

"I'm sorry. I'm sure that was a tough call to receive." Relief flooded through me. Laney had postponed her wedding and she no longer had a job in Chicago. Things were looking up.

"Surprisingly, I'm okay with it. I assumed it would happen, so I wasn't caught off guard. I know that coming home was the right thing to do."

"Agreed. Do you live with Charlie back in Chicago?" I asked.

"No. I have my own place. He's such a patient man. He wanted me to move in, but I wasn't ready. I'll move in with him after we get married."

I let out a long breath I hadn't realized I'd been holding. She wasn't ready to move in with him, yet she agreed to marry him? Something didn't add up. Laney Landers was a passionate girl. Always had been. Hell, she used to talk for hours about what our house would look like someday. She even named our future, non-existent kids. She wasn't big on taking it slow. Maybe she had changed in that sense. Or maybe Charlie just wasn't the right guy for her.

"So, tell me about him. How'd you meet? What's he like?"

She pushed back, turning to face me. "You really want to know?"

"I really do."

She crossed her legs, and reached for her bottled water, tipping her head back to take a long sip. "We met shortly after I moved to Chicago. Nat's boyfriend, Jared, was from there, and he'd grown up with Charlie. Nat was relentless about me meeting him, because I'd become a bit of hermit." She laughed. "So, I agreed to go on a double date, not expecting anything. But Charlie has a way of making you feel comfortable right away. We ended up talking for hours, and it continued for a few weeks. It was just a friendship at first. I don't know, he sort of brought me back to life, I guess."

I studied her. *What in the hell does that mean?* "Brought you back to life? In what way?"

"My last two years at Columbia weren't great. I don't know, I sort of slipped into this introverted cocoon." She shrugged and laughed. But I saw something behind those deep ocean eyes. Pain. Fear. Disappointment. I couldn't quite read it. "I needed a fresh start and that's what Charlie gave me."

"You didn't date anyone after we broke up?"

"Nope. I barely ever went out."

"Really? I assumed when you asked me to stop reaching out and refused to take my calls that you had a boyfriend," I said, leaning back and running my fingers over the blades of grass bordering the blanket. A light breeze moved around us, causing a few leaves to drop from the trees.

"You know what happens when you assume, Har." She raised one brow and smiled.

It was the first time she'd called me *Har* in five years. Something squeezed in my chest. Like someone reached inside and wrapped their fists around my heart.

"What about your sorority? You just skipped all the dances and events?" I asked. Wanting to know more. Needing to know everything.

"I dropped the sorority a few weeks after I got back to school. It was too time-consuming." She shrugged.

I shifted, stretching my legs out and rolling my neck. "Wow. That surprises me. You loved it so much."

"Things change. I was fine with it. Less obligation. I still hung out with Natalie. And I just focused on school."

I nodded. "All right. So, tell me how Charlie...what? *Saved you?*"

"Don't be an asshole." She laughed. "He really did in a way. I was not myself when I moved to Chicago. I'd been going through the motions for a long time, I guess. And he brought me out of the funk I was in. He introduced me to a new city. Took me to all the touristy spots at first, and then he started showing me all the local hangouts. We'd talk and laugh for hours, and I just kind of started to get my mojo back. It probably doesn't make sense, but he was a really good friend to me when I needed one most."

I cracked my knuckles. I wanted to hear about her fiancé, I really did. But it also sucked ass. Hearing that another dude had filled my shoes. The ones I'd always worn so proudly. "And then how'd you end up engaged to your new bestie?"

"If you don't want to talk about this, we don't have to. You keep asking, but at the same time, you seem highly annoyed." She narrowed her gaze, and a little crease formed between her eyes. Laney Landers always called me out on my shit, and I loved it. But right now, I didn't need her reading my mind.

"I'm not annoyed. I mean, I wouldn't say Charlie is my favorite topic, but I do want to catch up on the last five years, and apparently, he's a big part of that."

"Okay. So, we became really good friends. Great friends, even. We started hanging out every day. I mean, aside from Natalie, he was the only other person I knew there. He caught feelings long before I did, but eventually, he wore me down." Her head fell back, and she chuckled, and damn if I didn't want to flip her on her back and kiss her senseless. But unfortunately, we were still discussing her perfect best friend and fiancé. "He'd tell me every day how good we'd be together. We weren't dating anyone else, so it just sort of happened. He's such a good guy, Har. I mean, he's solid in every way. Loyal and kind. You'd actually really like him."

"Laney, you do realize you just described Duke to a tee, *loyal and kind*," I said, and we both burst out in hysterical laughter. Duke was the Landers' dog when we were growing up. Laney and I took him everywhere. He was an oversized border collie mix. He'd fetch the newspaper, run out in the vineyard with us, and follow us to school every day.

"Oh my gosh. Duke. Damn, I miss that dog." Duke passed away the summer before we left for college. He'd had a good run at sixteen years old. We'd both been crushed the day we found him on the side of her house looking like he was sleeping peacefully. Maybe in a way he was.

"Well, I think you found him in your fiancé."

She rolled her eyes. "Enough about me. Tell me about you. Did you get a girlfriend right away after I left for school?"

"No. Not even close. I mean, I waited a while before I even thought about being with anyone. You're irreplaceable, Laney Mae Landers."

She rolled her eyes. "Bullshit. You don't like being alone, Har. I know you. What's *a while*? A day? A week?"

"No. I mean, I was going to community college those first few months and I just spent all my time with Mom and Ford. We went to a bunch of Jack's games that first semester after you left, so life was busy, and we were all drowning in grief. And I missed the hell out of you. I'd never existed without you, at least not for any period of time that I could remember. And losing you and Dad, well, it was—tough."

She nodded and motioned with her hand for me to continue. I reached for my water and took a long pull, screwing the lid back on and setting it beside me.

"You didn't come home for Christmas that year, which was a huge blow. I'd had this plan to wait until you came back at winter break and then I'd woo you back. I figured you'd be okay with the idea of long distance once you settled into the whole routine at Columbia. But I ran into Sam and he said they were all heading to New York for the holidays. You weren't coming home. And that's when the panic set in that I'd really lost you."

With her lips pursed and her gaze narrowed, she studied me. "That's when you started calling me."

"Yeah. You kept sending me to voicemail and then you sent me that single text that said to stop bothering you, that you'd moved on. And I got the message."

She closed her eyes and tilted her face up to the sky. The sun glistened against her cheeks. "And then what? You started sleeping with all the girls in town?"

I chuckled. "Not quite, but I did sleep around a bit. The rejection stung. I didn't know what to do. I'd only ever been with you. I didn't like anyone else, so I just sort of slept around for the next few months."

"Ewww. I think I've got the visual. I don't need the nauseating details."

I laughed. "Yeah. It wasn't pretty. But I never lied to anyone. Hell, everyone in Napa knew us as *Harrison and Laney*, so I think everyone was aware I was just trying to get over you."

"You dumped me. I just assumed you were over me." She looked away.

"I've explained that to you. I was heartbroken, Laney. And then you told me you moved on, which is ironic now that I've learned you weren't dating anyone." I bumped her with my shoulder.

"Okay. So, you slept around and tramped it up. And then what? Who'd you date?"

I winced. "I briefly dated Bree Becker. The girl was relentless."

She pushed to her knees and gasped. "You did not. That little tart had been after you since fifth grade. She hated me in high school because she wanted you so bad. Remember how blatant she was at parties? She'd try to rub up against you right in front of me. Then we had that *girl fight* junior year in P.E. when she chucked the ball at my head in dodgeball. Let me tell you—she never tried that again. I dropped her ass right on the gym floor. Ugh. I can't believe you dated her."

We both burst out in hysterical laughter. "Yes, you got a two-day detention for that one, although Principal Donovan appeared to be pleased with you. I don't think you were the only one that wanted to take her down. Bree was a lot in high school. Who am I kidding—she was a lot even after high school. The whole thing was an epic failure. And your shoes were impossible to fill. It was super awkward, and she wanted it to be serious right off the bat. She surprised me and took me home to have dinner with her parents on our second date. She started talking about marriage and kids, and well, I jumped ship. You can only imagine how well that went over."

"Shut up, right now. You walked right into that. Serves you right. So that was a short relationship, huh?"

"Yeah. I hung in there for a solid month. I was miserable after day two, but I was actually afraid to break up with her. She'd gone so far into the future that I didn't know how to get out of it."

"Did you take her to Sunday brunch at your mother's?" She crossed her arms over her chest and waited for an answer. Laney had always joined us for Sunday brunch. It was a family ritual.

"I brought her once. She freaked everyone out talking about how she'd start taking every other Sunday and hosting at *our* house. Jack nearly fell out of his seat and Ford told her to slow her roll. That didn't sit well, so it was the beginning of the end."

She fell back on the blanket laughing. "You've got to love the Montgomery boys. So, who was your next victim?"

"I went back to playing the field for a few years, and then I dated a girl I met through some friends in the city. Nice girl. But she wanted more than I could give her, so we called it quits."

She nodded. "And now what? You just sort of sleep around?"

"I have some ladies I see on and off. They want the same thing as me. Nothing exclusive."

She covered her ears. "Okay, that's good. We're good. I've heard enough."

I smiled. I liked seeing her jealous and worked up because it meant she felt something. Or at least I hoped she did. I started packing up the leftover food and tossing our trash in the brown bag that had held the sandwiches. "Hey, you want to come see my house? You've never seen it. It's right up the road."

She bit down on her full bottom lip, and I looked away before my body started reacting to her again.

"I need to FaceTime Charlie, but I guess if it's close, I could see it before I head home."

"Cool."

"So, when did you buy your own place?" she asked, as we cut through the vineyard and made our way to my house.

"Three years ago, after I graduated. I couldn't very well bring women to my mother's house, and this one popped up for sale."

We stopped in front of the Parkers' old ranch house. I'd renovated the whole thing, but it was a house Laney was very familiar with. *"No, you didn't!"*

"Yes, I did."

So, maybe I bought the house that Laney always said we'd live in one day. Mrs. Parker was our school librarian and her husband had been the mayor of Napa for years. We'd go over every Halloween and they'd have hayrides and their yard was always decorated for the holidays. The house sat on a full acre of land, much more than I needed, but when it came up for sale, I snatched it up. There was a wraparound front porch with a swing, and I'd updated both the exterior and the interior.

"Wow. It looks amazing. I love the crisp white with the black shutters. Gorgeous. I can't believe you bought this place. What happened to the Parkers?" she asked, her eyes scanning every inch of the house.

"They moved to Florida to be closer to their grandkids. I made an offer the day it went on the market. I've just been slowly making updates."

"Amazing," she whispered, as we walked toward the front porch.

We stepped inside, and she stood in my entryway gazing around the room. I'd knocked a few walls down and opened up the living space. A knock on the door startled us both, and we laughed in response. I turned to open the door, and Jenna Gates stood on the other side.

Jesus. Her timing was terrible.

I'd been avoiding her texts and calls over the past few weeks. She'd grown up in Napa too, but attended a different high school than Laney and me. Since Napa was a small community, we all knew one another. I'd run into her every once in a while over the past year when I was out, and we had a casual thing going where we'd hook up every now and then.

Since Laney's return, I hadn't seen anyone.

Other than Laney.

"Jenna, hey," I said. Awkward didn't begin to describe the moment.

Her eyes doubled in size when she saw Laney standing beside me.

"Laney Landers? I heard you were back in town...I just didn't know." She motioned her hand between us. "I didn't know this was a thing again. I just, well, you haven't responded to my calls, Harrison, so I thought I'd check on you."

"Oh my gosh, no. *No*. This is definitely not a thing. I'm engaged." Laney held her hand up and flashed her engagement ring before she tripped over her own feet as she made her way to the door. I caught her arm and steadied her. "And wow. I didn't know *this* was a thing. But yes. Good for you. Okay. This is unbelievably awkward. Take care, Harrison. And it's good to see you, Jenna. Well, enjoy, I guess. I need to go."

I left Jenna on the doorstep and chased Laney down the walkway. "Hey, hold up. You don't need to leave."

"Yes, I do. What are we even doing, Har? I need to go call Charlie, and you need to—do whatever it is you do with Jenna Gates." She stormed away.

She was jealous. And that could only mean one thing.

She still cared.

I spoke to Jenna on the front porch and told her I just wasn't feeling it tonight. She asked if it had anything to do with Laney and I made it clear that it didn't.

Laney was engaged to another man. We were rebuilding our friendship.

And that was enough for me.

It had to be, right?

nine

. . .

Laney

I LAUGHED as Charlie continued to tell me about his crazy workday. I propped the phone on my desk and studied his handsome face. I'd just had the world's most awkward encounter with Jenna Gates. She and Harrison had a *thing*, apparently. He hadn't mentioned her. Jealousy had gotten the best of me, and I'd had a hard time hiding it. I hated the idea of him with Jenna. Hell, I hated the idea of Harrison with anyone. But that was natural. We had a history. Of course, I'd be protective over him.

"So, you worked late, huh?" he asked.

Guilt flooded through me. I'd had dinner with Harrison, again. I'd been hanging out with him more than I'd told Charlie. Unlike me, my fiancé wasn't a jealous guy. He trusted me. And I hadn't crossed any lines. Harrison and I were friends. Friends who got jealous over the other being with someone else, but still, friends. So why was I hiding it?

"Yeah. It's crazy busy at the winery. And then Harrison and I grabbed some sandwiches after, and I just got home."

He studied me through the phone screen, and my cheeks heated. "How's that going? You guys getting your friendship back on track?"

A part of me wondered at times if it was okay that Charlie never got jealous. I mean, he had no reaction to the fact that I was hanging out after work with Harrison. He didn't demand an explanation. Didn't appear fazed by it. Nothing. Nada. Was that normal?

"Yeah. It's kind of nice not to hate him, you know? We grew up together, so there's a lot of history there. He was such a big part of my life for as long as I can remember, so it's nice to catch up and hear what he's been up to."

"Good, Laney. I think that's important. What about your mom? You have an appointment at the surgeon's office tomorrow, right?"

He was such a good listener. And that was important in a relationship. Did Charlie and I have off-the-chart chemistry? No. But we were solid. If he were a flavor, he would definitely be vanilla. I'd learned that vanilla wasn't such a bad thing. There were no surprises. No risk. You knew what you were getting with vanilla, and that worked for me at this point in my life.

"Yes. I'm taking her to the city tomorrow morning, and hopefully, we can move forward and get everything scheduled for the reconstructive surgery."

"I miss you, Laney. I can't wait for you to be back," he said, carrying the phone with him as he moved through his apartment.

A heavy feeling settled in my chest. My mom was doing well. Dad was not teaching this next block of summer school and he could easily handle the caregiver position. But I wasn't ready to leave Napa. Sure, I wanted to be here for Mom. But that wasn't the only reason. It was good to be home. I felt like my old self again. And the guilt was all-consuming because I didn't want to rush back to Chicago. Guilt that I wasn't missing Charlie the way I knew I should be. Guilt that I missed lunch dates with my best friend, Natalie more than I missed spending time with my fiancé.

What's wrong with me?

"Yeah. I just can't leave her yet."

"Well, how do you feel about coming home next weekend for the annual company party? Everyone is hoping you'll be there. But only if your mom's surgery isn't scheduled before then. I've got miles, so I can get your ticket."

My stomach twisted, and anxiety coursed through every inch of my body. *I should go.* It was the least I could do. He'd been so supportive. Why was I feeling so panicked about leaving here? Maybe it was just because I was afraid to leave Mom? But my gut told me it was something more. Even more reason for me to do it.

"Yeah. That sounds great. I'll let you know after her appointment tomorrow. I would love to come visit and be there for you."

He chuckled. "Come visit? You mean come home?"

I waved my hand in front of my face and laughed. "Yeah, yeah, you know what I mean."

"All right. Good luck tomorrow. Call me after her appointment. I have a bunch of meetings in the morning, but I'll get back to you as soon as I can. I love you, Laney."

"I love you too," I said, ending the call. And I meant it. I loved Charlie. I really did.

My phone vibrated with a text from Harrison. I couldn't escape the guy. He was everywhere.

Harrison ~ Hey, I'm heading into the city tomorrow. Do you and your mom want to take the helicopter with me to save you the commute?

Shit. It would help because I could get to work sooner. But I needed to put some distance between us.

Me ~ Thank you for the offer, but I think we're going to drive. I could use the time with her in the car to talk and see how she's feeling. I'll let your mom know that I'll be in a bit later tomorrow afternoon.

Harrison ~ Are you sure that's the reason you don't want to go with me?

Me ~ I don't know what you're talking about?

I chewed on my fingernail as I waited for his response.

Harrison ~ Did it bother you to see Jenna at my house?

Me ~ Don't flatter yourself. Why would I care? We're friends, Harrison. I'm getting married, remember?

Harrison ~ Just making sure you aren't upset.

Me ~ Not even a little.

Harrison ~ Okay. Well, for the record, I sent Jenna home. She didn't come in.

My shoulders dropped in relief and I flopped back on my bed.

Which only made me more uncomfortable. Why did I care? We were friends. He could sleep with whoever he wanted.

Me ~ You can do whatever you want with whoever you want. You're single, after all. I mean, obviously I want the best for you. I don't think a cheap fling with Jenna Gates is necessarily it, but you're a grown man, so you'll figure it out.

Harrison ~ Thanks for looking out for me. You always did know what was best for me.

I sighed.

Me ~ Goodnight.

Harrison ~ Goodnight, Laney Landers. Sweet dreams.

———

Something startled me from sleep. Harrison Montgomery was climbing through my window and striding over to my bed.

"What are you doing in here?" I pulled the covers up and clutched them to my chest.

"I can't stay away from you, Laney. I miss you."

"You need to leave," I whispered, but the smell of mint and sandalwood settled around me and I only wanted more.

"If you really want me to leave, I'll leave. But your body is telling me something different," he said against my ear, leaning forward to hug me. His lips grazed my skin, and I gasped.

I pulled back to look into his dark eyes. Eyes that had always been able to see into my soul. "I can't do this. I can't."

"Do you ever think about us, Laney?" he whispered.

"Yes," I admitted, because I was half asleep and wasn't thinking straight. I'd lost all control of my senses. All control of my body. "All the freaking time."

He swiped at the single tear running down my face with the pad of his thumb. The contact set my body on fire. I hadn't wanted anyone like I wanted him since the day he asked me to leave.

I wanted him.

I needed him.

"I think about you, Laney. Every time I'm with anyone, all I see is you. All I feel is you. All I want is you."

"Harrison, please. We can't do this."

"I want to feel those lips against mine." He leaned over me, his hand moving up the back of my neck and tangling in my hair.

"You do?" I whispered, my lips skimming his.

"I do," he said, before he covered my mouth. He took control. Owning. Claiming. "Fuck, Laney, do you have any idea what you're doing to me?"

Before I could stop myself, I pulled him closer. Needing more. I hadn't felt this kind of passion since the last time I made love to Harrison Montgomery. Like he owned every part of me. He was the missing piece. The flame to my fire. The heat to my very core. He was it.

He was everything.

His tongue tangled with mine, and I couldn't get enough. It was too much. And not enough. I rolled him over, taking control. I was on top, straddling him now, as I sat up, and looked down at his beautiful face. He reached for the hem of my white baby doll night shirt and pulled it over my head. Exposing me in every way. His hands covered my breasts, and chills spread across my skin. The light from the moon shined through the opening in the curtains from my window, illuminating his handsome face. I rocked my hips back and forth, grinding against his desire. It was impossible to miss. I watched as his eyes rolled back in his head.

"Jesus, baby. This is what you do to me." He thrusted forward, and I trembled at the feel of all his hardness beneath me.

I tugged at his T-shirt and he yanked it up over his head, tossing it to the floor.

I continued to grind against him, as my fingers traced every hard line and muscle on his abdomen. *My god.* Harrison had always been in incredible shape, but this was ridiculous. He was chiseled and tan and hard. Everywhere. He reached for my head, pulling me down, his mouth claiming mine once again.

I kissed him hard. Our tongues fighting for control, as our bodies grinded in desperate need of relief. Even through my thin panties, I could feel his erection growing with each thrust. His mouth moved down my neck and I arched toward him before his lips covered one hard peak and I nearly came undone. He gripped the other with his hand.

"God, I missed you Laney."

That was all it took. I cried out my release and fell forward, dropping down beside him and rolling on my back, panting. I hadn't orgasmed in years. Harrison was the only man that ever brought that out of me, and we weren't even naked this time. Talk about hot and heavy make-out sessions. It took me a minute to catch my breath and when I opened my eyes to look at him, it wasn't his dark brown gaze that met mine.

It was the green gaze that I despised most in the world looking back at me and smiling. I shot forward. Gasping. Pushing back until my back slammed against the headboard. My skin was covered in a layer of sweat. It took me a minute to realize that it wasn't real.

My nightgown was still on.

No one was in the room.

It was all a dream.

I'd just dreamed about another man—and he wasn't my fiancé.

I was in deep shit.

———

I'd managed to avoid Harrison all afternoon. I couldn't look at him. Not after he'd starred in the most erotic sex dream of my life. I was heading home after a long day. I'd been in the city with Mom, we'd scheduled her reconstructive surgery in ten days, Charlie had booked my trip home to Chicago next weekend, and I was exhausted from my disturbing dream, slash nightmare.

When I came around the corner in the winery lobby, I slammed right into Harrison and all his hardness. That part was apparently not just a dream. The man was a chiseled god in his Armani fitted suit. He gripped both my arms to keep me from falling.

"Jesus, I'm sorry," he said, trying to steady me on my feet.

I waved my hand in his face. "No worries. I came in hot."

What? Great. Now I had diarrhea of the mouth. I couldn't look at him. Not after what we'd sort of done last night in my subconscious. No freaking way.

Charlie. Charlie. Charlie.

He leaned down, bending his knees a bit to meet my gaze. "Hey. You all right?"

"What? I'm perfectly fine."

"I looked for you earlier, but you had your office door closed. You sure you're okay? How did it go with your mom?"

"Yeah, just busy today. It went really well with Mom. She's having the surgery in ten days."

"That's great. Hey, are you hungry?"

"Um, well, I told my parents I'd grab them Romano's tonight. She's got her appetite back, so I'm going to pick up a pizza."

"Let's go together. I'll drive. I was going to stop by and check on your mom anyway. Do you mind if I crash your pizza party?" He cocked his head to the side and butterflies swarmed my belly. He was the most handsome man I'd ever laid eyes on. And I didn't know how to stay away from him. Obviously, my only chance for survival would be living far away from him. Which would happen soon. So, what was the harm in spending these last few weeks together, right?

"Sure. Of course, you're welcome. Are you kidding? My parents like you more than they like me, I think." I laughed and pulled away from his grasp as we walked out the door, making our way to his car. I'd been walking to work every day, and after the long drive to the city with Mom, I welcomed the fresh air.

I called in our order on the drive over, and we grabbed the pizza and made our way to my parents' house.

"Hey, do you still have that tree house in your backyard? I haven't been back there in years."

"Yep. It's still there. I doubt anyone's been in there since I moved away. It's probably a dusty mess. But Dad built it and I don't think they'll ever get rid of it," I said with a laugh.

"God, we had some good times in that house." He looked over at me and wriggled his brows. I smiled but tried to cover it with my hand. I was desperate to play it cool, act unaffected—and failing.

"Sure." I shrugged, trying hard to block out those memories as they flooded me all at once.

"I think I rounded second base up there."

I laughed, and my cheeks were suddenly hot. I needed to change the subject, and fast.

"Do you remember how I'd make you and Jack play house when we were like seven or eight? We'd spend hours in that tree house."

"Of course, I do. You always made me the dad and you the mom, and poor Jack had to be the dog, Duke." His head fell back against the seat as we pulled in the driveway and we both laughed hysterically.

"*Jack-ass* was such a good dog. Remember the way he'd bark when we'd ignore him?"

I bit the inside of my cheek and gazed out at the backyard, seeing the tree house in the distance. My eyes were wet with emotion.

"I do. He was a damn good dog," Harrison said with a chuckle as we slipped out of his car and made our way inside.

Of course, my parents were overly excited to see Harrison. We spent the next two hours laughing about old times and eating the world's best pizza.

And everything felt right.

Just like it always did when Harrison was there.

ten

. . .

Harrison

"WELL SOMEONE'S IN A MOOD," Jack said, as I settled in my chair in the conference room at Montgomery Media.

"You do seem particularly edgy," Ford added.

I rolled my eyes. "Sorry. Didn't get much sleep."

"Ahhh, you've got the Laney Mae blue balls." Jack winked.

Asshole.

"No, I don't. Where do you come up with this stuff?" I found it difficult to hide my irritation. It wasn't like me, but I couldn't help it. I'd been uncomfortable since the day Laney returned to Napa. Uncomfortable in the best way. I'd been seeing glimpses of my old self, and it was a reminder of all I'd lost.

"What's going on?" Ford brought the tips of his fingers together, forming a teepee as he studied me.

I dropped the pen I was holding on the table and shrugged. "I don't know. I'm just off."

"Har-bear, I know you. You're not off—you're frustrated. Just own it, man. Once you own that shit, you can fix it." Jack leaned back in his chair and sipped his coffee.

I wanted to tell him to shut the fuck up because that's what we always did. But he did know me. Maybe better than anyone, well, with the exception of Laney. She'd always known me best.

"All right. I can own it. It's difficult being around Laney. Makes me remember things."

"Remember things in a good way?" Ford asked, studying me intently. Ford was a fixer. He didn't like small talk. Nor was he one for long conversations. He preferred to attack. Go in strong and fix the problem.

"Sure. I guess, yeah. I think I forgot what it felt like to be happy. Since Dad died, I don't think I've truly been there. I mean—I'm fine. I'm getting by. But being around her. Man, it takes me back to a time when everything was great."

"I get it, brother. You two always did just fit," Jack said.

"So, if she makes you happy, what's the problem?" Ford asked, leaning back in his chair.

"Well, for one, she's engaged. She's marrying someone else."

"She isn't married yet," my youngest brother said, wriggling his brows.

"She may as well be. Her wedding is in four months. Laney's not a cheater, it's not who she is. There's nothing I can do about it."

"Bullshit. Jack's right." Ford paused and pointed at our baby brother. "That's the first and last time those words leave my mouth, so don't get cocky."

"Got it, ole wise one. Make your point."

"Well, she isn't married yet. I'm not suggesting she cheat on her fiancé. I'm just saying, there's time to equal the playing field. Maybe she isn't happy either. But she isn't going to jump ship if she doesn't have anything to jump for. Tell her how you feel and let her decide."

I studied him. This was way out of his wheelhouse, but here he was, talking it out with me. Harley had been good for him. He was more present these days. And he was probably the smartest dude I knew, so when he spoke—I listened.

"And how would I go about that?"

"Jesus, Har. I'm not a fucking therapist. I don't know. Storm the castle, man. Make it happen."

"Whoa, whoa, whoa. You were on track for about a minute there, genius. Nobody is storming the castle. Slow your roll. Har-bear may be in love with the girl, but I actually speak Laney Mae. Always have." Jack leaned back in his chair.

"Agreed. So, what would you do?"

"You're actually going to listen to him?" Ford rolled his eyes and thrust his thumb at Jack.

"Yeah. You should try it, know-it-all. I'm very wise when it comes to relationships because I actually interact with other humans." Jack smirked.

"Fuck you, Jack. I have Harley. She's a human."

I pinched the bridge of my nose. "Can we not do this right now?"

"Fine. We can discuss your lack of human interaction later. Right now, it's all about Laney Mae. We need a name," Jack said.

"A name for what?" I asked.

"The task. The operation. The mission. I've got it—Operation Blue Balls? Or, it could be, The Land Landers? Or, just keep it simple—Get the Girl Back?"

"Pfft." Our older brother pushed away from the table and crossed his arms over his chest.

I shook my head. "Who cares what we call it? What's the plan?"

Jack pushed to his feet and paced the room. "The plan. Yes. I've got it."

"And are you going to share it or keep it in that pea-sized brain of yours?" Ford raised a brow in challenge.

"Your relationship with Laney Mae changed in Tahoe, right? It was that summer before I started high school. I remember it vividly because you went from being best friends to sappy and sickening overnight." He laughed.

"Yep. That was the first time I actually told her I loved her. You know, *loved her*, loved her." I chuckled at the memory. I could still see her blue eyes going wide with surprise before they welled up with emotion. She'd said it right back. We'd both been fighting it. The attraction. The infatuation. I'd wanted Laney Landers something fierce back then, and nothing had changed.

"Okay. So, you take her to Lake Tahoe. We come up with a plan to get you there. Just for a day. A road trip. You need time alone with her

—where she can't run away. Bring back those memories. Get to know one another again." Jack dropped back down in his seat and nodded, like he was waiting for some praise for coming up with this crazy ass plan.

"A road trip? How in the hell am I going to get her to go to Lake Tahoe with me? She's engaged for God's sake."

"This isn't actually that bad of an idea. I think it could work. You need to spend some time with her alone. You know, nothing creepy. Just old friends getting to know one another. Show her what she's been missing," Ford said.

"I can't believe you're agreeing with him. This is a first. And how the hell do I get her to go to Tahoe with me? You expect me to just say, *hey, Laney, I know you're engaged and all, but I thought you might want to go alone with me to Lake Tahoe and talk?* Are you both fucking crazy? She will never go for that."

"Har, Har, Har." Jack shook his head with disappointment. "Of course, she won't go for that. She pretends that she actually likes to follow the rules. So, we have to trick her into breaking them. And deep down, no one loves breaking the rules as much as Laney Mae. So, we come up with a reason for you to go to Tahoe. Leave the details to me. I've got this. You just play along, brother. And I will get you both in that car tomorrow morning. Trust me."

"Well, he is a pro at the deceitful shit, I'll give him that. You've been pulling the wool over Mom's eyes since birth." Ford shook his head. "But why would Har need to go to Tahoe in the middle of the week?"

"Like I said, I'll figure out the details. You just show up and look pretty. Can you handle that?"

I rolled my eyes. "Yes."

I was making a deal with the devil, but I didn't care. I'd do just about anything to get Laney back. Even if it meant playing along with one of Jack's crazy schemes.

I was all in.

———

I made it to the winery early and Jack met me there. He'd asked me what time Laney was coming in this morning and told me to be ready. I did what I was told, because questioning my brother would be more work than just playing along.

"Morning, Sunshine," Jack said as he strolled in my office and dropped to sit in the chair across from me.

"Hey," I said, watching him suspiciously. He had that look he'd get when he was up to something. Hell, my brother was always up to something.

He mouthed the words, *she's here*, and thrusted his thumb at the wall beside me.

"I can't go with you," he said, louder than usual, catching me off guard.

I narrowed my gaze and whisper-shouted, "What?"

He shook his head and rolled his eyes, before pushing to his feet. "You've got to go, Har. We need this. And you've got to get out of here before Mom gets here and is suspicious. What the fuck are we going to do?"

He was shouting now, and I had no idea what I was supposed to do or say. I stared at him and he used his hand to cover his ridiculous grin.

"Everything okay?" Laney leaned in the doorway and looked between us, and Jack raised a brow at me and smirked.

"No, Laney Mae. Everything is not okay." Jack harrumphed, pacing around like he was in great distress.

"What's going on? Can I help?" she asked.

Jack came to a stop and studied her. "Actually, you just might be able to help."

"No, I've got this," I said, pushing to my feet, not even sure what we were talking about, but I had a feeling if I was too agreeable it would look suspicious.

"You're not driving there and back alone. It's not safe," Jack insisted, running a hand through his hair. And damn if my brother wasn't a brilliant actor, because he actually appeared concerned.

"Driving where? What's going on?" Laney whispered, like she was being let in on a grand secret.

"It's Dad's birthday in a few days. Har and I were supposed to road trip to Tahoe to get something for Mom, because it's the only thing that gets her through this day. You see normally we all go to Tahoe on his birthday, but this year we can't because we're swamped here at the winery and at Montgomery Media. Mom is going to be devastated without it. We can't have that. She's been through enough. So, we've got to get it." Jack was frantic now. Like his life depended on getting whatever bullshit he was talking about. We never went to Tahoe on Dad's birthday, nor did we have to retrieve anything from the house. But he was putting on a good show, and she was buying it.

"Oh my gosh. What is it? What do you have to go get?" Laney asked, looking between us.

Jack held his hand up to me and shook his head violently. "Don't, Har. We shouldn't. It's very personal. Something our parents shared, Laney Mae. It's too painful to talk about. Please don't make us."

She placed a hand on her heart. Jesus, he was pouring it on pretty damn thick. "Of course, I won't. I'm so sorry. So why can't you go now?"

"Because there's a political story that just broke this morning, and Ford needs me. This is the only day Har can go. I don't want him driving roundtrip by himself. It's not safe. He's been working long hours and I don't think it's a good idea."

"I'll be fine," I blurted and they both turned to look at me. "I'm going. Mom needs this."

We'd both probably rot in hell for lying—but I was okay with it if it meant she'd come with me.

"Why can't you take the helicopter?" she asked.

Great fucking question.

"Because Mom gets notified when we take it and where we go. We want to surprise her with this. She'd definitely be suspicious." My brother paced around some more and when I looked up, he winked before turning back to face Laney. "Maybe you could drive with him? You know, just ride co-pilot?"

"Don't be ridiculous. I'm a grown man, I can drive there and back on my own." I grabbed my keys off the desk and walked toward the door, unsure of what she'd do.

"Wait. Where would your mom think I was if I went with you?" she said, and I stopped at the door but didn't turn around.

"I'd tell her we needed you both in the city for an event for the company. Harrison goes back and forth all the time, so she won't question him going. You two can drop me at the helicopter and take off from there."

I turned around to see her chewing her thumbnail.

"Laney, I'm fine going on my own. You don't need to do this."

"That's a lot of driving for someone to do on their own. What if you doze off behind the wheel?" Jack threw his hands in the air and it took all I had in me not to laugh. I'd made that trip hundreds of times before.

"I'm not a child. I'll be fine."

"He's right. You shouldn't go alone. I can go with you. I haven't been in a long time. We'll be back tonight, right?" she asked.

"Yes. Are you sure?"

"Yeah. It's fine. I can work a little on my phone." She moved past me and walked down the hall toward her office. I glanced back at my brother who was doing some ridiculous dance and thrusting his hips around like a fool, while his arms swung above his head.

"We're going to burn in hell," I whispered.

"It's fine. We'll be together, Har-bear. I passed you the ball, now take the shot."

I nodded and we met Laney out in the hall. Mom was just walking into the winery. "What's going on? Where are you all off to?"

"Do you mind if we borrow Laney for the day? Ford has a big event he needs to put together for the fundraiser, and we need Har today for some help with that political story that's blowing up."

She waved her hand in front of her face. "Of course. No problem. As long as it's okay with Laney."

"Yep. Happy to go wherever I'm needed."

"Be safe. I'll see you all later."

"You're a natural bullshitter, Jack-ass." Laney laughed once we were outside.

She had no idea just how good he was. Mom wasn't the only one he'd deceived.

"It's a gift, Laney Mae."

We dropped Jack off at the helicopter and jumped on the freeway.

I had eight hours alone in the car with Laney to make some progress.

My brother got her here. Now I needed to make her stay.

eleven

. . .

Laney

WE DROVE in silence for a few minutes after we dropped off Jack.

"Thanks for coming with me. You didn't need to. I would have been fine." Harrison rubbed the back of his neck, as his other hand stayed on the steering wheel. I studied his profile. His chiseled jaw was peppered in day-old scruff. His dark gaze was trained on the road ahead, and his tongue dipped out to wet his bottom lip. I squirmed in my seat and looked away.

"It's fine. Jack's right. It's a long drive by yourself."

"Jack has the attention span of a Labrador. A drive to the neighbor's house is a long journey for him," he said, and my head fell back in laughter.

This was the problem, right? It was easy when I was with Harrison. We'd always just sort of fit and that hadn't changed. I'd never shared a comfort with another person like I had with him. Like I belonged there beside him. And that fact alone terrified me.

"Very true. Do you guys still go to Tahoe often? I know Jack said you go every year on your dad's birthday. Do you still spend summers there?"

"We go up more often in the summer, but not for long periods of time anymore. We're all busy with work these days. I go up on my own occasionally, when I need a break from the city. It's always been one of my favorite places, you know that."

There was more to his words than he let on. I'd always been an expert in reading him. He liked to put on a front like everything was fine—even when it wasn't.

"I used to love spending summers up here with your family. Those were some of my favorite memories."

He nodded. "Yep. We had some good times, right?"

"I haven't been since the last time I went with you. And you know we're going to have to stop and get snacks, right?"

He laughed. "It's nine in the morning. You want flaming hot Cheetos now?"

"Ah, good memory, Montgomery. And yes, I do. And a cola Slurpee."

"Don't forget the peach rings, or have you outgrown those?" He looked over at me and smiled, and my stomach did little flips.

How was that possible? After all these years? He'd always had that effect on me. Did Charlie make my stomach flip? No. Not even in the beginning. I felt content with him, and there was something to be said about that.

"Of course, I haven't outgrown peach rings. Pull over at the next exit."

He shook his head and clicked his turn signal to get off the highway.

Once we loaded up on snacks and got back on the road, I checked in on Mom before dropping my phone in my purse.

"Is she doing all right?" he asked, taking a sip from his water bottle and setting it down in the center console.

"Yeah. She's doing really well, considering all she's going through. She thought it was great that I was driving with you to Tahoe." I rolled my eyes. My mother wanted us to find some closure, so of course she thought the road trip was a good idea.

He chuckled. "And how do you feel about it? I mean, we're friends, right? We can spend a few hours in the car together."

He looked over and winked, and I turned away quickly to glance out the window.

"Sure. It's harmless." I popped a few hot Cheetos in my mouth and handed him one. "Come on. One Cheeto is not going to kill you."

He rolled his eyes and held out his hand. Harrison always ate healthier than I did, but he'd occasionally indulge. "I don't even like these. Why do you force me to eat them?"

"Because they grow on you over time." I laughed.

He popped one in his mouth and I was mesmerized as I watched him chew, making a face as if it were the worst thing he'd ever tasted. I popped a few more in my mouth and turned back to him, just as he dipped his finger in his mouth and sucked off the orange remnants. I could still remember how he tasted. The way his lips felt pressed against mine. The way he always took control when he kissed me. And damn, was it hot in here?

I tried to shake off the feeling just as a chunk of Cheeto lodged itself in my throat. I coughed hard, but I couldn't get it out. I reached for my Slurpee but couldn't stop coughing long enough to take a sip.

"Jesus, are you okay?" he asked, his arm reaching for my back.

I leaned forward trying to force it out. I needed air. I couldn't stop coughing. The car swerved violently and before I could process what was happening, Harrison was out of his seat and unbuckling me. He climbed over, pushed the door open, and leaned me forward. There were no notable sounds. My coughing ceased. One strong arm wrapped around me and the other pounded on my back.

Harder and harder.

"Breathe, Laney."

A piece of hard Cheeto shot out of my mouth and onto the ground, as tears streamed down my face.

Harrison wrapped both arms around me and held me close. "You're okay. How many times have I told you that processed food will kill you?"

I laughed as tears continued to fall. I mean, here was this sexy man holding me close, and I'd just puked up a piece of orange crap right in front of him. Yet I didn't want to move. I didn't want this moment to end. I leaned back to look up at him and pressed my cheek to his chest.

"It might be worth an early death though, right?" I asked.

He smiled, using his thumb to swipe the moisture from my cheek. "You okay?"

I nodded. I didn't have the heart to tell him that I was so mesmerized watching him suck his finger that I forgot to chew.

"Can you hand me my Slurpee?" I asked, as one hand wrapped around his forearm, keeping him there.

"No. Drink this water," he said, opening the bottle and handing it to me. "You don't wash down crap with more crap."

"So bossy."

"I did just save your life. I think you have to listen to me now." His voice was gruff, as his fingers grazed my collarbone.

What was I doing? Playing with fire, that's what.

I pushed forward and moved to stand. We were on the side of the highway, and a car sped by, looking over as it passed.

"You reacted awfully quick. I'm sure I would have coughed it up on my own, if you hadn't climbed on top of me like a crazy person." I placed my hands on my hips and studied him.

He laughed and stepped out of the car to stretch his legs. "What can I say? I have bat-like reflexes."

I rolled my eyes. "Okay, Batman. Let's get back on the road. Show's over."

I moved past him and slipped into the car. Maybe this wasn't a good idea. The closeness. He was everywhere. Surrounding me. His scent. His presence. It was too much.

"Do you want me to go around the car to get in or climb back over you? It may be safer to get in on this side," he said with a smirk, as he held the handle to the passenger door. His heated gaze took me in as his tongue swiped out to wet his bottom lip.

I shook my head. "Don't even think about it, Montgomery."

"Okay. I guess I'll just have to risk my life getting in." He laughed before leaning over me and tugging my seat belt across my body.

I slapped his hand away. "I can buckle myself."

"Were you waiting for an invitation?" he asked, before clicking it in beside my waist. I breathed him in before he pulled away. Cedar and jasmine filled my senses, and I closed my eyes for a minute and remembered how familiar it was. How familiar he was.

He got in the driver's seat and pulled out on the highway.

"Thanks, Har," I said, after a long stretch of silence.

"Don't be silly. There's nothing I wouldn't do for you." His eyes were trained on the road, but I didn't miss the tick of his jaw.

"I'm glad we were able to put everything behind us."

"Me too."

"So, how do you feel about your dad's birthday coming up? Are you doing okay with everything?" I asked.

"Yeah. I just miss him."

So honest. I'd always loved that he'd tell me how he felt. He kept a mask on for others, but never with me. I was glad that hadn't changed.

"I get that. I was so scared when Mom called and told me she had cancer. The thought of losing her—it terrified me. And I know how close you and your father were. Grieving sucks."

He smiled and nodded. "Glad to see you still just say what you think, Laney."

It had been a while since I'd felt like myself, but these past few weeks had been good for me. Being home—it was good for me.

"Always."

We continued our conversation for hours. It was easy. It'd always been easy. My phone buzzed with a text from Charlie.

Charlie ~ How's work going?

I gazed out the window wondering if I should tell him. But why would I hide it? I wasn't doing anything wrong, and God knows, Charlie never seemed to be the slightest bit concerned.

Me ~ Hey. Actually, on my way to Tahoe to get something for Monica Montgomery. It's a quick trip there and back. I'll be home tonight. How's your day?

Charlie ~ Well, aren't you just living the life? My day is not nearly as exciting as yours. Meetings. Nothing exciting. Certainly, no trip to the lake.

Me ~ LOL. I'll call you tonight.

Charlie ~ Love you.

Me ~ Love you, too.

I dropped my phone in my purse again.

"Was that your mom again? Is she okay?" Harrison asked.

"No. It was Charlie."

"Ah." He paused before glancing over at me. "Does he know about our, uh, history?"

I intertwined my fingers and squeezed. "Um. Not everything. I mean, he knows you and I used to date. That's all he really needs to know, right?"

He shrugged. "I don't know? I mean, I'd want to know everything about my fiancée, I guess. But that's just me."

I huffed. I wasn't in the mood to be judged. "We aren't like that. We don't need to tell one another everything. We have a mature relationship. We trust one another."

He nodded and stared out at the road in front of us. Large green pine trees on one side, and yellow flowers scattered across tall peaks on the other. "Who are you convincing, Laney? Me or you?"

"I'm not convincing anyone. It's the truth."

"All right. We can agree to disagree. Tell me about Chicago. Do you like living there?"

I was thankful for a safe topic. "I love it there. Nat's there, so that's a plus."

I paused to think about my life in Chicago. I had Nat and Charlie, a few friends from work, Taco Tuesdays up the street. That was about it. It didn't sound like much of a life when I said it aloud.

He nodded. "Nice. Do you ever miss home?"

"Honestly, I really never thought about it. But being home now, I realize how much I miss it."

"Yeah?"

I bit down hard on the inside of my cheek. The way he looked at me when he glanced over had my stomach doing all sorts of twists and turns. I lowered my window to let some air in, and my hair blew around wildly.

He chuckled and turned the air up. "You warm?"

His tone was all tease and I tried to keep it together before I put my window back up. "You know I always get a little carsick."

"Well, maybe if you didn't eat all that orange crap, you'd feel better."

"Do you still want to get married and have a family someday?" I asked, suddenly desperate to know what his plans were for the future. Friends talked about that stuff, right?

"That was quite a segue." He chuckled, and his gaze stayed on the road. "I don't really know, Laney."

"What do you mean, you don't know? You've always known what you wanted, Har."

He shrugged and glanced over at me. "I guess I changed too."

"How so?" I pressed.

"You want to do this? Because if you want me to share, then you have to do the same. Wasn't that always *your* rule?"

I rolled my eyes. "This is not truth or dare. It's conversation."

"And it works both ways. I'll tell you something if you tell me something."

"That's very juvenile." I folded my arms over my chest. "But fine. How have you changed?"

"I don't know that I changed, per se, but what I *want* changed."

"Go on."

"I used to want all those things, because I wanted them with you. Without you, none of those things sound appealing." His tone remained even, but I didn't miss the tick in his jaw. Nor did I miss the sound of my frantically beating heart. I took a moment to process his words. They were honest.

Raw.

And heartbreaking.

"Okay," I whispered, before shaking my head and looking out the window. It wasn't the answer I expected. "So, just because my parents thought I should go back to school, you decided that meant you needed to break up with me? Why?"

I'd been dying to ask this ever since he'd opened up about hearing that conversation with my parents all those years ago. But I hadn't worked up the nerve.

"Well, think about it, Laney. Would you have left if I hadn't?"

"I don't know. I wasn't given the opportunity," I said, turning to face him.

"You wouldn't have, and we both know it. There was a lot of truth to what your parents said that night. Hell, my mom said the same thing. They all knew you would stay for *me*. You'd always done what was best for me. And it hit home. I thought I was doing the right thing, I really did. And I wasn't much good for anyone at that time. I was drowning in grief and didn't need to bring you down."

I chewed on the inside of my cheek as I processed his words.

"You never brought me down, Har." My voice cracked, and he glanced over and looked at me before returning his gaze to the road.

"Okay. I gave you an answer. Tell me more about this big change of yours," he said.

"I told you…I'm less trusting."

"That's your big change? You're less trusting? Bullshit, Laney. Tell me how you've changed."

I leaned back and thought about it. "I don't know. Mom says I lost some of my light, and maybe she's right."

"I don't think so. I see it there. It's always shining."

I fought back the tears that threatened to burst. I *had* lost my light. But maybe he was right. Maybe I was getting it back after all this time.

"Thanks for telling me the reason why you broke up with me. Even all these years later, it helps to know what happened."

"Yeah, I never told anyone about it. It was one of those secrets I thought I'd take to the grave. But you deserved to know."

"How does it feel, getting it off your chest?" I asked.

"Pretty good, actually." He laughed. "At least it helps me explain to you what I was thinking back then. But hell, after Dad's accident, I don't think anything made sense to me."

I nodded. "Yeah. I get that. Sometimes things happen that change you forever."

"Forever is a long time, Laney. Nothing, not even grief, lasts forever. It just takes time. I'll never stop missing him, but I've learned how to live without him."

"I'm glad to hear that."

"You got any secrets you want to unload on me?" he teased, and my chest squeezed. Because if I could say the words aloud to anyone, it would be Harrison.

"Nope. Nothing juicy to share." I laughed.

We continued to talk all the way to Tahoe. And for the first time in forever, I was exactly where I wanted to be.

twelve

. . .

Harrison

I HATED THIS DAY, almost as much as the day Dad died. His birthday had always been a huge celebration at our house. Mom liked to plan these elaborate surprises for him. My father was social and loved by many, and I still felt the loss of him every single day. But his birthday was a reminder of a life taken way too soon. We still had more to do together.

Jack had spent the night in Napa last night at our family home, as he usually stayed at his apartment in the city, but he didn't want Mom to be alone. Mom asked me to come over for breakfast, and Ford and Harley surprised us all when they walked in.

"Hey," Ford said, walking straight for our mother and wrapping his arms around her. It was a rarity for my brother to miss a morning at the office in the city, but Harley was good for him. I'm sure this was her doing, as he'd been spending a lot more time with all of us since he'd met her.

"This is such a nice surprise," Mom said, and Lorena came out with two more place settings.

"Harls, thanks for coming and making this one show his face during work hours." Jack pointed at Ford, and everyone chuckled.

"How do you know it wasn't my idea?" Ford raised a brow in challenge.

"Because you're an asshole by nature," our younger brother said.

"Are you really going to start with me?" Ford moved in Jack's face. These two liked to set one another off every chance they got, and I wasn't in the mood today.

"Was it your idea?" I stepped between them, forcing them to each take a step back.

"Hell, no. My better half is far more thoughtful than I am. I just didn't know you all knew it too." Ford moved toward Harley and took his seat.

"We are all very aware." Jack smirked.

"Come on, brother. It's not the day to start shit with him," I said, steering him toward the other side of the table.

"Got it," he mumbled.

I wasn't in the mood to babysit these two. I'd been doing it my entire life, and my patience was running thin today.

"Well, now that we've established that I'm the *wiser half*, and Ford's just my arm candy, let's eat," Harley said.

Laughter filled the room, and it was nice to escape the doom and gloom of the day, if even for just a moment. We passed the platters around, scooping waffles and bacon and fresh fruit onto our plates.

"So, Harrison, how did things go with Laney Mae in Tahoe?" Ford asked.

"It went well, actually. It was nice to have uninterrupted time to catch up." Laney and I were making progress. We'd spent the entire day together, and even took the boat for a spin up at the lake before we drove back. We caught up on years of conversations that we'd lost and I was surprised when I pulled into her driveway that I wasn't ready for our trip to be over yet. I don't think she was either.

Jack moaned and buried his face in his hands. "Catch up? This wasn't a girls' night out, Har. You were supposed to take the shot."

"You have to set the shot up before you take it," I grumbled and scooped fruit onto my plate.

"What shot? When were you in Tahoe?" Mom asked, and we all looked at one another before Jack answered her.

"It was nothing. Just helping Har-bear out with Laney Mae." Jack spoke around a mouthful of food.

She shook her head. "Finish chewing before you speak, Jackie boy. Is something wrong with Laney?"

"Nothing is wrong with Laney. Can we please change the subject?" I hissed. My mood was darkening by the minute.

"Don't wait too long. You need to do something about it before she marries someone else." Ford dabbed the corner of his mouth with his napkin. "This is not the time to play peacekeeper, brother."

I scoffed at the mention of the nickname Dad gave me years ago. Yeah, I was the peacekeeper amongst this group of crazy. Neither of my brothers had a patient bone in their body, nor did they think before they acted most of the time. I played it safe, sure. But it had gotten me far in life. Unlike the two hotheaded guys at the table.

"And what is it you think I should do?" I set my fork down and stared at my older brother.

"Something. Anything. Tell her how you feel," he said.

"There's obviously still feelings there. Even I see it, and I've only just met Laney. By the way, I like her. A lot. She's good peeps. You need to make that happen, Har-bear." Harley cocked her head and met my gaze, and a big smile spread across her pretty face.

I tended to listen to her much more than I did my brothers. They acted first, thought later. Harley was more rational. Even-keeled. Wise.

"Yeah, I think that ship has sailed." My chest tightened as the words left my mouth. The truth was—Laney was marrying someone else. I'd put myself out there, and she hadn't given me anything back.

"That ship hasn't sailed. Blow that shit up. Tell her how you feel. Make some fucking noise," Jack said, turning to face our mother and opening his mouth wide to show her that he had swallowed his food.

This is the guy I'm supposed to take advice from?

"Language, sweetheart," Mom whispered, and we all chuckled again. She'd never stop trying to keep Jack in check. He was her wild card.

"She's happy. I'm not a selfish prick. I'm not going to complicate things for her."

"Do you still love her?" Mom asked, surprising everyone with her question. I didn't think she'd be chiming in on this too.

I leaned back in my chair. "I'll always love her. Doesn't mean I'm supposed to mess her life up."

"Yes, it does, honey. It may complicate things, but she has a right to know."

"She told me she's happy. Multiple times. I'm just glad she finally stopped hating me. We're friends," I said, scrubbing a hand over my coarse scruff.

"Why did she hate you all this time?" Harley asked, scooping some fruit onto her plate.

"I broke her heart."

"But didn't you try to reach out a few months later? She never spoke to you again?"

"Not until now. She was angry. I get it."

"You can't be that angry unless there's real feelings there, right?" Harley and my mom shared a glance.

"Shake shit up, man. Stop being the good guy for once in your goddamned life. Make some waves. Make some noise. Break the rules." Once again, Jack spoke around a mouthful of bacon.

Mom threw her hands in the air in defeat and we all chuckled.

"Dude, I did that once. Remember? I broke up with her. That definitely shook shit up." I tossed my napkin on the table because I was done with this conversation. It was Dad's birthday. They were agitating me. I needed space.

"That was you trying to do the right thing," Ford said to my back as I left the room.

I didn't need them to psychoanalyze me or try to figure this out. I didn't need advice. Laney Mae Landers was the center of my universe throughout my adolescence, and I'd grieved that loss just as I'd grieved the death of my father. But some things weren't in our control. Dad's accident. Laney's engagement. What was I supposed to do? Tell her not to marry Charlie? She loved him. I was her past. He was her future. And me having a temper tantrum wasn't going to change that.

I made my way to the office. Every muscle in my body tensed. I walked because I was fairly certain I wasn't going to remain sober past noon today. Mom was going into the city to have dinner with Jack, Ford, and Harley. I had already declined and said I'd be busy at the winery. I didn't want to drag this out. I'd have a few shots of whiskey and sleep it off. Tomorrow would be a better day.

I sat behind my desk taking care of payroll, orders, and looking over the events scheduled for the next few months. I had a com call with our marketing director about a few ads we were running, and lunch had come and gone. The knock on the door startled me as I stared at my monitor reading an email.

"Yeah. It's open," I grumbled.

Laney stood on the other side of the door. Her hand gripped the knob as she spoke. "Hey. Haven't seen you today. How are you doing? I know it's a tough day."

"I'm fine."

"You're not fine, Har." She stood there awkwardly, as I didn't respond. I didn't have the energy to convince one more person that I was okay. "Do you, um, have anything fun planned for your birthday?"

She remembered my birthday. Three days after Dad's. This girl knew me. Knew everything. Every secret. Every fear. Every dream.

"Yeah. I don't celebrate my birthday all that much these days."

"You know I loved your dad, too. I say a little prayer and talk to him every year on his special day."

My father adored Laney. He hadn't been close with Ford's ex-girl-friend, Madison, at the time of his passing, and Jack always had a slew of girls he'd introduced to him—but Laney—she was his favorite. She'd been part of the family ever since we were kids.

"I'm sure he loves that." I chuckled. "He loved to mess with Laney Mae Landers."

He always called her by her full name, and he teased the hell out of her every chance he got. My heart ached. I missed him.

She laughed. A full-bodied, deep soulful sound moved around the room. "You know, he wouldn't like you moping around and skipping your own birthday, right?"

I nodded.

"Yeah, I'll keep that in mind. So, what are you up to?" I asked because she appeared nervous as she moved to sit in the chair across from me.

"Um, nothing. I just wanted to let you know I'm not working tomorrow. I already spoke to your mom. I meant to tell you when we went to Tahoe, but I just, I don't know. I forgot to mention it."

I studied her. She avoided my gaze and messed with her skirt as she sat there quietly. Laney wasn't ever at a loss for words.

"Does your mom have an appointment?"

"I'm flying home in the morning. To Chicago. Charlie has a work event he wants me to go to, so I'm taking a long weekend."

Of course, she fucking was. Because just when I thought this day couldn't get worse, it did. This was a slow painful torture—spending all this time with the girl I loved, only to watch her walk away and marry someone else. What the fuck was I even doing?

I pushed to my feet and stormed toward the door. "This is your fucking home, Laney. You're the only one that doesn't know it."

"What are you talking about?" she said from behind me, and I turned around to see her on her feet, huffing behind me.

This time she didn't get to be upset. Sure, I'd fucked up five years ago. I'd ended things for the wrong reasons. But none of that mattered now. She was marrying someone else, and I was living in the past. And I was fucking sick of being haunted by the ghosts of my past.

"You heard me. Go run to Charlie and keep pretending you don't belong here. I don't give a shit anymore."

I slammed my office door behind me, which made no sense because I'd just left her alone in there. But I needed space.

Distance.

Quiet.

Whiskey.

I walked to my house and grabbed the bottle of liquor and slammed back two shots before I dropped to sit on the couch and calmed the fuck down.

Dad was dead.

Laney was marrying someone else.

And fuck if the pain wasn't overwhelming. My phone continued to vibrate on the coffee table, and I threw it up against the wall. I grabbed the bottle of whiskey and cut through my backyard, leading to the winery. I trudged all the way to the barn where I knew no one would bother me. This had always been a place of comfort for me since I was a kid. Memories of Dad and memories of Laney filled my head as I tipped the bottle back and let the cool liquid make its way down my throat and through my body. Numbing and warming all the places that needed it most. Yeah, call it what you will—my own pity party—but fuck it, I needed it. I yanked off my tie and my dress shirt and tossed them on the hay barrel, leaving me in just a T-shirt and dress slacks. I stumbled to sit down and take off my shoes. This was as good of a place as any to sleep it off. Hell, the horses weren't half as annoying as my nosy ass brothers. If Mom saw me, she'd worry. It would be better if I was out of sight tonight. And Laney, well, she was packing for her trip home. To her new home. Her home wasn't with me anymore, and it was time I realized that. I dropped to sit on the filthy floor and leaned my back against the hay bale.

The horses moved around in their stalls, and I heard a few grunts, and the sound of hay crushing against the floor. I tipped my head back and took a few more long pulls.

My father had always praised me for keeping my cool under pressure. I'd been proud of the nickname he'd given me. But where did that get me now? Alone in a barn.

A drunk, numb, peacekeeper.

Sorry, Dad.

———

Someone shook me, and I jerked up to see who it was. I was lying facedown on the cool floor covered in hay and dirt. My head pounded. My mouth was dry. A bit of light from the moon came through the opening of the doors in the barn. And that's when I saw her.

Laney.

She pulled me up and dropped to sit beside me so I could lean against her. "Jesus, Har. What are you doing here? Your mom is frantic. Jack called me in a panic. Your mom found your phone smashed at your house, and no one knew where you were."

"But you knew where I was, didn't you?" My slurred words were barely comprehendible, which made me laugh, so I continued. "Yeah, you knew, Maney Lae Manders."

Holy shit. I butchered her name, which made me laugh even harder and caused me to fall forward. She leaned over and pulled me up to sit again, wrapping her arms around me. She brushed something from my face, and her warm hand rested on my cheek. I put my hand over hers, needing to touch her. I turned a little, and my face rested on her chest.

"God, you have perfect tits," I said before laughing again. I didn't give a fuck. She was leaving tomorrow to go see her fiancé, so what did I have to lose?

"Okay, drunkard. Let's get you to your feet. Do you think you can walk?" Her voice was my favorite sound. I didn't want to move. I didn't want this to end.

"No. Stay here with me." I turned so I could breathe in her lavender scent, nestling my face in her cleavage.

"Oh my god, Harrison. *Stop.*" She turned my face away, so my cheek was resting against her chest.

"What, Laney? You don't like me to tell you how I feel?"

"You can tell me whatever you want. You can't put your face in my boobs. Fair?"

I laughed so hard tears sprang from my eyes. I didn't know if I was laughing or crying anymore. I held her hand against my cheek, needing her more than I wanted to admit.

"I'm sorry. I'm so sorry for hurting you. Can't you forgive me this one time? Come back to me. I want you back, Laney. I want you back so bad I can't see straight."

"Harrison," she whispered, and two tear drops landed on my forearm, so I knew they'd come from her.

"I made a mistake. A stupid mistake that ruined my life," I mumbled, as I closed my eyes and drifted off in her arms.

"It's okay. I forgive you," she whispered, and I kept hold of her hand on my cheek and reached for the other one resting in my lap. I held both her hands, as if I could keep her there forever if I held on tight enough.

Laura Pavlov

"I love you, Laney. I'll love you forever. Come back to me." I swiped my tongue out to wet my bottom lip and tasted the salty tears that had rolled down my face. Both mine and Laney's.

I drifted away after I'd confessed everything to her. I was at peace.

Always the peacekeeper.

I jolted awake as the sun hit my face. I squinted through the obscene amount of light as cars honked in the distance. It was ridiculously loud. My god, was someone setting off fireworks? My head pounded, and I turned my face to see my brother. Jack. He was carrying me.

What the actual fuck?

"Put me down," I shouted, before my ass hit the seat of his truck.

"No problem, asshole. You're not all that light to lug around."

I pulled the door closed and waited for him to get in the driver's seat. "Why the fuck are you carrying me?"

"Well, let's see...you had Mom in a panic, convinced that something happened to you. We had to call Laney Mae because Ford and I were in the city last night. She found you around 1:00 a.m. and stayed with you until I could get there this morning to pick your drunk ass up. She had a plane to catch and barely made it to the airport." He pulled out on the road and drove toward my house.

"Shit. She stayed there till this morning?"

"Yep. She wouldn't leave. Ford and I were going to get on the helicopter last night, and she insisted she'd just sleep in the barn till morning. But I doubt she got any sleep with your drunk ass lying in her lap and clinging to her the way you were." He had an evil grin on his face, and I rolled my eyes.

"Jesus. How was she this morning?"

"She didn't say much. Poor thing had to sleep sitting up. Once I got there, she hurried to her car and said she had to get to the airport."

My head fell back against the seat and I closed my eyes.

"Oh, fuck."

"What?" he asked, pulling into my driveway.

"I think I told her I loved her."

He turned to face me, letting his seat belt slap back toward the door. "Well, that's one way to set shit on fire."

112

I pushed the door open and nearly lost my balance getting out of the truck. Jack hurried around to the passenger side and hooked my arm over his shoulder. He helped me through the door and dropped me on the sofa. He walked to the kitchen and clanked a few cabinets before starting the coffee.

"Remind me to never take your advice again," I called out.

"No one told you to drink a bottle of whiskey before you told her."

"Now she probably hates me again. I think I begged her to take me back. Fuck. Why'd I have to drink so much?" I asked, rubbing my temples, as he set a mug of black brew in front of me.

"Maybe it's the smartest thing you've done in a long time." He dropped to sit beside me, taking a sip of coffee and nodding.

"How do you figure?"

"You finally put it out there. You told her how you felt, Har-bear. Now let's see what she does with it."

"I was drunk."

"You were honest."

"She's going to run, trust me." I set my mug down on the coffee table and leaned back against the sofa.

"I don't know. She looked pretty concerned about you this morning. Not sure how many engaged women spend the night with their drunk ex-boyfriend on the floor of a barn."

I let out a long, slow breath. "Jack?"

"Yeah, brother."

"I miss Dad and I miss Laney."

"There you go. Was that so fucking hard? I know you do. Now you've got to fight if you really want her. Because Dad's gone, brother. We can't change that. But Laney—she's alive and well."

"What should I do?"

"Well, I think when she comes back from Chicago, you need to tell her the same things you said last night when you're sober."

"Okay," I said, sliding down to lie on the couch. I was fucking tired. But I'd slept in Laney Landers' arms, and I'd sure as fuck give up sleep any day of the week to do that again.

I'd give up everything.

thirteen

. . .

Laney

"GIRL, spill it. I can tell there's something on your mind," Natalie said, as she glanced over to see Charlie and Jared standing at the bar with a few of their coworkers. Jared worked at the same company as Charlie, which made their work events all the more fun.

"What? I told you my mom is doing really well, and all is good back in Napa."

"Mm-hmm. Right. So, you got in this afternoon? I never heard back from you last night." Nat worked in marketing, but I'd always teased her that she would have made a great CIA agent. She had a gift of prying information out of me.

"Yeah, I got in this afternoon. We grabbed a late lunch and then it was time to get ready for tonight."

"You're avoiding my question about last night. Where were you? I texted you a couple times."

My gaze moved to Charlie, who was still standing at the bar talking. I leaned in close to her. "I ended up sleeping at the Montgomery barn because Harrison got plastered and his family was worried about him."

Her brows cinched together. "And they called you to find him?"

Nat knew about my history with Harrison as she'd known us as a couple our first two years at Columbia. She'd seen me fall apart after our breakup, and she'd always been there for me. And she'd help put me back together when she introduced me to Charlie.

"They were in the city and they were worried about him. And I knew he'd be at the barn. That's always been his go-to place." I fiddled with the napkin in my lap. We sat at a round table in the back of the outdoor tented area. Chatter and laughter filled the air, and the smell of barbeque drifted around us.

"And what happened when you got there?" Nat's dark gaze danced with curiosity. She was probably the one person who knew the depths of my relationships with both Charlie and Harrison.

"He was really drunk. I couldn't get him up, so I just sat there with him to make sure he was okay."

"Did he talk to you? Tell you what he was upset about?"

I nodded and bit down on my bottom lip. "He was upset about it being his dad's birthday."

"And…"

Damn, this girl knew me too well. There'd only been one secret in my life that I'd ever successfully kept from her.

"He also told me that he missed me," I paused to look around, my eyes landing on Charlie before returning to my best friend. "Actually, he said he missed me, and he loved me."

She gasped and slapped the table. "What the actual hell? And you waited this long to tell me?"

"Um, kind of been busy spending the day with my actual fiancé." I shook my head with disbelief. How was this my life?

"I knew that Tahoe trip was bullshit. I mean, he went all the way there to grab a T-shirt from the drawer. It made no sense. Well, it sure as hell does now. He wanted to spend time with you, Laney."

I rolled my eyes. "I don't know. Maybe you're right."

"Listen, Laney, I'm going to say something to you, and you can take it or leave it. But as your best friend, it's my duty to do so." She clapped her hands together and intertwined her fingers. "I know how long it took you to get over Harrison, which is why I pushed so hard for you to get back out there and date when we moved here. I wanted you to be happy. But if Charlie doesn't do that for you, you aren't doing you or him a favor by dragging this out. He's a great guy, but if he's not the right guy, you need to say something. I've been listening to you these past few weeks since you've been home, and you've sounded really good. Full of life. And if that's because of Harrison, then you need to do something about it."

I shook my head and dabbed at my eyes with my napkin. "How? How do I do that to him?"

"I know it's going to suck, trust me. I love Charlie. But I love you too, and I don't want you to spend your life regretting a decision you made out of guilt. Life is short, Laney. You deserve to be happy. And Charlie deserves to marry someone who loves him as much as he loves them. And you and I both know that it's not you."

This wasn't our first conversation discussing this very issue. Long before Harrison Montgomery came back into the picture, Nat thought something was missing, and I couldn't convince her differently. Because I knew it too.

"He deserves better," I whispered.

She placed a hand on my shoulder. "You both deserve better."

"What's going on over here?" Charlie asked, setting a glass of wine in front of me and squeezing my shoulder.

"Oh, you know, just girl talk." I forced a smile.

"How is it possible that you two talk every day and still have this much to talk about?" Jared asked, sliding in the seat beside his girlfriend.

"Laney was just asking me when our lazy butts were going to pick a wedding date," Natalie said, with a huge grin spread across her face before throwing me a wink.

"You've got to be exhausted from traveling and all the running around we did today. Are you ready to get out of here?" Charlie asked.

"Yeah, sure." I pushed to my feet and promised to call Nat tomorrow so we could hang out.

The drive home was quiet, and my mind wandered to my conversation with my best friend. And then it wandered to Harrison.

Always Harrison.

He consumed my thoughts. He owned my heart. And I now understood that he was the reason I'd never been able to move on. Not really. I was one foot out the door with Charlie from the moment we met. I'd agreed to marry him out of guilt. But he deserved more. I was selling us both short, keeping up with this charade.

We walked into my apartment. I'd asked him if we could sleep here tonight so I could organize a few things this weekend before going back to Napa. My stomach twisted with nerves. Guilt consumed me.

Charlie wrapped his arms around me when we entered my bedroom. His lips lingered against my ear. "I missed you so much, Laney."

"I missed you too," I whispered, fighting back the tears that threatened.

He turned me around in his arms and kissed me. It wasn't like the kiss that he'd greeted me with at the airport. Nor the one that he'd given me before we walked out the door to head to the party. This kiss was heated. Passionate. Needy.

He dropped to sit on the bed, pulling me down on his lap. His fingers tangled in my hair, and he groaned against my mouth.

My mind raced with thoughts of home.

Home.

The place I'd been running from for a long time.

I'd missed it so much more than I realized.

And I wasn't eager to return to my life here in Chicago. Maybe it was because I'd found my home in the process. And I wanted to go back.

Maybe it was Harrison. And what he'd said last night. He was drunk, but his words were raw. Honest. I'd known he still loved me before he'd said the words. I felt it. Deep in my soul.

And I felt the same way about him.

I loved him. I'd never stopped.

But what did that mean?

I didn't have a clue. I didn't know how to move forward because I was stuck. Living under a cloud of secrets and shame.

But I knew one thing for certain: Charlie deserved better. I owed him the truth.

I pressed my hands against his chest and pushed back to look at him, his heavy breaths the only audible sound. The truth lingered just above.

"What is it? Are you okay?"

I shook my head. "I'm not."

He took my hand in his and pressed my palm to his mouth.

"Talk to me, Laney."

I shook my head. I didn't know how to say it. How to rip his heart out. I didn't want to hurt him. He'd been so good to me. But I wasn't doing him any favors by lying.

"Charlie," I said, and the single word broke on a sob. "I'm so sorry."

His puzzled gaze searched mine. "Sorry about what?"

I tipped my head back and closed my eyes, searching for strength from anywhere. I moved off his lap to sit beside him.

"I gave my heart away a long time ago, Charlie. And I never got it back. Not really. And I think if you're really honest with yourself, you'll agree." My voice trembled, and he let my hand fall to my lap.

"Is this about Harrison? You still have feelings for him? Did something happen? Were you unfaithful?" He pushed to his feet, pacing in front of me.

"No. I didn't cheat on you. I wouldn't do that. But that doesn't mean everything is okay. I'm in love with someone else. I don't want to be, I promise you, I don't. I wish this wasn't happening. You've been so good to me. You brought me back to life, Charlie. I love you, I really do. But not in the way that I should." I covered my face and sobbed.

"Jesus." He bent down in front of me, pulling my hands away from my face so he could see me. "Maybe you're just confused? Being home might have stirred up those feelings. Is this something we can fix?"

Shit. Why did he have to be so nice? Why wasn't he screaming at me? Angry with me.

I pushed to my feet and he stood up with me. "I can't change how I feel about someone else. I've just been running from it all these years."

"You're in love with him?"

"Yes. I never stopped loving him." I covered my mouth with my hand to muffle the sobs escaping my throat.

Raw and painful.

"And are you in love with me?"

I looked into his kind blue eyes. How do you hurt someone you care so much for? "Charlie." I bit the inside of my cheek. "You've been so good to me. You mean so much to me. I love you. I do."

He moved closer, towering over me. His gaze locked with mine. "That's not what I asked you, Laney. Are you in love with me?"

I didn't speak. I didn't need to. He saw it there. Written all over my guilty face.

"Wow. Okay. Well, I don't think there's much more to say. I don't want you to marry me because I'm good to you. Or because you feel obligated."

"You deserve better," I croaked.

"You're right, Laney. I do. And you're not who I thought you were."

He turned and walked out the door. His words stung. Because he was right. I hadn't been true to myself or to him. I dropped down on my bed and curled up in the fetal position. Exhaustion and stress set in and took me under.

The room was dark. I'd fallen in and out of sleep, tears waking me several times. I moved to my feet and walked to the bathroom. Flipping on the light, I needed a minute for my vision to focus. I stood in front of the mirror and took in swollen eyes, with dark bags settled beneath. My lips were chapped. My hair was still curled from the party, and I pulled it back in a hair tie at the nape of my neck. I changed into a night shirt and washed my face, squeezing a blob of moisturizer into the palm of my hand and rubbing it over my face. A heavy weight sat on my chest. The look in Charlie's eyes would forever haunt me. Two tears streamed down my cheeks, and I swiped them away.

I moved back to the bedroom to check my phone for the time. It was two o'clock in the morning. There were three texts from Harrison, apologizing about last night. It felt like days had passed since I'd seen him. So much had happened over the past twelve hours. There were a half dozen texts from Nat asking me what happened, as Jared had spoken to Charlie.

I sent Nat a quick response that I'd call her tomorrow. I didn't respond to Harrison. It didn't seem right. I didn't know how to handle my feelings for him. I knew I couldn't marry Charlie, but that didn't mean I was going to run to Harrison with open arms. We were still finding our way with one another. I didn't even live in Napa anymore. There was too much up in the air. I'd have to break the news to my parents that I wasn't getting married. I didn't know what I was doing anymore. I'd ended my engagement, I'd lost my job, my lease was up in a few weeks, and I had no idea what I wanted to do with my life.

My head pounded as I made a cup of tea and sat in the dark crying as I looked down at my mug. My world was spiraling. And I didn't know where I should land.

————

The knock on the door startled me from sleep. I'd dozed off at some point a few hours ago on the couch. I pushed to my feet, looking like a lukewarm mess, I'm sure. Hot mess was too kind a description for my current physical state.

I shuffled my feet toward the door and found Natalie on the other side.

"Hey," I said, and the tears started to fall again.

She shut the door behind her and pulled me in for a hug. "It's going to be okay, Laney."

She guided me to the couch, and I dropped down to face her. "I don't think it will be, Nat. He hates me."

"He doesn't hate you. But it sure looks like you're beating yourself up pretty good all on your own. Listen, Charlie was at our apartment last night. He slept on the couch. He's angry and hurt. But he also owns his part in this."

I pulled my knees up and wrapped my arms around, hugging them tight. My chin rested there. "His part?"

"He talked a lot about when you first met. He said you were very open with him that you weren't looking for anything serious and that he'd fallen hard and fast. Looking back, he feels like he pushed you at every turn."

"No. This is my fault. Not his," I said.

"Laney, he said he knew you didn't want to marry him the day he proposed. You hesitated, and he saw the panic in your eyes, but he wanted it so bad that he let you agree to it. He thought he could love you enough for the both of you. I agree with him. Your heart was never in it. That's the truth. You and I talked about it. You didn't want to move in with him. You didn't want to plan your own wedding. You're a wedding planner, Laney," she said, reaching over and rubbing my shoulder.

"I thought maybe things would change. That I'd grow to love him the way I should over time. I wanted to. But being around Harrison showed me that I am capable of loving someone the right way. I was just trying to force it with Charlie." My words broke on a sob.

"You can't marry someone because you think he's a good guy. It's not okay for either of you. Give him time to heal. He's just hurt right now. He wishes you would have been honest with him sooner, but he said he's glad you told him before you guys got married. The truth is, Laney, he isn't shocked. None of us are, and that's a red flag. You did the right thing."

I swiped at the tears running down my face. "I'm so sorry. I do love him, Nat. I don't know how to fix this."

"Maybe you don't need to. Not right now. I think you guys need to cut off contact for a while. And maybe someday, you'll be able to be friends again. Who the hell knows? But Laney, you need to do some soul searching of your own. You need to figure out why you let things get this far. Why you would have married someone you weren't in love with. I think Charlie played therapist for too long, and you both got comfortable with him being that person for you. You know, the one who kept telling you everything would be okay. You need to be that person for yourself. And then find your happiness. You're one of the best people I know. You deserve to be happy."

"What do I do? Should I call him? Make sure he's okay?"

"He was still there this morning, and he knew I was coming here. He told me to tell you that he'd call you when he was ready. Give him time."

My chest was heavy. And tight. The lump in my throat so thick I stifled the sob as it escaped. "Okay," I said, as the tears blurred my vision.

"We'll keep an eye on him. He's going to be okay, and so are you."

I let her words sink in. I hoped she was right.

I spent the rest of the day in bed, and Nat went and got us a tub of ice cream and hot Cheetos. It was our *go-to* food when either of us were upset about something. I barely moved for hours. I cried, and she listened. I was sad about Charlie. Disappointed in myself. And confused about my future. About where I belonged and what I should do. I realized Charlie was right. It was time to start figuring out what I wanted. Sort through my issues. My fears. My anger. And it wasn't going to happen this weekend. It was a process.

"You're going to be okay, Laney. You took the first step. I think this was a long time coming." Natalie handed me a tissue and I pushed to sit forward.

"Yeah. How did I let it get this far?"

"I think you've known for a long time. You were just stuck. Maybe going home was exactly what you needed."

"Being around Harrison makes me feel things I thought I'd never feel again. It doesn't mean I should be with him, but it made me realize that something was missing with Charlie and me. Something big."

She wrapped an arm around my shoulder. "I'm sorry, Laney. I know you tried, there's no doubt about it," she said, her eyes wet with emotion.

"Thanks for being here," I sobbed. Everything was changing so quickly and the loss of control over my own life terrified me.

Nat and I talked and cried for hours. And then we cried some more. She and Jared had dinner plans with his parents, and I urged her to go. Alone time would allow me to clear my head.

I'd FaceTimed my parents and filled them in on what happened with Charlie. They didn't appear as surprised as I'd expected. I cried, and they listened. They were supportive as always. They begged me to get on the plane and come home so I wouldn't be alone. I agreed to return home the following day.

Harrison's birthday.

I owed him a text back, but I hadn't found the words yet. I didn't know what to say or how much to tell him. I knew I couldn't call him —he'd always been able to read me, and he'd know something was wrong. I asked my parents to keep what happened with Charlie to themselves. I didn't know if I wanted to tell Harrison yet. I feared he'd want to dive back in, and I needed to figure myself out first. I knew I loved him, and that was the reason I'd ended things with Charlie.

The next call I made was to Jenny Lane, a family therapist in Napa. I'd found her online and made an appointment for next week. It was time to reclaim my life, and this was a step in the right direction.

———

I'd been back in Napa for a few hours, and I finally sat down to text Harrison back. I was in a better place now. He'd never know I'd spent the last forty-eight hours crying in the fetal position. And that's the way I wanted to keep it.

Me ~ Happy Birthday! What are you up to today?

I chewed on my fingernail as I waited for him to reply.

Harrison ~ Took you long enough to respond.

I laughed.

Me ~ Sorry. It was a busy couple of days.

Harrison ~ Are you mad at me about my drunken crazy antics? I'm really sorry about that.

Me ~ Not at all. I promise. How's your birthday?

Harrison ~ Just another day, Laney. I told you I don't celebrate. Well, my pain in the ass brothers came by this morning, and I had lunch with Mom. But I'm just ready for the day to pass. I think I might still be hungover from the other day.

I hated the idea of him being alone on his birthday. I chewed on the inside of my cheek as I contemplated what to do.

Me ~ Stop sulking. Get your butt up and meet me at the tree house in an hour. Can you do that?

Harrison ~ Are you serious? Are you going to make me be the dad or the dog?

Me ~ I'll decide when I see you.

Harrison ~ What are you up to, Laney Landers?

Me ~ Nothing. Just some birthday fun.

I hurried to the kitchen to let my parents know I was running out to grab a few things for Harrison's birthday. They were deep in a *Rocky* movie marathon and waved as I ran by.

What was I doing?

We were friends. Friends celebrate one another, right?

I ran to the store and grabbed a few things and hurried up to the tree house to get everything ready.

fourteen

. . .

Harrison

I WALKED OVER TO THE LANDERS' house and followed the paved path to the backyard. Laney sent me a text telling me to meet her at the tree house. I wasn't in the mood to celebrate my birthday. Hadn't been since we'd lost Dad. But being with Laney was enough to get my ass up and I was willing to do just about anything. I hadn't spoken to her since my drunken ass fell asleep on her before she left for her trip. She hadn't responded to my texts and I'd been out of my fucking mind the past few days. What was I expecting? She'd gone to be with her fiancé.

"Hey," I yelled up to see if she was there.

"Happy Birthday. Are you coming up?"

I laughed and climbed the wooden ladder her father had attached to the tree when we were kids. I paused about halfway to the top when I noticed the letters I'd engraved in the trunk. HM + LL. God, I was a sappy bastard back then. Laney brought that out of me. I'd do just about anything to make her smile. Not much had changed, seeing as I was climbing this ridiculous ladder to find her sitting in the little house her dad built.

The tree house was pretty spectacular. Dave Landers was a crafty dude. He'd built it himself, and Laney had designed it. He'd built wooden stilts onto the back, as it was too large to be supported by only the tree. There were faux wood floors and two windows. One wall had been painted in chalkboard paint, and it clearly still worked because the words: *Happy Birthday, Harrison* were written in pink script. There used to be furniture in here, but they'd cleared it out when we were in high school. It had just become a cool fort to hang out in at that point.

Laney had a blue blanket spread across the floor, two sandwiches from Johnny's, which happened to be my favorite, and a small cake in the middle with my name on it. There were two sparkling waters, a little tub of fruit, and a bag of potato chips in the middle.

"Wow," I said, crawling through the door. It was a bit tighter than I remembered, but we hadn't been in here in years.

"Still like these sandwiches?"

"Yep. Still my favorite." And so was Laney.

"Well, I figured we'd just drink water. Seeing as I've already spent the night holding your drunk ass, I passed on the alcohol." She laughed, but a flush of pink covered her cheeks.

Damn. She was so beautiful. Her blonde hair was pulled back in a messy knot at the nape of her neck, and her ocean blues were rivaled only by the color of the deepest sea. She wore a pair of jean shorts and a white tank top, and I wanted to run my fingers along her sun-kissed skin. Stunning.

"Yeah, I won't be drinking for a while." I sat down on the blanket, leaning my back against the wall near the door. Laney and I both dug in and started eating.

"It's a tough day, I get it. Losing your dad was devastating, Har. There's no shame in being sad." She took a long pull from her water. The cool liquid moved down her throat and I sat there mesmerized as I took her in.

"Grief sucks. It's taken us all a long time to move on. I mean, Mom doesn't date, but she does her best to put a smile on her face every day. Ford meeting Harley has been life-changing for him. He's finally in a better place. And Jack, well who knows what goes on in that head of his? I wonder if he regrets not pursuing his dream to go to the NFL, but he doesn't talk about it."

"It's a tribute to your father, really. It shows how much he meant to all of you. The loss of one life affected so many people. That's the power of a good man. He touched so many, and his loss rocked your world. Hell, it rocked my world, and I was just the girl who lived up the street. But I loved him. And when you truly love someone, you can't replace them, you just have to learn to live without them."

I studied her as she spoke. There was a lot more meaning behind that statement than she was saying. And I understood it.

"Wise words, Laney Landers. And you're right, you just have to keep moving forward. I think the fact that I lost Dad and then I pushed you away—well, that combo was, hell, I can't even tell you how tough it was. How tough it's been."

"You don't have to. I know, Har. I lived it too. You know you always hear about first loves and how they never last," she said, pausing and gazing out the little window so she wouldn't have to look at me. "But what you and I shared was—rare. I mean, finding *your person* when you're in kindergarten…it's not normal." She belted out in laughter then and turned to face me.

"Well, normal is overrated. I'll take what we had any day. You know you used to believe that there was one person for everyone. I remember you telling me that when were like, what? Eight, nine years old. You were a bossy little thing even back then." I chuckled.

A wide grin spread across her pretty face. "And what exactly did I say?"

I swallowed my food, savoring every last bite. "Damn, this is good."

"You don't remember, do you?"

I raised a brow in challenge. "I remember everything, Laney. You said that everyone had a perfect match, and we were lucky that we'd found ours. You said that your parents didn't find one another until college. And we weren't even anything more than friends at the time. But you knew."

"What did I know, Harrison Montgomery? I was just a stupid kid spewing her nonsense."

"I don't think so. I think you were spot on." I leaned forward and tucked a loose strand of hair that sprung free from her bun behind her ear. She closed her eyes and sat very still.

"I don't know if I know anything anymore," she whispered.

"Where is all this doubt coming from? Trust yourself, Laney. God knows I do."

Her eyes popped open and her striking gaze locked with mine. "Thanks for having faith in me."

"That's never been in question."

"Same. I have faith in you, too. Always have."

"Even when you weren't speaking to me?"

She laughed and the sweet sound trickled around the small space. And I swear to Christ, if I died right now, I'd leave a happy man. Everything I needed was right here. In this tiny little tree house.

"Even when I wasn't speaking to you, I had faith in you. I was just hurt, I guess."

"You had reason to be." I tipped my head back and chugged my water.

"Well, I'm glad we found our way back, I mean, where we aren't hating each other anymore. And I'm happy I get to spend your birthday with you."

"Me too. I was pretty miserable today, and you managed to turn all that around."

"Good. Now let's try this cake."

"Sounds good. So how was Chicago? How's Charlie?"

She nodded. "He's good. It was nice to go back and get some things organized at my apartment. I got to spend some time with Nat. She says hi by the way," Laney said, handing me a plate with a large slice of cake. She avoided my gaze as she spoke, which made me think something was up. Maybe she was just uncomfortable discussing her fiancé with me. Maybe there was more to it.

"Tell her I said hello. I always liked her."

"Yep. She's good peeps." She laughed, and her tongue swiped out to lick some frosting from her top lip and I fought the urge to swipe it from her sweet mouth myself.

Laney and I sat like that for the next two hours. Talking and laughing just like we always did. Like no time had passed. Like the past five years hadn't been real.

And I reveled in it.

In her.

———

Laney's mom had surgery yesterday, and I hadn't seen her since the tree house. And now that I'd been spending time with her, it was almost harder to be away from her. I missed her. Craved her.

I stepped off the helicopter in San Francisco, in need of a distraction. I was meeting Ford and Jack for lunch. We had a few things to catch up on for work, and I needed to get Laney off my mind. I was happy she didn't hate me anymore, but now it was difficult to stay away from her. But she was fucking engaged to another man.

I'd opened up to her on our drive to Tahoe and I'd played my cards the night she'd found me drunk in the barn. She'd made light of it when we ate in the tree house. She'd given me nothing to show there was any sign of hope that she felt the same way. Hell, she probably wanted to forget all of it. And I should do the same. Be thankful to have her back in my life and move forward as friends.

I arrived at the Montgomery building and stopped by Harley's bakery downstairs. It sat in the bottom corner suite. She was a phenomenal baker and there was always a line out the door. We'd invested in her company when she'd first opened, and there were talks of her opening a second shop up the street. She'd hired several employees, as her best friend, Molly, had helped her get DeLiciously Yours off the ground, and Molly had left for law school this past fall.

"Hey, you just missed the rush. You guys are going to lunch, right?" she asked when I stepped inside.

"Yep. Just thought I'd come and say hello before we go." I wrapped my arms around her and pulled her in for a hug.

"Ford just texted that he and Jack will be down in a few minutes," she said. "Sit. Let's chat. Tell me what's happening with Laney."

I laughed. Harley was like the sister I'd never had. I dropped down in the chair across from her. "All's good."

"Don't pull that tough guy shtick with me, Har-bear. I know you. You're crazy about her. Have you brought up what you said when you were a drunk fool?"

"Drunk fool's a bit harsh." I barked out a laugh.

"Hey, I call 'em as I see 'em."

"Touché. No. I mean I've apologized for her being there, but we haven't talked about what I said. Obviously, she was here. She heard me. But she's engaged, so I'm sure she doesn't want to make it awkward by bringing it up. And we're finally talking again after all these years, so I don't want to ruin the friendship we've formed."

"You're a good guy, Harrison. But sometimes you've got to put yourself out there. Once she's married, it won't be an option."

"She's got a good guy. I don't want to mess that up for her. And I don't want to lose what I've got with her. We went a long time without talking."

"Rarely does reward come without risk. Trust me. Loving your brother did not come risk-free."

I nodded. "It's not only that."

"What is it?" She leaned forward, her fingers joining together to form a teepee.

"Maybe there's a little fear of being rejected. I mean she's made her choice. She chose him."

"I get that fear, I really do. But she chose him when she didn't have all the information. She didn't know why you pushed her away all those years ago."

I shook my head. "Maybe I'm just destined to be alone. Live the life of a miserable playboy and grow old by myself."

"Nah. That's not your endgame. You deserve to be happy. And if you don't think you can find that with anyone but Laney, you best get your game face on and start figuring out a way to win her back."

I laughed. "Thanks, Harley. We'll see what happens."

"You know you can always talk to me." She pushed to her feet when the door swung open and my brothers stepped in.

Ford lifted her off the ground and spun her around and her laughter filled the bakery.

"Damn, baby, I missed you. And now I have to go eat with these two." Ford thrusted his thumb in our direction.

"We can hear you." I rolled my eyes.

"I'm starving." Jack went behind the counter like he always did and helped himself to a cupcake.

"We're going to lunch," Ford hissed.

"I can walk and eat. It's not that difficult. Stop pastry-shaming me." Jack barked out a laugh and came back around and hugged Harley. "Love you, sis. See you later."

Ford kissed his wife. She reached for my hand and pushed up on her tiptoes and kissed my cheek. "You'll figure this out. I have faith in you."

My chest squeezed thinking how Laney had said those exact words to me.

We decided on Jack's favorite Italian restaurant up the street, because, well, he was the loudest. And the most passionate. My mind was elsewhere, and I didn't really care where we ate.

We settled at a table in the back and ordered.

"All right, we need to talk about Mom." I dropped my napkin in my lap and rested my forearms on the table.

"What about her?" Ford asked.

"Her fiftieth is in six weeks," I said.

"Jesus. Mom's fifty?" Jack said, shaking his head in disbelief.

"Yes. That's what comes after forty-nine, moron." My older brother rolled his eyes.

"Do you always have to be an asshole?" Jack snarled.

Jesus. These two couldn't go five minutes without an argument. "Come on. This is about Mom. Stop poking at one another, and let's discuss this like adults."

Ford raised a brow at Jack, and he nodded in return. This peaceful moment would last for maybe the next few minutes if I was lucky.

"My point being, what do you want to do? Should we take her on a trip? Throw her a party?" I asked, as the waiter set our plates down in front of us.

"Well, having all of us leave at the same time is always tricky," Ford said.

The savory smells of warm bread and garlic wafted in the air around me. Chatter and laughter filled the upscale restaurant.

"I think we should throw her a kick-ass surprise party. She's never had one. She's always throwing events for everyone else." Jack nodded as he spoke.

"I like the idea of a party too. What do you think?" Ford asked me.

"I think she'd love it. We have enough time to organize it. We could fly out all of the family. I'm sure they'd want to be there for her." Our mom had three sisters and two brothers, and they were scattered all over the US. They were very close and having them there would make her really happy.

"I'm sure Grammie and Pops and Nana and Poppy would all come as well," Jack said.

"Yeah, but how do we pull this off without her knowing?" Ford asked.

"We use a kick-ass event planner named Laney Mae. You can oversee it all, and Mom won't have a clue," Jack said, looking at me with a dumb grin.

"Yes, that'll work. But how long is she here?" Ford directed his question to me.

"I don't know. The hotel she worked at in Chicago had to replace her, so I don't think she's in a rush to get back. At least not until her mom is out of the woods. I'll talk to her today." The idea of working closely with Laney definitely had my pulse beating a little faster. This would be a huge event. "We couldn't do it at the vinery, because there'd be no way to set up without Mom knowing."

"Let's choose a cool venue."

"I'll get started on this today," I said.

"I'll bet you will," Ford said with a smirk.

"You'll need to put in some long hours with Laney Mae. You think you can handle that? I mean, without passing out drunk in her lap?" Jack said and he and Ford burst out in laughter.

"Thanks for the reminder."

"We're just giving you shit. All right, let us know what she says. If she can't do it, we'll need to find someone who can."

"I think she'll do it." I nodded. "So, what else do we need to talk about?" I was eager to finish this meeting and call Laney.

"We need to talk about Monroe Buckley." Ford set his fork down and wiped his mouth with his napkin. One of my brothers had impeccable manners.

"She's Buck's little sister," Jack spoke around a mouthful of food. Obviously, this brother did not share Ford's strength in etiquette.

Miles Buckley was Jack's best friend. They'd played for rival high schools in northern California, and then they'd gone on to room together at SC and play for the same team all four years. Jack was quarterback and Buck played receiver. They were a powerhouse team during college. They'd remained tight, and he was a good guy. We'd been to several games with Buck's family, and I'd met Monroe a few times.

"Yes. I remember her. Nice girl."

"Yeah. She's brilliant. Just graduated from Stanford and won some big journalism award. Buck claims she got the smart gene." Jack howled out a laugh.

Ford rolled his eyes at our younger brother. "Apparently, she's a phenomenal journalist, and she's interested in working for us, but word on the street is that CBS wants her and she's interning there now. She was the chief editor for the Stanford student paper. She sent her resume over this morning and it's very impressive."

"Buck wants her to work for us because if she takes the job with CBS, they want her to move to New York." Jack tore off a piece of bread and popped it in his mouth. Buck lived in Los Angeles, but obviously preferred his sister to remain out west.

"Well, let's make it happen," I said, looking at Jack "You know her best, so work your magic."

"Yeah. About that. She kind of hates me."

"Of course, she does. Tell me you didn't fuck her?" Ford hissed, his hands fisting on the table.

"God, no. Buck would kill me. He's warned all of us, especially me —Monroe is off-limits. Plus, she's not my type. But we may have taken a guys' trip down to see her race two years ago. She ran on the Stanford cross country and track team. Ended up winning nationals last year." Jack shook his head like he'd just remembered she was a freaking superstar.

I shook my head. "And?"

"Buck and I hooked up with two of her teammate, and she called us pigs. She's barely acknowledged me since." He shrugged and popped another piece of bread in his mouth. "But hopefully she's over it now. Anyhoo, Buck's protective as hell, so we'd need to look out for her if we brought her on."

"Keep your dick in your pants, Jack. I'm not kidding. I don't need any more HR headaches from you." Ford waved the waiter over and asked for the bill.

Jack pointed his finger at our older brother. "You don't have to worry about me. Buck would kick my ass. But we need to watch out for some of those shady fuckers you've got in the newsroom."

My head fell back, and I chuckled.

"Who? Hal? Wesley? They're like a hundred years old. What are you even talking about?" Ford's face was red. He'd hit his limit with Jack, and this was where things tended to go sideways.

"The interns, dude. They're shady fuckers. They cruise around the newsroom like they own the place, hitting on all the young chicks. And Wesley just celebrated his seventy-ninth birthday and the dude slays. But he's no predator."

Ford rolled his eyes, and I covered my mouth with my hand to try to hide the smile. It was impossible not to when it came to Jack. He was batshit crazy, and by far the most entertaining person I knew.

"Okay, then. I'll keep my eyes out for predators. I'm sure she can handle herself. Babysitting doesn't come with the gig. But if you hear of anyone acting inappropriately, I'd appreciate if you told me. I mean, aside from yourself." Ford pushed to his feet.

"I dated two chicks that worked in the newsroom. They're my age and they hit on me. I also wasn't working in that department at the time, so no harm, no foul. I haven't touched a single chick in that newsroom since I started overseeing it."

Ford shook his head with irritation, and I stepped between them as we walked out to the curb and moved into our waiting car, before I spoke. "First off, don't call them chicks—they're women. Come on,

Jack. Secondly, you do own the company, so it would be wise to remain professional. Can we please stay focused on Mom's party?"

"Have you heard the saying, *don't dip your pen in company ink*?" Ford scrolled through his phone before smirking at our younger brother.

"Hell yes. Which is why I haven't acted on any of the women who have hit on me since I took over that department. And trust me, it happens on the daily. Just hard to deprive all the ladies of my charms."

I laughed and shot a text to our pilot to let him know I was ready to leave. "Jerome, can you drop me at the helicopter on the way back to the office?"

"Sure thing, Harrison."

"Someone's eager to get back to Napa," Jack said, a stupid grin across his cheesy face.

"I have work to do. Stay out of my business, and try not to kill each other this afternoon," I said, opening the door when we pulled up to where the helicopter was parked.

"Let us know what Laney says," Ford shouted.

"And stop being a pussy. Tell the girl how you feel, asshole." That came from Jack.

I slammed the door and made my way to the helicopter pad. I shot Laney a quick text before we took off.

Me ~ Can you meet me at the office in an hour? I have an important project to discuss with you.

Laney ~ Sure. I'll see you soon.

A smile spread across my face as the helicopter left the ground.

Now I just had to sell her on sticking around for six more weeks.

Once we were on the ground, I drove the short ride over to the winery and dealt with yet another ridiculous issue that happened in the kitchen. Mom called to let me know that Donovan and Robb, who were our chef and assistant chef, had gone to blows and were both threatening to quit if we didn't fire the other. The entire argument was all over the new server we'd hired, Elise. Wasn't it always about a girl? I spoke to Elise first, because I'd learned over the years that it was best to go to the source. I then met with both of the guys and let them know that Elise was not interested in either of them. They both stormed around blaming the other, before I informed them that Elise had given me permission to let them know that she didn't date men. She was in a long-term relationship with her partner, Tara. Both men pouted for a minute before fist bumping the other and apologizing.

Another day in paradise. If it wasn't one thing, it was another. Thankfully, my brothers had trained me well when it came to putting out fires.

I found Laney sitting in my office. I shut the door behind me and laughed.

"Wow. Someone's prompt." I moved past her and dropped down to sit at my desk.

"You piqued my curiosity."

"Good. I just had lunch with Ford and Jack, and we wanted to talk to you about planning a party for Mom. She's turning fifty in six weeks. We want to have a big blowout for her. Obviously not here, because she'd know. But we need to find somewhere special to have it. We'd fly in all of her family and friends. It will be a lot of work, and I didn't know how long you were staying and where you were with your wedding plans. But we all three want you to do it if you're available."

She leaned back in her chair. Long blonde waves cascading around her shoulders. Ocean blues dancing with excitement. Her yellow sundress and white cardigan were sexy as hell.

"Really? What would we tell your mother I was doing?"

I formed a teepee with the tips of my fingers and thought this over. "We'll come up with something at Montgomery Media. We'll say you're overseeing a large event for the company. She won't ask much because she's not super involved with that side of the business. Ford can handle that end of things."

"Okay," she said, looking off as if she was deep in thought.

"Are you going to stick around for six weeks?"

She pushed to her feet. "Yes. I think I am."

I couldn't hide the stupid shit-eating grin on my face if I'd wanted to. I nodded. "Charlie okay with that?"

She paused at the door and turned around to face me. Her gaze locked with mine for the first time since we'd talked in the tree house.

"Oh, we're not together anymore. The wedding's off. I'll go check out some venues and let you know what I come up with."

My pulse raced at her words.

What the hell?

And just like that, things were looking up.

fifteen

. . .

Laney

"SO, you're going to stay on for a while to plan this event for Harrison's mom?" Jenny asked. It was my second time meeting with her, and so far, she'd impressed me. She was a family therapist and she didn't push. She let me share what I was comfortable with, so it felt more like I was visiting with a friend.

"Yep. I told him I'd take it."

"I'm sure your parents are thrilled that you're staying. I think it's good, Laney. Allowing yourself the time to figure out what you want to do. And your mom is doing well, so that helps."

"Yes. I'm so relieved. She's been so strong through all of this, which in a way has actually inspired me."

"How so?" Jenny asked.

"Well, she faced cancer head-on. I need to do the same. And I think breaking off my engagement was the first step. It still hurts when I think about Charlie. The pain I caused him." I shook my head. "But I know it was the right thing to do."

"Agreed. For both of you. Marrying someone out of obligation wouldn't have been fair to either one of you. And yes, you hurt him. And you'll learn from it. But not allowing yourself to explore things with Harrison doesn't take the hurt away from Charlie. It punishes you. In a sense, not following your heart does a disservice to him."

I pushed forward, resting my elbows on my knees. "How so?"

"Well, you called off your engagement because you knew it wasn't right. Harrison is the one who showed you that, correct? The way you feel about him is very different from the way you felt about Charlie?"

"Yes. That's true."

"So not exploring that means it was all for nothing. You hurt Charlie, but you didn't allow yourself to be happy either—making it all for nothing, right?"

I nodded. "I guess. It just feels too soon to jump into anything."

"It's been a few weeks, Laney. You told Charlie you were in love with Harrison. You ripped the bandage off, and then you ran for cover. Why do you think that is?"

"I don't know. Maybe I'm afraid of getting hurt. I honestly don't know," I admitted.

"Maybe you don't think you deserve to be happy. Is that possible?"

I licked my lips and reached for the bottle of water sitting on the side table. Jenny's office was chic. Decorated in whites and blush pink. White sofa, white coffee table, pink floral art on the walls. A large crystal chandelier hung overhead. Feminine and gorgeous. I instantly felt comfortable here. But right now, I had my haunches up.

"Why would I not deserve to be happy?"

"I think that just might be the million-dollar question. I want you to think about it before we meet again next week."

"Okay. I can do that."

"Dig deep, Laney. The root of everything is there. It's the reason you were going to marry someone you weren't in love with. It's the reason you stayed away from Harrison and your home for so long." Her dark brown gaze drilled into mine.

I shook my head and whispered, "I was heartbroken."

"I believe you. But why? That's what I want you to think about."

My skin was warm as I pushed to my feet. I clenched my teeth. She'd hit a nerve. One I wasn't ready to expose.

"All right. I'll see you next week."

I turned my phone on when I got in the car and saw a text from Harrison.

Harrison ~ When will you be back? I've got a few bids to discuss with you.

So needy. And I loved it.

Me ~ On my way now.

When I arrived at the winery I walked straight to Harrison's office.

"Can you pull the door closed behind you? Mom's around here somewhere. I just saw her walk by."

I shut the door and took the seat across from him. He removed his glasses and set them on the desk. He only used them for reading or when he was looking at his computer, and he looked sexy as hell when he wore them. His dark hair was a bit disheveled today, a little longer in the front with a clean fade on the sides. He had day-old scruff peppering his chin, and my fingers longed to brush against it. I tucked my hands beneath my legs on the chair to keep them in place. His white dress shirt exposed his T-shirt beneath, the tie loosened, and two buttons undone. Very un-Harrison. His jacket hung over his chair and his chocolate brown gaze locked with mine.

"You okay?" I asked.

"I'm fine. Where were you? You took a longer lunch than usual. Did you have date?" He rubbed the back of his neck with his hand.

I barked out a laugh. He was a frazzled jealous mess. "No."

"You can tell me. I mean, you are single now, right?

I smiled and pushed to my feet, Jenny's words ringing in my ears. *If you don't give it a chance, it was all for nothing.*

He studied me as I came around his desk. I reached for his hand, holding it between both of mine. Tears threatened as I pushed the lump in the back of my throat away.

"I ended things with Charlie because I have feelings for someone else. So, no, I'm not dating anyone. I was actually at an appointment. I'm seeing a therapist. I want to work through all of those feelings, but there is one thing I know for certain."

He pushed to his feet and looked down at me. "What's that, Laney?"

"I love you. I've never stopped. I don't know what it means, and we need to take this slow because I'm terrified, Harrison."

"What are you afraid of?"

I shook my head, tears streaming down my face. "Of my feelings. Of how strong they are. Of my future. Of my past. Of the way I hurt Charlie, and how I allowed it to go that far."

He placed his fingers beneath my chin, forcing me to look up and meet his gaze. "No more being afraid, okay? I'm here for you. I love you so fucking much I can't think straight."

He used his thumbs to swipe away the liquid beneath my eyes. And he stepped closer. One hand moved behind my neck, tangling in my hair. His lips hovered just above mine. Close enough that I could feel them. Mint and sandalwood flooded my senses. I fisted his dress shirt in my fingers, wanting him in a way I didn't know was possible.

"Are you going to kiss me already?" I whispered.

His mouth crashed into mine. My heart exploded like fireworks blasting through the sky, my desire and need almost overwhelming me. He dropped to his chair and pulled me onto his lap, without losing contact. I straddled him, yet I still couldn't get close enough. He tilted my head to the side, taking the kiss even deeper. It still wasn't enough. Like a starved animal, I took and took and took. Tasting and savoring every single second. Every single sound. He moaned into my mouth, his tongue dancing wildly against mine. I pressed into all his hardness, and his desire fueled me even more. It wasn't enough. Not even close. He pushed my cardigan off my shoulders and it fell to the floor. His lips moved down my neck and I leaned back to give him better access. His finger tugged at the spaghetti strap of my dress, and one shoulder broke free. His mouth covered my breast and I gasped as I tugged at his hair.

Wanting more.

Needing more.

A knock at the door brought me out of my sex-driven trance and I fumbled to pull myself together. Harrison tried to help me, but we both lost our balance and fell to the floor. The door flew open, and he sprawled out on top of me, using his hands to keep his weight from crushing me.

We were panting and crazed.

A startled Monica Montgomery stared with disbelief before she quickly apologized and hurried out of the room.

We both broke out in a fit of laughter. This was not the first time his mother had caught us in a compromised position. But it was certainly the first time in a long time. And the only time it had happened since I'd been employed by her.

And oh my god. *What does she think of me right now?*

"Shit. Does she know I'm not engaged anymore?"

"Yes. I told her the day you filled me in. She encouraged me to tell you how I feel." He pushed the hair back from my face and moved to his feet, offering me a hand.

"Please tell me my boob wasn't out when she walked in," I said, frantically trying to right my clothing.

Harrison laughed, moving closer and putting his hands on my shoulders. "She didn't see anything."

I stepped back and held my fingers up, making the sign of the cross. "Stay back, you *sexy beast*. I can't do this at work. This is so unprofessional."

His head fell back with a wicked laugh. "I own the place. We love each other. I don't give a shit who knows it. And that was some kiss, Laney. Five years of wanting you right there."

I placed my hands against my cheeks, feeling the heat against my skin. "Oh my god. *Stop.* You can't talk like that. Not here. And we're taking this slow."

I fumbled over to the door and hurried out in the hall. And then I remembered I was there for an actual meeting.

Shit.

I knocked on the door.

"It's open," he purred.

"We had a meeting, right?"

"Yes, we did." He dropped down to sit in his chair and patted his lap for me to sit.

I pushed the door all the way open, dramatically raised a brow, and pointed my finger at him. "No. And the door stays open."

I dropped to sit in the chair across from his and reached for my notebook still sitting on his desk.

"Laney?"

"Yes," I said, in my most serious voice.

"Your sweater is inside out."

I closed my eyes and took a breath before quickly yanking it off and putting it back on correctly.

"Are we good?"

"We were always good." He winked. "But I've got a bit of a situation down here."

I pushed to stand and leaned over his desk to look, and he pointed to his lap.

"That's quite the boner, my friend." I chewed the inside of my cheek.

"Those are some perfect tits you're flashing me right now, *my friend*," he mocked, leaning forward and slipping his hand beneath the front of my dress.

I slapped it away, and nearly fell for a second time, before making it back to my seat. "Okay, where were we?"

"About to round third, I think," he said, and his tongue came out to swipe his bottom lip. I squirmed in my seat. I hadn't felt like this since Harrison and I were teenagers.

Wanting and needing him so much I couldn't think straight.

"Oh, good, is this a better time?" Monica said from behind me.

I couldn't turn around. My cheeks would certainly give me away. But I'd known this woman most of my life, and she'd seen me at more embarrassing moments than this.

Scratch that.

Equally embarrassing moments. Today could rival the worst of them. After all, she'd just seen me sprawled on her son's office floor with him on top of me, and possibly one boob exposed. This definitely ranked number one at the moment.

"Monica. Hello. So sorry about that." I waved my hand in front of me as I turned to face her. "I was just giving something to Harrison, and I tripped. And then he tripped. And, well, yeah. We both tripped."

"You certainly did." She smiled and patted my shoulder. "Did you give it to him?"

I bit down on my bottom lip and tried not to laugh.

"Oh, she gave it to me, Mother. And boy, am I glad she did," Harrison said.

"I can see that, sweetheart. Okay, well, I was just coming to see if you'd both like to have dinner with me tonight?"

"I would love to," I answered quickly because I needed this conversation to end before I exploded.

"Great. I'll see you around six tonight."

"Count on it," Harrison said as she walked to the door.

"Oh, I will." Monica had a huge grin on her face as she waltzed out to the hallway.

"Please make it stop," I mumbled, covering my face with my hands.

"Please don't ever let it stop," he said, and the heat in his gaze had me flushing all over again.

"Let's start over. What did you want to discuss with me regarding the party?" I kept my voice low just in case Monica was close by.

Harrison leaned in and handed me a few pieces of paper. They were bids from different venues in the area. I looked each one over and nodded.

"So, I had another thought. These will work if you want to go this way. But your mom is all about family."

"Right," he said, watching me with a look of confusion.

"I just think these venues won't be very personal. We'll have to use their food and beverage, and we'll have restrictions on head count and time frames. This is her fiftieth. She's been through a lot. I say we hit it out of the park with lots of personal details. All Montgomery wines. We can order all the pastries from Harley. Get the food catered from her favorite restaurant. Have as many people as we want and bring in all the personal touches."

"I like the sound of that. But we can't have it here without her knowing." He raised a brow in question.

"Your property sits on an acre. It's the same backdrop as the winery because it's close enough. We can tent it off, bring in our own restrooms, dance floor, the whole nine yards. In the most beautiful setting."

He leaned back in his seat. "I like it. Let's do it. It's much more her style."

"It'll be a bit more work for us to get it all set up, but I really believe it will be better in the long run. Not so cookie cutter."

"I like that. You sure you can handle pulling that off in six weeks?"

"Are you doubting me, Montgomery?"

"Never," he said, with a smile. "But you know this means we'll be spending a lot of time together at my house."

I laughed. "We're taking it slow. I can handle myself, can you?"

"Weren't you the one who just came over here all hot and heavy?" he teased.

I covered my face with both hands and moaned. "It takes two to tango."

"Damn straight. I can't wait to tango again."

I pushed to my feet and shook my head. "I'm going to get to work on this. I'll be in my office if you need me."

"Hey, Laney," he called after me when I hit the doorway and I turned to face him.

"Yeah?"

"I always need you."

Lord, give me strength.

Because I'm in deep trouble.

sixteen

. . .

Harrison

LANEY AVOIDED me the rest of the afternoon and sent me a text saying she needed to run home and she'd meet me at my mom's for dinner. I knew she was freaking out about what happened between us in my office. I wasn't. I was just hoping it would happen again soon.

Lorena was busy in the kitchen when I walked in, and my mother was placing fresh roses from her garden in a vase.

"Hey," I said, reaching for a few grapes out of the bowl on the counter.

"Hi, sweetheart. Jack's on his way. Where's Laney?"

"She ran home to check on her mother. She's on her way."

"You two seem to be getting on well." Her cheeks pinked, and I knew she was embarrassed that she'd walked in on us earlier.

"We're taking it slow," I said, and Mom and Lorena shared a look. Nosy little birds. Thankfully, the doorbell rang, so I escaped the slew of questions that were sure to follow.

I needed a minute with Laney alone before my mother and brother started getting in our business. I opened the door and reached for her hand and hustled her down the hallway to the bathroom.

"Well, hello to you too," she whisper-shouted.

I pulled her into the restroom and shut the door. "It was a kiss, Laney. Don't blow it up and overthink it."

She crossed her arms over her chest and rolled her eyes. "What makes you think I'm overthinking it?"

"Because I know you. And you avoided me all afternoon."

"You do know that I actually have a job to do. I'm not just at the winery to have make-out sessions with you."

I moved closer, invading her space as she backed up against the sink and dropped her purse and cardigan on the counter.

"You sure about that?" I asked, getting lost in her lavender scent.

She put a hand on my chest and licked her lips. "Yep."

Our mouths were so close, my lips grazed hers as I spoke. "Glad you finally took that sweater off." I traced over the spaghetti strap of her dress with my finger, and goose bumps covered her skin.

"Well, it's definitely hot in here." Her little breaths were the only audible sound.

"It sure is." My mouth covered hers and I lifted her off the ground, setting her ass on the counter. I moved between her legs and her fingers tangled in my hair.

Our tongues dueled for control and I pushed one strap down on her dress and started on the next. She moaned into my mouth, and it nearly undid me.

"Harrison," the word came out breathy and full of need.

The door burst open, and Laney and I fumbled to right ourselves.

Fucking Jack. He came in and closed the door behind him.

"Hey, kids. What's going on in here?" He laughed, biting into an apple. "Laney Mae, your nip's out. I mean, I'm fine with it, but I figured you wouldn't be."

"Dude, get out of here," I hissed.

Laney yanked her strap up, fixed her dress, and moved to her feet. "These are the times I really hate you, Jack-ass."

"What? Lorena said you two snuck off to the bathroom, and I assumed it was to discuss the surprise party. I'm definitely out of the loop on what's happening here, but I'm not upset about it at all. This is good stuff."

"Out." I pointed at the door.

He dropped the apple core in the trash and reach d for the door. "Should I leave this open? Doesn't appear you two can be trusted behind closed doors."

"We're coming with you." Laney laughed and tug ;ed at my hand before leaning close to my ear. "Behave yourself."

"That was all you," I said, following her out to the c ining room.

"Ah, good, you're all here. Dinner's ready." Mom took the seat at the head of the table, and Jack sat acro s from Laney and me.

"This looks amazing, Monica. Thanks for inviting n e."

"Are you kidding? I'm thrilled to have you back n town, even if just for a short time."

I tensed beside her at my mother's words. Woul Laney still go back to Chicago? We hadn't talked about anythin yet. Hell, we weren't anything yet. But I was damn sure going to do my best to change that.

Laney slipped her cardigan over her shoulders and nodded.

"Are you cold, Laney Mae? It is a little *nippy* in ere," Jack said with a smirk. He loved giving her shit.

Laney coughed, and my mom pushed to her feet. Oh, is it cold in here? I'm so sorry."

"No, no, it's not cold at all. I'm totally fine." She ; lared at Jack as my mother moved across the room to adjust the th rmostat. Laney looked down to make sure her dress was in place ar d I tried not to laugh.

Jack beamed and I shot him a warning look. H e was enjoying himself.

"So, are you still playing tennis?" Mom asked Lan y, as she passed the salad around the table.

"No, I haven't played in a long time."

"Well, you two were always so good together. You should get the rackets out, Harrison."

I glanced at Laney. "Yeah, we haven't played in a w ile."

"And, you have those *blue balls* you could use." Jac leaned back in his chair and tried to cover his dumbass grin.

Laney full-on choked now, and I patted her back as she coughed it out.

"You okay?" Mom asked with concern, handing the roasted potatoes to Jack.

"Yes, just went down the wrong pipe." She shrugged, trying to cover her smile as she glanced at my brother.

"So, I just read an article about this. There is a reason that they use the yellow balls in tennis. It's all about the visibility. Apparently, they used to use white balls, but they were more difficult to see. I haven't heard of using blue balls. Is that a new thing?"

I set my fork down and tried hard not to laugh. Laney's hand found mine beneath the table and she squeezed it. I knew she was trying to contain herself as well.

"Oh no. It's not new at all. Har-bear's had the blue balls for years," my brother said.

"Really. Have you used them, Laney?"

Laney set her wine glass down, and her eyes were trained on her plate. "Nope. I haven't tried those yet."

"Oh, I thought you gave him the blue balls." Jack raised a brow at Laney and her cheeks flushed pink.

"Well, the yellow ones have been working for as long as I've been around. I don't think I'd switch it up, sweetheart," Mom said, reaching for the bottle of wine to refill her glass.

Classical music piped in softly around us, and Lorena came out to let us know she was getting dessert ready. It was time to mess with my brother a little bit. He was begging for it.

"You know who I ran into the other day?" I said.

"Who?" Mom asked.

"*Bobby Carpenter*." My gaze locked with Jack's and I fought back laughter. He hated the guy.

"Boogie Bob," Laney and Jack said in unison. They both had issues with Bobby. This would be fun.

"Why does he have that name again?" my mother asked, trying hard to keep up.

"Laney gave him that name," I said, shaking my head.

"He was always digging for gold, if you know what I mean?"

Laney said. "He sat beside me in third grade and he was really going for it one day and he turned and wiped his boogie on my notebook. It was one of those cute ones with the horses on the cover. He literally wiped his boogie on my book."

The table erupted in laughter.

"You had a problem with him too, didn't you, Jack?" Mom asked once she pulled herself together.

"Funny you should mention it. *Brother dearest* here is quite familiar that Boogie Bob is a trigger for me." He wiped his mouth and dropped his napkin on the table.

"He did ask how you were doing when I saw him. He just bought his family home from his parents. They moved to Arizona to retire. He's living up the road, so I'm sure you'll be seeing more of him." I raised a brow and tried to cover my smirk.

"I can't stand that guy," Jack hissed. "He's the one who stole my underpants freshman year."

More laughter came from the table.

"Oh yes. I had to come to the school to pick you up. Why did he do that again?" Mom asked.

I glanced over at Laney, and her eyes danced with mischief. She loved this story and she adored my brother. My chest squeezed with something. Nostalgia, maybe? Hope?

"Coach decided to make me the starting QB my freshman year, and Boogie Bob was a junior. He'd been starting the two years before and he was pissed. Hell, I get it. It sucks. But that's football. The little punk stole my drawers when I was in the shower."

"There was also the issue with his sister, right?" Laney prodded, biting down hard on her bottom lip as a grin spread across her face.

"Ah, yes, thank you for the reminder, Laney Mae. His sister, *Little Boogie* was a pistol. That chick had a serious *Jack attack*. She climbed me like some sort of spider monkey under the bleachers. I rejected her, and she got pissed. You know I don't like when ladies get too aggressive, Mom. Nothing worse than feeling violated."

Mom rolled her eyes and shook her head, but her smile was impossible to miss. "So, he got mad at you about his sister and you taking his spot on the team and that's why he stole your underwear? That's not very mature."

"You're right about that. So, the family jewels were just—out there." He motioned with his hands out to the sides. "And rubbing up against my jeans was not tolerable. So, I went to my *brother* for help. And he turned his back on me." Jack shook his head.

"You barreled into my science class telling me you were in pain. Walking like you were carrying a load. I told you to go to the nurse." I couldn't take it any longer and I burst out in laughter, and Laney and Mom fell over the table doing the same.

"It's called chafing, Har-bear. Have you ever chafed your balls, brother? It's not pretty."

"Well, you always were the one with the most sensitive skin," Mom said, trying to rescue the big baby. "And you sure did love Nurse Pathi. But I remember you weren't happy with her that day."

"Yeah, you were always going to her for everything," Laney said, shaking her head. She looked fucking beautiful too. Sitting here beside me.

Jack closed his eyes as if the memory was too painful for him. "Yes, Laney Mae. Usually Nurse Pathi would let me lie down and tell her my woes when I needed an escape from math class. But that day was different. I told her I had some *discomfort downstairs.* She had that fancy ice machine in her office, and she grabbed a bag and filled that mother-fucker to the top. She dropped it on my crotch, applying pressure, while she made small talk with her assistant. *Four fucking minutes* she made me ice my balls. You know how I know?"

We were all on the verge of losing it, and Laney was the one who got out the one word he was waiting for while trying to contain her laughter. *"How?"*

"Because I counted to sixty. Four fucking times. While Nurse Pathi nearly froze my oversized di—um, sea monster right off my body."

That was it. My hand came down on the table and I couldn't hold it in anymore. Hysterical laughter filled the room, and even Jack finally joined in. And damn if it didn't feel good to laugh like this again. Laney had brought her light back into our house. Reminding us of happier times before Dad passed away.

"I remember Dad going up to your room and sitting on the bed, all serious. You were convinced your manhood had been damaged for life." Mom swiped at the tears that were streaming down her face. Happy tears. I studied her, seeing the lines around her eyes that had formed as she grieved for our father these past few years.

"You may want to *earmuff* what I'm about to say, Mom." Jack held his two hands over his ears, showing our mother how to protect herself from his words.

She smiled. "I'm all right. I've raised three boys. Nothing shocks me anymore."

"Well, let's just say my *sea monster* recovered quickly. But even thinking back to that day makes us both want to shrivel up and die. No pun intended."

I shook my head as everyone continued to chuckle at his antics. Laney glanced over at me and smiled, and I fought the urge to pull her onto my lap and kiss her senseless. She was what was missing in my life. This girl. She filled a void no one else ever could.

"Sounds like we're having some fun out here," Lorena said, carrying out a tray of chocolate eclairs.

Jack howled. "They're *boobiful*, aren't they, Laney Mae? Excuse me, I mean *beautiful*."

Her head fell back, and I knew she was enjoying his banter. She looked—lighter.

Happy.

"You sure are on one tonight, Jackie boy." Mom passed the tray of pastries to my brother.

"Always. Did you say Boogie Bob bought his parents' home?" my brother asked.

"Yeah. I'm sure we'll be seeing lots of him, so you might want to give your *sea monster* a heads-up." I was enjoying this. Nothing better than torturing my little brother.

He nodded. "What's that you used to say when someone pissed us off, Laney Mae?"

"Payback's a—" She glanced at my mom. "*Biotch*?"

"You can say *bitch*, sweetie. I raised this one." Mom thrusted her thumb at Jack. "I can take it."

More laughter.

More smiles.

More Laney.

"I don't think we ever paid ole Boogie Bob back properly. I mean, you had to throw out the horsey notebook and I was tortured slowly by the little prick."

"I think you're right about that," Laney said, a mischievous grin spread across her face.

"Doesn't sound like his daddy's home anymore." Jack raised his hand and pretended to be dinging a bell. "Ding, ding, ding."

It was code for ding-dong-ditching. Also known as Laney Mae Landers' favorite thing to do. The girl would get us all on board, even Ford joined in a few times back in the day.

She nodded and shrugged. "I haven't done that in a long time."

"You aren't going to ring on that poor guy's door and run, are you?" Mom asked with disbelief.

"He chafed my balls, Mother. He has it coming. You're not a chicken are you, Laney Mae?"

She looked over at me and smiled. "Never. But Harrison's going to have to give me a piggyback ride through the vineyard because I'm wearing wedges."

"I don't think he'll mind that at all." My brother winked.

"I'm in."

"You kids are ridiculous," Mom said, pushing to stand from the table and coming around to give us each a hug. Just like she always did.

We all helped Lorena clear the table and sat outside drinking wine and shooting the shit until it got dark.

"Okay. It's time for Operation Boogie Bob," Jack said, and we said goodbye to Mom.

Laney was riding on my back, and her nearness had me in a constant state of discomfort. But I wouldn't trade this moment for anything. She was coming around, and that's all that mattered.

"What if he's with someone? Like a woman," Laney whisper-shouted.

"Oh man. That would give me joy," Jack said.

"Why?" I asked with disgust.

"Because the thought of him getting his game on and us interrupting him when I ring his doorbell forty fucking times. Priceless."

"Payback's a bitch, Jack-ass," Laney reminded him, resting her chin on my head.

"That's right, girl." Jack crouched down behind some bushes when we were one house away. "Okay, so who gets to ring the bell?"

"You two can be my guest. I'll stand guard." I rolled my eyes. I was only going along with this ridiculous stunt because it meant more time with Laney.

She hopped off my back and bent down to take her shoes off. "I'll most likely need to sprint from the crime scene, so you hold these. But once we're in the clear, I'm hopping back on."

"I feel so dirty. Like you're using me as the getaway car," I said.

She turned to face me. The moon was full and shining all its glory down on her. Her eyes danced with mischief. She pushed up on her tiptoes and kissed me. It wasn't fast. It wasn't soft. And it took me by surprise. Jack howled beside us. Let's just say his ability to stay incognito was slim to none.

She pulled away and smiled before taking off with my brother for the door. I watched as they walked up to the front porch and took turns ringing the bell. *Over and over.* I mean, they took this to a whole new level.

"Jesus. Let's go," I whisper-yelled.

The door flew open and Laney and Jack were in a full sprint toward me. We all took off through the wine fields laughing. I tugged at Laney's arm once we were far enough away that we couldn't hear him shouting anymore.

"Hop on. I don't want your feet to get cut up."

She jumped up and her legs came around my waist, her arms around my neck—goodness surrounded me everywhere. I put a hand over hers, and we walked the rest of the way.

"Man, that was awesome. I think you got in more rings than me, Laney Mae," my brother said.

"Did you hear the dogs barking and Boogie Bob shouting after us?" Her body vibrated against me as she laughed.

"Fucking awesome. Just like old times," Jack said, as he walked beside us.

I tilted my head back and she kissed my cheek. She was feeling it too. When we got to the end of the vineyard, Jack headed to Mom's to get the car and head back to the city for the night. I walked Laney back to her parents' house. Something I'd done more times than I could count when we were young—but this time it meant everything. We were getting back on track. Back to what we had. Something neither of us had found since.

She dropped down to the sidewalk and slipped her shoes back on, insisting on walking the short distance to her house. Our hands linked of their own volition and we swung them between us.

"That was fun, huh?" she asked.

"It was. You two are insane."

"Yeah. I forgot how many happy memories lived here."

"Yep. There's a lot. So, what's your plan? I mean, now that you're not engaged, do you think you'll still go back to Chicago?"

She led me up to the front door. "I don't really know. I haven't thought that far ahead, which is very unlike me. But I just need to see how my mom is doing before I can make any decisions."

We both knew that wasn't the reason, but I'd let her say what she needed to. Her mom was doing great. Laney was just lost right now. And I was desperate to help her find her way.

"Okay. You know if you need to talk to me about anything, I'm here."

She nodded. "Yeah, I know. Thank you so much for taking it slow. I've flashed your mother and your brother all in one day."

My head fell back in laughter. "Yeah, it was quite a day. Sure brought back a lot of memories. I don't think you've changed nearly as much as you think you have."

"Maybe you're right. Maybe I haven't." She pushed up on her tiptoes and gave me a chaste kiss.

"I love you, Laney."

She reached for the door handle. "I love you, too. That was never the problem."

What was the fucking problem? She'd ended things with Charlie.

Laura Pavlov

Why were we taking it slow? We'd been apart for five years, what was the hold up?

She walked inside and shut the door.

I thought about all that had happened today. She may be holding back, but the bottom line was—we were making progress.

She was coming back to me.

And that's all that mattered.

seventeen

. . .

Laney

THE NEXT TWO weeks went by in a blur. Mom was doing well, and she'd recovered like a champ. She was getting ready to go back to school. I was keeping busy at the winery planning Monica's party and spending every spare minute with Harrison. I'd kissed this man so much over the past two weeks that my lips were permanently chapped. The thought made me smile. The way he made me feel. The way he kissed me. But we hadn't taken things further and it wasn't because neither of us didn't want to. But I wanted to take it slow, and he respected that.

Everyone continued to inquire about my plans as far as staying in Napa or going back to my life in Chicago. Hell, I was just as curious as everyone else. But I didn't have a clue. My position at the W Hotel had already been filled, and what surprised me was that I didn't care. I wasn't upset.

I liked being here. I walked into Jenny's office. I saw her twice a week now and talking through everything with her helped.

"So, how are you? Did you think some more about what we talked about?" she asked.

I settled on her white couch and held the floral throw pillow on my lap as I thought it over. Jenny and I continued to delve into the conversation about why I'd stayed away. Why there'd been this shift or change after Harrison and I broke up all those years ago.

"Yes. I've been thinking about it a lot."

"That's good. And are you talking more with Harrison?"

"Yep. He's being really respectful about taking it slow. I know he's confused. But there's just—I don't know. So much has happened. I've accepted that I was with Charlie for the wrong reasons. I think even Charlie knew it. I was never all in. And the guilt about hurting him still sits heavily on my shoulders," I admitted.

I felt terrible for what I'd done to him.

"Well, you owned it, right? You knew he deserved better and you called it off. And it sounds like he understood from the conversation you had with Natalie."

"Yeah. I just hope one day he'll be able to forgive me."

"I'm sure he will, Laney. But I think right now, you're the one who needs to forgive yourself. Which brings us back to the question. Why were you in a situation where you felt you owed Charlie—what? Your love? He'd been there for you, so you felt obligated to marry him?"

I sucked in a long breath and leaned back on the couch. I chewed relentlessly on the inside of my cheek and clutched the pillow in my lap.

"I've thought about a lot of things lately. It's not like I haven't made mistakes in my life before this. I have. But I was never someone who ran from the consequences. I've always owned them. God knows I was grounded plenty of times for my shenanigans growing up. Hell, I'd break curfew and sneak out of the house with Harrison. I even took the family golf cart four-wheeling once. But I always owned it. I never hid things from my parents. I faced my mistakes head-on."

"And you don't think you do that now? I think that's exactly what you did with Charlie." Jenny sat in the chair across from me and crossed one leg over the other, adjusting the notebook on her lap.

"I just think that there are things you can't come back from."

"You don't believe in second chances or redemption?"

I moved the pillow off my lap and set it beside me. "No. Of course I do. And I know there are consequences for our actions. I just think sometimes those consequences take you away, if that makes sense."

"Okay. I'm following. When you were in high school, you got into normal mischief, and the punishment was maybe losing your phone or being grounded."

I nodded. "Right."

"But as you get older, such as what happened with Charlie, the stakes are higher. So, the consequences are going to be different. Tell me, what kind of crime leads to a consequence that forces someone to avoid going back home?"

I glanced out the window at the blue sky, as the sun shone down. "Shame, guilt, uncertainty."

She nodded. "I understand shame and guilt but explain what you mean by uncertainty."

"Just about knowing who you are anymore. I don't really know?"

"Try, Laney. Tell me more about these consequences," Jenny said as she reached for her bottle of water and took a sip.

"I guess it depends on each person. But I think sometimes feeling all that shame and guilt, you know, like you're drowning in it. Like you've been sentenced to a lifetime in purgatory, but no one in your life knows it, and you can't be set free."

She studied me and remained quiet for a moment. "That's a heavy price to pay for an accident. I don't even think our criminal justice system condemns anyone to a lifetime of purgatory for an accident."

I nodded. I knew logically she was right. But my head and my heart weren't on the same page. "Well, we are our own worst critics, right?"

"If that's the case, then I guess it all comes down to you. It sounds like you're the judge and the jury. So only you can set yourself free."

I clasped my hands together and nodded. "I think you're right."

"What I want you to do when you leave today is to think about what you want. What would make you happy? And then we're going to figure out how to get you there, or why you don't feel deserving of it."

I released a breath that I hadn't realized I'd been holding. "Okay. I can do that."

"Yes, you can." She smiled and pushed to her feet.

I gave her a hug because we'd grown close over the past few weeks and Jenny felt more like a trusted friend.

But some things you couldn't trust anyone with.

Because that would mean saying it aloud.

———

Harrison brought the popcorn over to the couch and we were in the midst of deciding what movie to watch. We'd spent the day out on his property measuring and configuring the layout for the party. This event was going to be epic, and I was thrilled to be part of it.

"Okay, so how do we possibly decide between *Jason Bourne* and *Sweet Home Alabama*?" He rolled his eyes. He wasn't a big rom-com guy, and I wasn't in the mood for action and suspense. It was Friday night and we'd had a long week. We'd spent every day together, and I'd been thinking a lot about what Jenny said. I'd come to the conclusion that Harrison Montgomery made me happy. He always had. He was the missing piece in my life. We'd had more steamy make-out sessions this past week, but I was still holding back. And he wouldn't push me. I appreciated it, but the sexual tension was getting to me. I hadn't wanted anyone the way I wanted him since—well, since I was last with Harrison. No one else had ever known me the way he did. What I liked. What I needed.

"We could skip the movie if you want," I said.

He opened his mouth and I popped in a few pieces of popcorn and studied his handsome face. I ran my fingers over his scruff, loving the feel of his prickly stubble against my fingertips.

"Yeah? What do you want to do?" His heated gaze nearly dropped me to my knees.

"*What do you want to do?*" My lips grazed his as I repeated his words back to him.

He pulled me onto his lap, and I straddled him. "All I want to *do* is you, Laney Landers."

My head fell back in laughter and he kissed his way down my neck.

"You don't have any family members that are going to bust

through the door and catch me the minute you take my top off, do you?" I didn't recognize the sound of my own voice. It was breathy and gruff, and he chuckled against my skin. Chill bumps covered me, and I tangled my fingers in his dark, thick hair.

"No one's coming through that door. It's locked, so we're safe. But does this mean you're going to let me take the whole thing off? You're not going to torture me with one shoulder at a time?" He continued to graze his lips against my skin as he kissed his way across my neck and came back up to meet my gaze.

"No more teasing. I'm ready."

"What are you ready for, baby?" His dark eyes locked with mine. Intense and hungry. Full of desire.

"I'm ready for you. All of you."

The corners of his mouth turned up. "Do you know how long I've wanted to hear those words?"

"A couple of days?" I teased.

He put one hand on each of my cheeks and held me there. "Five fucking years, Laney. That's how long. From the minute I pushed you away, I missed you. Needed you. You're it for me. And I want all of you."

"I've always belonged to you. We just had to find our way back to one another."

"And here we are."

"Here we are," I whispered.

He reached down and tugged the T-shirt over my head, pausing to take in my pink lacy bra. He reached behind my back and unsnapped it, and it fell to my lap.

"Jesus. You're so beautiful. I just want to look at you," he said, and his eyes were wet with emotion.

"I missed you, too." My voice trembled. Goose bumps spread across my skin as his hands cupped each breast, and I fell forward with a desperate need to kiss him.

He pushed to his feet, not losing contact, and my legs wrapped around his waist. He groaned against my mouth as he placed me down on the bed. He pulled back to tug his shirt over his head, and I studied him. His chest was more muscular than it used to be. Strong arms and chiseled abs. He'd always been fit, but this was a whole new level.

When I looked up to meet his gaze, he was watching me. The heat in his eyes was impossible to miss. He leaned down and unbuttoned my jeans, tugging them off of my body and dropping them to the floor. I pushed to sit forward and reached for the button on his jeans. His erection threatened to break through the denim.

"Someone's excited to see me," I whispered as I carefully freed him from both his pants and his briefs. I let out a long breath as I took him in. "Wow. Was it always this big?"

His head fell back in laughter and he looked down at me. "I think he's just *really* excited that you're here."

He pushed me back on the bed and propped himself above me. "I'm going to take my time with you, Laney. It's been way too long."

My breaths came hard and fast. This was happening. I was in Harrison's bed. The love of my life. There were still so many things that hadn't been said. So much time had passed.

"Hey, are you okay?" he asked, and the concern in his eyes made my chest squeeze. He pushed the hair back from my face and stroked my cheek. "You're shaking."

"I'm sorry. It's just been a long time. What if it's different? What if I'm different?"

"There's no part of you that I don't love."

"I love you, too."

"Let me make you feel good, baby." He kissed my forehead, my eyelids, my nose, my cheeks and my lips. All the worry left me as his lips traveled down my neck, heating and scorching parts of me that had been dormant for years. His mouth covered my breast and I arched into his touch, needing more. He made his way down my body and his lips lingered over my panties. His fingers slipped beneath the silk fabric and he slowly moved them down my legs. I writhed beneath him as he settled between my legs, and his warm breath hit my most sensitive area.

I squirmed with need and the feeling was so unfamiliar that panic coursed through my veins. I hadn't even liked sex after Harrison. I'd gone through the motions with Charlie. But this—this was different.

Because I didn't know I could feel this way again. And it was everything.

Harrison Montgomery lit a match and set my soul on fire. He awakened me in every way. He buried his head between my legs and the sensation was so overwhelming, so freeing, I didn't stop him. I allowed myself to feel every single thing.

And, oh my, did I feel it.

I whimpered and squirmed before I cried out my release. Pleasure rolled through me as I tried to calm my breathing. Harrison propped himself above me and swiped at my falling tears.

"Hey. Was this too much? We can stop."

I shook my head, as a sob left my throat. "No. I don't want to stop."

"Laney, you're crying. You're upset."

"No. No, Har, I'm not. These are happy tears."

"You sure? Tell me what's going on." He dropped to lie on his side, and I turned to face him. He stroked my hair and searched my gaze.

"I just haven't felt this much in a long time. I didn't think I could anymore," I said, and his thumb caught the last tear as it fell.

"That's a good thing, right?" he whispered. His eyebrows cinched together, causing a worry line to form between them.

"It is. You brought me back to life."

He smiled, and my heart threatened to explode. "You've always been there, Laney."

"Only with you," I said.

"Always with you."

"I don't want to stop," I whispered, my fingers running over his muscled chest and dropping between us to grip him.

"Tell me what you need," he said, and his words were strained.

"Just you. And I don't want to wait another minute. We've waited too long."

"You've got me, baby." He pushed back and reached in his night-stand for a condom, tearing the wrapper with his teeth and covering himself as I gaped in awe of him.

Everything was better with Harrison in my life.

He settled above me and his dark gaze locked with mine. "I love you, Laney Landers."

"I love you, too," I smiled up at him, overcome with emotion.

He moved forward, filling me inch by glorious inch and nothing had ever felt so good. We moved together in perfect sync, just like we always had. I tangled my fingers in his hair and his mouth covered mine. Connected in every way. We moved slowly until the building pressure was too much to take.

The sensation so overpowering, I called out his name as waves of pleasure racked my body. Harrison went right over the edge with me as a moan left his throat and his body shook and quaked.

He fell to his back and we both gasped for air. But when he turned to face me, he reached for my hand and interlaced our fingers.

"No more time apart. Promise me," he whispered.

"I promise."

Because this was where I belonged.

And I was never leaving.

eighteen

· · ·

Harrison

"SO WHERE ARE we with the party?" Ford asked, as we settled at the table of one of our favorite restaurants in the city.

"Things are set. Laney's sending the invites out this week."

"You two seem to be picking up where you left off," Jack said, tearing off a piece of bread and popping it in his mouth.

"Yeah, we're figuring it out."

Ford narrowed his gaze. "What is there to figure out? She called off her engagement and you're together."

"And the attraction is obviously still there. I've walked in on you two too many times to count. I've been flashed a little tit, caught you with your drawers down—and that can never be unseen," Jack said, shaking his head as Ford and I both laughed.

"Well, if you could just stay in your own goddamn lane, it wouldn't keep happening. Stop opening doors that are closed."

"Or you could put a tie on the door. Something to give me a heads-up."

"I'm a grown ass man, I'm not putting a tie on my door when I'm with my girl. This is not a fraternity house. That's insane. Just try knocking on a door before you enter." I rolled my eyes and thanked the waiter as he set our food down in front of us.

"That's not really my style." Jack reached for his burger and took a bite.

"You don't fucking say," Ford said with a smirk. "So, what's the deal? Sounds like everything's great? What's there to figure out?"

I finished chewing and took a sip of water. "Thing *are* great. I just feel like she's holding back a little. She hasn't given up her place in Chicago yet, and I think she's keeping something from me. But I could be reading into it."

"Why don't you tell her to give up her place in Chicago? Take charge. Be a dick. Girls love that," Jack said, turning his gaze to follow a blonde woman as she strode past our table. She stopped, turned around, and waved at the asshole. "Excuse me, boys. I'll be right back."

"Jesus," I said under my breath. "He can't make it through lunch without hitting on someone."

Ford set his fork down. "Why don't you just talk to her? You've known her your whole damn life."

"I don't want to pressure her to give up her place. Hell, we just got back together. The last thing I want to do is fuck it up."

"Sometimes you've got to fuck things up. I didn't handle things perfectly with Harley, but we figured it out. I pissed her off more times than I can count but look where we are. Sometimes you've got to ruffle some feathers to get what you want," Ford said.

"Yeah, that's not really my style."

He chuckled. "I'm quite aware. I know there's a badass under that exterior. The day I took your bike without asking—I got a little preview."

"Dude, that bike was brand new. You rode it before I did."

"I recall you diving on top of me and tackling me on the driveway. Remember? Dad laughed his ass off because we'd never seen you lose your shit. And brother, you lost your shit that day. What did Dad say? I remember afterward you felt really bad and he said something about it being all right to go a little crazy sometimes."

I leaned back in my seat as I thought about it. My father was so even-keeled, and I always admired it. I'd felt pretty shitty because Ford and I had rolled around on the ground and thrown punches. Mom was screaming and shouting. "He bent down and got eye level with me—you know like he always did. Made you feel like an equal when he spoke to you. I can still remember it like it was yesterday," I said, pausing to take a sip of water. "He said, *'Harrison, a strong man knows when to walk away and a strong man knows when to fight. You just showed me that you're a strong man, Son.'* And then he went on to tell me something about how you would probably never fuck with me again."

Ford chuckled. "I hope I have half his wisdom someday. And he was right. I never touched that fucking bike again. Not sure I can say I never fucked with you again, though."

I nodded. "You're right about that."

"Got the digits." Jack set his phone down on the table and reached for his burger. "What did I miss?"

"Just reminiscing about that time I pissed ole Har-bear off and stole his bike."

"Dude. You lost your shit, big-time. I remember standing there with my jaw on the ground," Jack said, and then he pointed his finger at Ford. "It was a lame thing to do. You took the *Ninja Six Ghost Rider* before he got to ride it. That was a dick move."

We all laughed now. I'd not only worshipped that bike, I'd named it.

"No doubt. And if memory serves, Laney punched me in the stomach for it later. What were you guys, in third grade?"

I nodded, trying to hide the smile on my face. Laney had lost her shit on Ford when I told her what happened. She was this little blonde in pigtails, but she always had my back. She never backed down. Not then, and not now. "That was badass. How many third-grade girls walk up and punch a fifth-grade boy?"

"That's Laney Mae for you. She's punched me, kicked me, and bit me a few times over the years. Let me warn you…do not mess with the Har-bear. She won't tolerate it." Jack fell back in laughter. "It's been really nice having her home. So, don't fuck it up. I'd really like to keep her. It wasn't the same when she was gone."

"She's not a dog, you dumbass. She's a human being. You can't *keep her*," I hissed, and a big grin spread across Jack's face.

"No. But *you* can. So, don't fuck it up." He waved over the waiter and asked for dessert menus and Ford and I both groaned because we were ready to leave.

"Let me do this my way. She's not going anywhere. She just needs some time to figure out her plan."

"Mom said Melanie isn't coming back from maternity leave. So, you know there's a spot for her at the winery if she wants it. Not that it would matter if Melanie came back. We'd always make a spot for Laney Mae." Ford tossed his dessert menu on the table when the waiter brought them out.

"Yeah, Mom already talked to her about it. She's interested. She's been putting in a lot of hours working on this party. Wait till you see how she's transforming the outdoor space. She drew up some sketches to help me get a visual for it, and Mom is going to love it."

"And we have everyone flying in the night before or the day of, right?" Jack asked.

"Yes. Laney arranged all the travel and the hotel accommodations as well."

"Good. Sounds like she has it all under control," Ford said.

We waited for Jack to finish his crème brûlée. *The guy could eat ten pounds of sugar a day and not put on an ounce, unbelievable.* I took the helicopter back to Napa. I thought about what my brother had said, and I contemplated how to bring it up with her. Something was nagging at me. Something she wasn't telling me. I'd seen the internal struggle beneath her blue gaze more than once.

I stopped by her office and paused in the doorway. "Hey, how's your day going?"

She looked up from where she sat behind her desk and pushed to her feet. She lunged at me and I caught her, wrapping my arms around her.

"What's this? Are you okay?"

"Yeah, of course," she said, pausing to look up at me. "I just missed you."

"I missed you, too."

I moved to sit in the chair across from her desk and pulled her onto my lap. "Tell me about your day."

"I was just going through all those boxes of photos you guys got out of storage for me to make the slideshow for your mom. Seeing us on our first day of kindergarten, and through the awkward days of middle school, and every high school dance…it just gave me all the feels, I guess."

"Yeah, we've been through a lot together, huh?"

She nodded and ran her fingers over my scruff. "We have."

"How was your mom's appointment today?" I asked as I pulled her closer and her head nestled just under my chin.

"It went really well. Everything is looking good. She'll have to go back often this first year, but everything came back clear. She asked me what my plans were, you know, for the future."

"What did you tell her?"

"I said I didn't know, I was just taking it one day at a time," Laney said, pushing back to look at me. "But that you and I are together, no matter what."

"What does that mean, baby? We're together, but you're keeping an apartment back in Chicago, too? Sounds like you're still one foot out the door, if you ask me." It came out with more bite than I intended. I didn't understand what the hesitation was about.

She pushed to her feet. "Of course not."

"Is that what you told Charlie?"

I knew I shouldn't have said it the minute the words left my mouth. What she and Charlie had was different, and I knew that. Knew it in my gut. But I needed to press her on this because I didn't understand what the problem was.

She gasped and huffed around the room. "Seriously? Did you really just say that?"

"I did. I need to understand this."

She moved over to the window. "I love you more than anything, there's nothing to understand. I'm going to get rid of the apartment, I just think we need time to get to know one another again before we move in together and jump all in."

"Get to know one another? Are you fucking kidding me?"

"Don't raise your voice at me. I'm just telling you how I feel." She placed her hands on her hips and glared at me.

"I didn't raise my voice. The only one doing that is you. Listen,

Laney, I know you. You know me. I have no secrets. Can you say the same?"

At that, she rolled her eyes and her face flushed. "Sure. But I don't know everything you did while we were apart."

"I don't know everything you did. And I don't give a shit about it. What matters is *now*. We've lost enough time already. What do you want to know? You want a list of everyone I slept with? Is that what this is about?" I pushed to my feet and moved over to where she stood, crowding her space.

She reared her head back. "There's a list? How many were there? This is what I'm talking about, Harrison. I don't even know who you've been with, and who I need to hate moving forward."

"Twelve. Twelve women in five years. And only two were repeat customers. How about you?"

"I'm not doing this with you." She stormed past me and walked right out the door, slamming it behind her.

What the hell is going on with her?

I glanced out the window and saw her get in her car and drive off.

"Hey." Mom peeked her head inside. "I saw Laney run out of here. Is everything okay?"

I let out a long breath. "I don't know. I mean, everything is great, but there's something she's afraid of. And she won't fucking tell me. Maybe it's just that she doesn't fully trust me yet. I don't know."

"You guys seem like you're getting along great. What brought this on?"

"I don't really know. It's any time I talk about the future. She claims it's because she doesn't know what I've done the past five years. But who cares? We're together now."

Mom dropped in the chair next to mine. "Women don't really work that way, sweetheart. Of course, she wants to know what you've done, who you've dated. That's fair. So just sit down and talk about it."

"I will. She just overreacted. It'll be fine. Just a lot of change for her pretty quickly with her mom getting sick, finding out why I broke up with her, and ending her engagement."

"You're the most patient man I know, next to your father." She chuckled. "Just give her time."

"I will."

"How were the boys today?" she asked.

"Good. Jack managed to get two phone numbers between our walk to the restaurant and lunch. Ford and Harley seem to be doing well. I dropped a box of Harley's pastries in the kitchen for you."

She pushed to her feet and patted my cheek with her hand. "So thoughtful. I love you. I'll see you later."

I walked over to Laney's desk to turn off her computer and saw the box of photos tucked underneath. I pulled it out and placed it on the desk. I went over to shut the door so Mom wouldn't catch me by surprise.

She was right. Laney had been a part of our family from the very beginning. She was in as many of these photos as I was. In fact, there were very few of me without her. If I wasn't with Laney, I was with my brothers.

I realized the photos stopped after Dad died. Or maybe we just settled for pictures on our phones after that. The Christmas card photos we took every year when Dad was alive had stopped, and so had all the family photo shoots. I sat back in Laney's chair thinking about all that Mom had lost. At least Ford, Jack, and I would marry and start our own families. She'd lost her best friend. Her soulmate.

Her Laney Landers.

I flipped through a few more photographs and laughed at the one from our senior prom. Laney was in a formal gown but somehow managed to take a picture riding piggyback. I ran my thumb over the print as I studied it. Our smiles were larger than life. We were getting ready to leave for college. We had a plan. A future. And I'd fucked it all up.

I'd be damned if I'd allow that to happen again.

nineteen

. . .

Laney

"LANEY, HI, COME ON IN," Jenny said, leading me back to her office.

"Thanks for squeezing me in."

"Of course. You sounded upset. What's going on?" she asked as she dropped in her chair and I settled on the couch across from her.

"Harrison and I just had a fight."

"Okay. Do you want to tell me about it?"

Tears sprung from my eyes. "I'm really not normally such a baby. I don't know why I'm crying all the time these days. Most of the time they're happy tears anyway."

I hated being a blubbering wuss. That was not my style at all.

She laughed. "You're not being a baby. I think a lot of things you've avoided were waiting for you here. And you came back home to face them."

I shook my head. "But I didn't. I came back home to help my mom. I didn't want to dredge everything up."

She set her notebook on the side table beside her. "Listen, Laney, for whatever reason, you're here. And sometimes the things we don't want to face are the things holding us back. Maybe if you just talk about it, you'll feel better. Get it all off your chest."

"I'll lose him," I whispered. "He won't look at me the same."

"I thought you said he loves you more than anyone ever has."

"He does." I chewed the inside of my cheek and swallowed down the taste of metal as the blood broke free.

"When you love someone, you love them regardless of their mistakes, Laney. We're all human. And you forgave him for pushing you to go back to school and breaking up with you. Why can't you give him the same opportunity?"

"It'll hurt him too much. I know him."

She nodded. "Okay. Then find a way to tell him that will hurt him the least. Because it sounds like you're going to lose him if you don't get this off your chest. Secrets always surface. And if you keep them in, they'll eat you alive. You need to just tear off that bandage. I'm here if you want to unload on me. You know that, right?"

"I do." I said, tears streaming down my face. "I've never said it aloud. Not to anyone. Because when I do, it's going to be real."

"You know that just because you haven't said it, it's still real, Laney. And it's hurting you in a different way. What are you going to do?"

"The only thing I can. I'm going to tell him," I said, pushing to my feet.

It was a long time ago. He deserved to know. I'd never told a soul. I'd buried this secret for so long, I didn't know how to even say it. I thought I'd take it to the grave with me. But Jenny was right. I had to tell him because this was the reason I was still holding back. I'd have to find a way to tell him without devastating him. There'd been enough of that for a lifetime.

Harrison was the most important person in my life. I couldn't risk losing him again. I drove straight to his house. I parked in the driveway and sat there for a minute trying to gather my thoughts. I swiped at my face with the sleeve of my shirt before I pushed out of the car and made my way to the front door.

He opened it immediately and took one look at me and pulled me into him.

"Hey, what's going on? I've called you a dozen times." He hustled me inside and we both dropped to sit on the couch. "Baby, I'll tell you whatever you want to know. I'll even write you out a list of women I've been with since we've been apart. Whatever you need."

I pushed back so I could look at him, shaking my head as I did. "That's not it."

"What is it?"

"There's something I need to tell you, but I don't want to."

"Why?"

"Because you're going to look at me differently. Hell, I look at me differently," I said.

"Nothing could ever make me look at you different y. Never."

I nodded. He was about to find out how wrong he was.

"Har, I've never told anyone this. Not a single soul."

He held both my hands in his, and his dark gaze locked with mine. And all I saw was—*love*.

"You can tell me, baby. I promise it'll be fine."

I let out a long breath. "When I returned to school, you know, after we broke up. I was so upset. A few girls from my sorority were going out the day after I got back, and they convinced me to go."

He nodded. Patiently waiting for me to crush his world. "Go on."

"We were at this club and we were drinking. I was emotional over our breakup. And there was this guy, and he seemed really nice, and I was blubbering on about you. He was with the group we were with, and we were just talking, nothing more. I had zero interest in him."

Harrison shifted on the couch, and I sensed his discomfort.

"We'd been talking for a while. Well, I talked, he listened. But then I started to feel really nauseated out of nowhere, so I ran to the restroom. I vomited a few times. I was so sick. And when I stood up in the bathroom, I struggled to stay on my feet. My vision started going blurry and I panicked. I stumbled out of the restroom to go find my friends, but that guy, he was there, waiting for me. He said he was worried when I ran off. I struggled to walk, and he held me up. I asked him to go get my friends and he said he'd call them, but he wanted to get me home right away." I looked up to meet Harrison's gaze, but I had to turn away. I didn't want to see what I knew would be there.

"What happened, Laney?" His voice remained even.

"I honestly don't remember the details. I started crying because I couldn't see at all. My vision was completely gone. Everything went black. I remember him pulling over so I could open the door and vomit. He told me that he'd called my friends and they were going to meet me at his house because it was closer."

I moved to my feet and grabbed some tissue to blow my nose.

"Tell me what happened next," he said, reaching for me to come sit back down. His eyes were glossy, and I could tell he was doing everything in his power to remain calm.

"I don't know, Harrison. That's the last thing I remember. I woke up the next morning and I didn't know where I was," I said through my sobs. "I was naked. And there was a used condom on the floor."

"What the fuck," he hissed, pushing to his feet and pacing in front of me. "Was he there?"

I nodded, covering my mouth to stop the sobs. "He was—and it was awful."

"What does that mean? Did you confront him? Did he threaten you?" He bent down in front of me and reached for my hands, and anger stirred in his dark gaze.

"I panicked, I mean, I was naked. I hurried to get my clothes on and accused him of drugging me." My whole body started to shake.

He ran his hands up and down my arms. "And what did he say?"

"He laughed. He didn't even try to deny it. He just said I could never prove it, and that I needed to loosen up because I'd wasted his whole night talking about my ex-boyfriend and he'd done me a favor. He said that I didn't say *no*. He kept saying it over and over—that I hadn't said no, and that I'd enjoyed myself. He said no one would believe me because everyone saw us talking earlier and that I shouldn't make it a big deal. We had a good time."

"Jesus fucking Christ." He pushed to stand again and ran his hands through his hair. "Did you get the hell out of there?"

"He wanted to give me a ride, but obviously I refused and called an uber. I got out of there as fast as I could."

"Did you go to the police?"

I shook my head. "No. He was right, Harrison. I'd put myself in that situation. I got in the car with him. I went to his place. I'd been drinking. And God only knows what happened after I was unconscious. I have glimpses, flashbacks, of him touching me. Of me begging him to stop. My body frozen and unable to move. But I don't know if those are real or something I've imagined."

The lump in my throat dissipated, and I was completely gutted. *Empty.*

"Jesus, Laney, you should have fucking reported him." He stood in front of me, his hair standing on end from where he'd tugged on it.

"For what? Everyone would have found out. My parents. *You.* My friends. Teachers. He would've claimed I went to his place willingly and I would have looked guilty."

"So, what did you do?"

"I went to the hospital and told them I thought someone had slipped something in my drink the night before because I'd been so sick. I tested positive for ketamine. They asked if anything happened to me, and I said no." I shrugged, as the tears continued to fall. "I was afraid. I didn't know what to do. I'd never been with anyone other than you. I couldn't think straight. I panicked."

He dropped back down to sit beside me and reached for my hand again. "That's the day you called me. *Three fucking times.*"

He dipped his chin down and closed his eyes.

"Yeah. I didn't know what to do. I couldn't call my parents. You were not only my boyfriend—you were my best friend."

A tear streaked down his cheek when he looked up to meet my gaze. He'd only cried in front of me twice in all the years I'd known him, and that had been at his father's funeral and the night he was drunk in the barn.

"You needed me, and I wasn't there for you."

I chewed the inside of my cheek. "I'm not telling you this to make you feel guilty or for you to try to fix what happened. I'm telling you because if I don't—I think it's going to destroy me. Something changed in me that day, Harrison. Maybe I lost my ability to truly trust, I don't know. But the shame and guilt I feel is eating me alive, and I don't know how to let it go."

He pulled me onto his lap and wrapped his arms around me. "There is absolutely nothing to feel ashamed of, or guilty about. You were a victim, Laney. And you've been holding this in all this time. Is that why you quit your sorority house?"

I rested my cheek against his chest and breathed in all his goodness. "Yes. I just focused on school. I never went out again. I was a hermit those last two years. I didn't want to be around anyone or anything. I was disgusted with myself for letting it happen. Putting myself in a situation that allowed someone to use me that way. It makes me sick to think about."

"This is not your fault. Not in any way, shape, or form. Do you have any idea who he is? Did you ever see him again?"

I'd shared as much as I needed to. The details wouldn't help either of us.

"No. I saw him from a distance a few times on campus, but I steered clear. I filed an anonymous report to the campus police about what happened, and I included his name and address. I used the library computer to report it so they couldn't trace it back to me. I don't know if anything ever came of it, but at least I felt like they would be made aware if anyone else ever reported him. I wasn't thinking clearly at the time. I was not in a good place. Sometimes I wish I'd handled it differently, but it's taken me five years to even tell anyone."

"You would have told me that day. And I would've flown there and gone to the police with you. This is on me, Laney. I failed you. I'm so fucking sorry. I will spend the rest of my life making this up to you." His voice was smooth like steel. Laced with something I didn't recognize.

"How are you not going to look at me differently?" I broke on a sob.

He pulled back and placed a hand on each side of my face, forcing me to meet his gaze. "You're right. I do look at you differently. Because I had no idea just how strong you were, Laney Mae Landers. You've carried this on your shoulders for all this time, never asking anyone for help. You're a brave fucking warrior. So yeah, I have even more respect for you now, which I didn't think was even possible. But in no way would I ever blame you for any of this. Do I wish you would tell me who did it, so I could seek my own fucking revenge on the sick bastard? Yes. I do."

I shook my head. "No. Please. I want to put this behind me so badly, Harrison. Please. Promise me you won't tell anyone or do anything. Promise me."

He wrapped me up in a safe cocoon. "Okay. If that's what you want."

"That's what I want. But I'm glad I told you. I don't want there to be secrets between us."

He kissed the top of my head and we sat like that for a few hours. I cried and he held me. I fell asleep in his arms and woke up when he carried me to his room and set me on the bed.

"What time is it? I should go home." I pushed to sit up.

"I texted your mom and let her know you were staying here tonight. Get some sleep." He kissed my forehead and leaned me back on the pillow. He sat beside me on the edge of the bed. "I love you so fucking much, Laney."

"I love you," I whispered.

I dozed off and didn't wake up until the sun brightened his room. When I sat up, the bed was empty. I replayed the events of last night and buried my face in my hands. Was it good that I'd told him? It actually felt good to get it off my chest. To share my nightmare with someone who wasn't the man who violated me. Someone I trusted completely. Up until now, he was the only other person that knew what had happened to me. Now Harrison knew everything. And we could move forward with no secrets. No lies. I stopped in the bathroom and looked in the mirror. My face was swollen. Eyes puffy and red. But there was a peacefulness that I hadn't seen in a long time. I walked out to the kitchen to find him pouring two cups of coffee.

"Hey," I said.

He turned around, and the sadness in his eyes nearly brought me to my knees. "Good morning, beautiful. I was just going to bring you some coffee. How do you feel?"

"I feel okay. How about you?" I asked. I couldn't read him. He was containing a whole lot of emotion under that stoic front of his.

He pulled out a bar stool for me and then took the one beside it. He set our coffees down and turned to face me. "Listen, Laney, I'm really glad you told me everything. I'm really sorry that you've been carrying this around all this time. Alone. And I'm most sorry that I wasn't there for you. So fucking sorry."

"I knew you would blame yourself, and that's why I didn't want to tell you. But it's a hard secret to keep from the man you love." Two tears streaked down my cheek. "And a part of me feared that you might look at me differently. Because I haven't felt like the same person since it happened."

"I don't know why you would possibly think I'd look at you differently. Jesus. You were a victim in this sick fucker's game. And he didn't change you, Laney. No fucking way. He violated you—caused you to lose your trust in others, sure. But who you are..." He placed his palm over my heart on my chest. "He didn't change a fucking thing."

"Do you know how many times my parents told me to make sure I never left a drink unattended when I went out? I let my guard down, Har. I should have been paying attention."

"Don't you dare fucking do that to yourself." His fist came down on the counter and his voice boomed, startling us both. "This is not on you. This is on some sick fucker who gets his rocks off drugging girls and raping them. Don't ever blame yourself again."

I nodded. "I know logically that makes sense. But I own my part. I've never put myself in that position again. Never."

He pushed to his feet and wrapped his arms around me. "I promise that I'll always be there from now on. I promise, Laney."

"I know you will," I whispered.

"You want to go for a bike ride? Get some fresh air?"

"Yeah. I'd like that," I said, scooting off the chair.

We took our time getting ready, and he kissed me no less than a dozen times before we made it out the door—slowly. With compassion and care. We were going to be okay. I felt lighter in a sense now that I'd told him. Like a weight had lifted off my shoulders.

And that was because he'd taken that for me. His reaction had blown me away. He'd been supportive and kind. He didn't judge me or beat me down, the way I'd done to myself so many times over the past five years. I wish I'd found a way to tell him the t uth a long time ago. I should have taken his calls when he reached o it months later. Maybe that's just the part of life that we have to accept.

You may not be able to change the past.

But you could control the future.

twenty

. . .

Harrison

TO SAY that this week had been a whirlwind of emotion was an understatement. So much good had come out of Laney opening up to me about what happened to her. She was now staying at my house every night, and we were talking about the future. Like she'd been a prisoner to her own secret, and she had finally been set free. I was happy about that. I wanted to take some of that burden from her if I could. We were moving forward, and I couldn't ask for more.

But that burden came with a different set of problems. One being the fact that my girlfriend was drugged and raped and violated. No way was I okay with that. So, I was at a crossroads. I'd promised Laney I wouldn't do anything about it or tell anyone about what happened either. Obviously, five years later, it would be impossible to go after the piece of shit who did this to her. We couldn't prove jackshit. But what I felt inside—it burned like a fucking forest fire. Rage. Anger. A need to make someone pay.

I was a smart guy. Revenge had its upside and its downside. The upside being the satisfaction of beating the shit out of the guy who'd hurt her. Whether or not we could prove what he did legally, it didn't matter, because I just wanted to hurt him. The downside being hurting Laney more by doing so. But I hadn't been able to shake it. And I couldn't talk to anyone because I'd given her my word that I wouldn't. What kind of fucked up promise is that? The woman I love was violated and I couldn't do or say anything about it. The only thing keeping me from acting on my rage, was the fact that she'd called me when it happened. Three fucking times. And I'd ignored her call.

Fuck.

I punched the wall as I stood in the bathroom at the winery. I'd come in here to clear my head. Pace around a room without anyone asking why I was doing it. I leaned over the sink and rinsed my knuckles as the water forced the blood down the drain.

She'd needed me and I hadn't been there. And where the fuck were my friends that night? I'd asked Big Joe to watch out for her. He was my closest friend back at school, and he'd said he never saw Laney out after I left. She'd obviously gone out one night, and no one had been there to protect her. The one time I wasn't there. I leaned my back against the wall and buried my face in my hands. I didn't know what to do with all this anger. It was foreign to me—not being able to tamper it down. Sure, after Dad died, I was angry at the world. But this was different. This was injustice at its finest. A sick fucking predator preying on the innocence and trust of the girl I loved. I wrapped the paper towels around my hand when someone knocked on the door.

"Harrison?" It was Laney.

"Yeah, I'll be right out." I dried my hands and headed for the door.

Laney and I were good. Golden, even. I think her finally telling me this secret that had been haunting her for years finally allowed us to get back to where we'd been before. And for that, I was grateful. Now I just needed to get myself under control.

"Hey, what are you doing?" I tucked my hands in my pockets to hide my battered hand.

She smiled. "It's time to head to the city. Did you forget?"

"No. Just lost track of time."

We were going to San Francisco for the afternoon. Laney was meeting with Harley to go over the desserts for the party, and I was going to hang out with my brothers to discuss a few things at Montgomery Media, and then we'd all go to dinner together

"Your mom just left for an appointment, so it's perfect. She won't even know we're gone," Laney whispered.

"Ah, very sneaky," I winked.

We drove over to where we kept the helicopter, and Laney leaned against my shoulder once we were up in the air. "It's been a crazy couple of months since I came home, hasn't it?"

"I wouldn't expect anything less," I teased.

"Remember when we flew to the city for my mom's appointment? I was barely speaking to you then."

I laughed. "Yeah. And I was crazy in love with you and didn't know what to do about it."

She pushed up to face me. "I was crazy in love with you, too. I just didn't know how to handle all those feelings."

"Well, seeing as you were engaged to someone else and all...that made it challenging."

She winced. "Yeah, that was when I realized something wasn't right with Charlie. Well, I think I knew it before that, but after seeing you, it forced me to deal with it."

Laney had put me back together in ways she couldn't begin to understand. I was finally whole again. And I wanted to make all her bad memories go away. Erase that night for her. But I didn't know how to do that.

"Hey, where'd you go?" she asked.

"I'm right here."

"You sure?"

"Of course, why?"

"Well, ever since I told you what happened to me, I find you dazing off into space a lot. You want to tell me what you're thinking?" she said, intertwining her fingers with mine.

Damn, this girl knew me.

"Obviously, I won't break my promise to you, but I'd be lying if I didn't admit I wanted someone to pay for what happened. I want to take all that pain away for you."

And beat the living shit out of the guy who did this to you.

"You already are. Just telling you helped a lot. Seeing myself through your eyes made me look at the situation differently. I never saw myself as a victim. I honestly believed it was my fault for a long time. But you've helped me close the door on those feelings. Anger isn't healthy, Harrison. We need to let it go. I've los enough of my life."

I pulled her close and wrapped my arms around ier. "Of course. Love you, baby."

"I love you, too." She swiped at her cheeks and smi ed.

She was right. And it was the least I could do. I n eded to do this for her. I'd failed her once. Never again. I'd bury this hit deep inside and leave it there.

She flipped my hand over and noticed the skin n issing from my knuckles. "What happened?"

I didn't want her to worry. "I was getting some woc d from the barn and scraped it."

She nodded, looking up at me and studying my gaz before smiling and resting her head against my chest.

Once we were on the ground, we headed over o Montgomery Media. It was an iconic building on the busiest corne in the city and we made our way to see Harley at the bakery. My brother always wanted her to hire more help because he thought she v orked too hard. Ford was protective by nature, but when it came to Harley, he bordered on the ridiculous. I loved it. Loved seeing hi n love big—the way he did with his wife. It was the kind of love our parents shared. The kind of love I shared with Laney. So, I got it. I und rstood his need to keep her safe.

When we arrived, Jack was already at the bakery w th a cupcake in hand.

Shocker.

"Laney Mae, bring it in, girl." He shoved the past y in his mouth and scooped my girl off her feet.

"Are you getting crumbs in my hair, Jack-ass?" s ie said through her laughter.

"Maybe a little," he spoke around a mouthful of cal .

"Stop harassing the customers." Harley swatted m brother with a dish towel before wrapping her arms around n y middle and hugging me.

"Busy day?" I asked.

"Yeah. Always."

"That's why I'm here," Jack said, moving behind the counter. "Keep things moving."

"He's here because the new girl I hired is cute." Harley smirked and hugged Laney. "I'm glad we're going to dinner. We need to catch up."

"Yes. So much to catch up on," Laney said.

"I'll be back in an hour and we can head to dinner. I'm going up to see Ford. Jack, are you coming with me or staying here?"

"What do you think he's going to do?" Harley rolled her eyes.

"I'm staying," he sang out from the kitchen.

If I could spend a day in the life of Jack Montgomery, I might never return to reality. He'd been like that since the day he'd entered the world. Loud and proud—and annoying as hell.

I tipped Laney's head back and kissed her hard. "I'll see you soon."

"You will." She held onto my hand until I was at the door.

Ford's assistant Sam greeted me when I stepped off the elevator. "He's waiting for you. Where's the doofus?"

Yes, Jack had a reputation.

I laughed. "Where do you think? Eating cupcakes."

"He was supposed to bring us up a box an hour ago."

"He probably ate them all." I knocked on her desk and made my way to Ford's office.

"Hey," I said, walking in and dropping in the chair across from his desk.

"What's up? Are Laney and Harley going over the details for Mom's party?"

"Yep. And Jack's down there chasing tail and eating cake." I laughed.

"I don't get it. The kid eats more baked goods than anyone I've ever seen, yet he's never gained a pound. Where the hell does he put it?"

"He's always been a freak of nature."

"Yeah, he has. So, I just sent you the forecasting for next quarter. You can go over the numbers whenever you have time and let me know if everything looks good." He leaned back in his chair. There was something lighter about him, and he wore it well.

"Sure. I'll get back to you later in the week."

"Great. And we're all set for the party?"

"Yeah, I think Laney's got it all dialed in," I said, drifting off again like I'd been doing so much lately.

"Good. And everything's going well with you two now? Did you talk to her about letting go of her place in Chicago?"

That seemed like a conversation from a hundred years ago now. I understood why Laney hadn't made a decision about the future at that point, because she was living with something she didn't know if she could share.

"Yep. She already gave notice. She accepted the position at the winery. We're going to fly to Chicago and move her out of her place after the party."

Ford leaned forward in his seat and folded his hands on his desk. "That's great. When did this all go down?"

I shrugged. "The last few days."

"What's going on with you?"

"What? Nothing? I'm happy."

"I know you, brother. I believe you're happy, but something's going on. Spill."

"I don't know what you're talking about." I rolled my eyes.

"You know how everyone always teases you for being the peaceful one? What Dad called you, the peacekeeper?" He laughed.

"Yeah?"

"Well, you break up fights and settle us all down when we're being irrational. But you wear your heart on your sleeve, and I know when something's eating away at you. You haven't taken my calls this week. You didn't tell me Laney took the job. What the hell is up?"

"Listen, I can't talk about it." I looked up to meet his gaze.

"Unfortunately, you're also the most loyal motherfucker on the planet. So, you can't talk about it because god-for-fucking-bid you ever break a promise," he said with a smirk.

I already broke the most important promise to keep Laney safe. I made that promise to her when we were five. I broke it the day I turned my back on her. It would never happen again.

"What can I say? I take it to the grave, brother."

He studied me. "So, you can't talk about it, but it's eating you up, right?"

"No comment."

"You're struggling with the promise though, aren't you? Let me help you. You don't have to tell me what it is. Just, I don't know, draw me a picture." He chuckled.

Ford was a man of few words most of the time. But he loved his family, and he always put us first. I appreciated that about him. Our father would be proud of the way he'd filled his shoes.

"Has Harley ever asked you to do something for her that went against everything in your nature?"

"Yes." He didn't even have to think about it.

"And you honored it?"

He reached for his water bottle and took a long pull. "Does what she's asking you to do put her in danger?"

I thought it over. It didn't. I was too late to step in and rescue her. This was about revenge. Holding someone accountable.

"No."

"Then let it go, brother. Honor her when you can. There may come a time when it's not an option."

I nodded. "Have you ever been so angry that you needed to get it out?"

"All the fucking time." He barked out a laugh. "Come with me to the boxing gym. You can beat the shit out of a bag. Don't risk your relationship, Har. You just got her back. Whatever it is—leave it alone."

He was right. Acting on my anger would be serving myself. Sure, I wanted to defend her honor, but what would that do for Laney? Nothing. All I needed to do was love her every day from here on out, and that would be easy.

I pushed to stand. "You're right. I'm actually going to take your advice."

He smirked. "You always do."

"I'll let you keep thinking that," I said, following him out of his office and onto the elevator.

When we arrived at the bakery, Laney and Harley were smiling, and Jack was holding a spatula and singing into it like a fool. I realized right then, I had everything I wanted. I couldn't change what happened during the time that Laney and I were apart, but I could damn well make sure every day after was perfect for her.

"What the hell are you doing?" Ford said as he opened the door, and everyone laughed.

Laney hurried over to me and wrapped her arms around my middle. "Missed you."

"Missed you, too." I kissed the tip of her nose.

"Missed you three," Jack shouted, wrapping his arms around both of us and squeezing tight.

"Break it up. I'm starving," Ford said over the chaos. Harley flipped out the lights and we walked down the street to the steakhouse.

We placed our orders and the waiter brought out our drinks.

"So, Priscilla is totally into me," Jack said, tearing off a chunk of bread and popping it in his mouth.

"Who the hell is Priscilla?" Ford asked.

"She's the new girl that started today." Harley elbowed her husband. "And she has a boyfriend, playboy. Don't make her leave me before she even gets started."

"That's her way of saying, *keep your dick in your pants, asshole*. We don't need any drama. And I'll tell you why," Ford said, setting his wine glass down.

"Why what?" Jack asked with annoyance.

"Why we don't need any drama," he barked at our younger brother.

"Oh. Do tell." Jack perked up and we all waited.

"Tell them, baby," he whispered to Harley.

She kissed him before turning to the table. "We're preggers. Well, I guess I'm preggers. Big Daddy over here helped, though."

I gasped. Laney clapped her hands together. And Jack jumped to his feet.

"I'm going to be an uncle," he shouted and threw his hands in the air, as everyone in the restaurant turned to stare at him. We all laughed.

I pushed to stand and made my way over to Ford and hugged him tight. "I'm happy for you. Congrats. You're going to be a kick-ass dad."

"Thanks. I'm damn well going to give it my best shot."

"No doubt about it, brother."

Laney hugged Harley and Ford and we all made our rounds.

When I returned to my seat, Laney leaned against my arm. I looked down to see her swipe at a falling tear.

"You okay?"

She looked up at me, her gaze full of emotion. "Yeah. Things are just coming together, huh? Everyone is moving forward. It just gives me so much, I don't know, what's the word? Hope? Yep. Hope."

And she was right.

Life had a way of forcing you to move forward.

And that's exactly what I planned to do with Laney.

twenty-one

. . .

Laney

"OH MY GOSH, when did you become such a baby?" I said with a laugh as we walked up the path toward Jenny's office.

"A baby?" he gasped. "Did you just therapy shame me?"

I shook my head, trying to hide my smile with my hand. I'd come to see Jenny the day after I told Harrison everything. For some reason, now that I had told him what happened, I was okay sharing it with her. I hadn't felt this good in years.

Free.

At peace.

But my boyfriend, as much as he liked to pretend that he was okay —he wasn't. He wasn't sleeping, and he was constantly distracted. I'd dropped a bomb on him that I'd been dealing with for five years. It was new for him. And for Harrison Montgomery, seeing the people he loved hurt was worse than being hurt himself. It was a big part of the reason I hadn't told him for so long. I knew this would wreck him, and I didn't want to go there. So, Jenny suggested we come together to therapy. He'd fought me on it, insisting he was fine. I'd pulled out the big guns and said I'd consider moving in with him if he was willing to talk this out with her—and he'd agreed to come today.

"Hey, if the shoe fits." I smirked.

"I just don't see the need to be here. I told you, I'm fine. But if it helps you, then I'll do it."

Whatever he needed to believe to get him here was fine with me.

"Great," I said, knocking on the office door.

"Laney, hey there. You must be Harrison?" Jenny said, offering her hand to him.

"Yep. Nice to meet you."

We took our seats on the sofa and she offered us each a water, which we accepted. I sat close to him, our fingers intertwined and rested between us.

"So, Harrison, I understand this is your first time in therapy?"

"Yes."

Ford had been going since their father passed away, but Harrison always insisted that he was okay. That was his role—always being okay.

Even when he wasn't.

"Well, nothing to be nervous about. We're just here to talk through what Laney shared with you, and then later with me. It's a lot to process."

"Yeah. I mean, it's horrific what she went through. I'm not sure why I'm here, but if it helps her, I'm happy to do it."

Jenny nodded and glanced at me. "I get that. But it's also not an easy thing to hear that someone you love was violated either, right?"

"Sure. But I didn't go through what she did. I wasn't violated. Laney was. So, my concern is with Laney." His hand let go of mine and fisted as he moved it to his lap.

"Right. Exactly. But sometimes when our loved ones experience something horrific, it's very difficult for us to process those things. To know what to do with that anger."

"Yes. That makes sense. But I also think you have to *man up*. She's the one who had to deal with what happened. The least I can do is just be here for her."

"She did. And I do think finally sharing what happened with you has been a huge weight off her shoulders. She's also five years ahead of you with this news, so she's had time to process what happened. This is all new for you."

"I'm glad she told me, and I'm happy to take any weight I can from her shoulders."

"I'm sure you are. But taking some of that burden from Laney does not mean that it can't cause you pain either."

"Meaning?" he said, his posture stiffening beside me. He was irritated and making every attempt to hide it, but I knew him.

"Meaning, helping Laney with what happened doesn't mean you can't feel it also. You're entitled to your feelings, Harrison. And hearing that the woman you loved was violated will obviously bring up a lot of anger."

He nodded. "Okay. Sure. I'm angry. I'm fucking pissed."

"Of course, you are. It's okay for you to be *angry*, to be *fucking pissed*. Do you feel like you aren't allowed to express that?"

"Pfft," he threw his arms in the air, "how do I express that exactly? I can't talk to anyone because it's a secret. And I get that I can't go after the guy. I can't punch anyone or break anything, right? *I'm that guy*. I keep my shit together. So, do I feel like I can express what I'm feeling? Hell no. And that's okay. That's the price I have to pay for what happened. For my role in this. I wasn't there for her. It's the least I can do." He reached for my hand again, and I turned to face him.

"It's not because you weren't there for me, Harrison. It happened. Life happens. I've been holding all this in for so long, and now that it's out, I feel—free. Better than I have in years. And that's because of you," I said, tears streaming down my face. "I thought that if I told you…you would look at me differently. Like I was weak or at fault. But instead, you looked at me with so much love, I found a way to look at myself that way again. I'm learning to love myself again because of how much you love me. Do you see how much you're helping me, just by being here?"

"I love you so much, Laney. But yeah—this is killing me. I want to break something. Hurt someone. Make him pay for what he did to you. I want him to suffer the way you did."

I placed a hand on each of his cheeks and forced him to look at me. "I felt that way for a long time too. But the truth is— he's a miserable human being. He's suffering, Harrison, in his own way. I don't doubt that for a minute. And there are days I'm ashamed of myself for not coming forward because I was weak and scared. But I reported him to campus security. I'm sure they followed him. They were made aware. I wasn't in a place to do more than that, and that's something I have to live with. But I've also learned that living with that anger—it isn't healthy. So, if you need to talk to Ford and Jack so you can get this off your chest and make peace with it, you can do that. I trust you. And I trust them. I realize now that it wasn't fair of me to drop this bomb on you and not expect you to need to talk about it. To share that pain with someone other than me." I nodded, as the tears continued to fall.

He studied me for a long moment and pulled me close to him, wrapping his arm around me. "Laney Mae Landers, you've always been wiser than your years."

"I can see that as well. And I think you two are going to be just fine. I don't know that I've ever seen two people put the other first quite like this," Jenny said.

Harrison kissed the top of my head. "It's been like that since day one."

"That's what I've been told," Jenny said with a chuckle. "I also understand you only agreed to come here if Laney considered moving in with you?" She had a smirk on her face as she directed the question to my boyfriend.

"Damn straight. I'm not above blackmail if it means I get to wake up with my girl every day."

"And I might be the world's best poker player, because I already made my mind up about moving in with you before I made this deal," I said, swiping at the last of my tears and looking up at him. His dark determined gaze locked with mine. Strong. Kind. Loyal. I saw it all right there, just like I always had.

My rock.

My love.

My everything.

"You've always been a bit devious."

"I'm fine with that." I laughed.

He dropped a peck on my lips, and we talked more about what happened and how to move forward. But I knew in that moment that we were going to be okay.

There was no other option.

I wasn't living without this man again, so getting past it was something we'd do together.

———

It was the day before Monica's fiftieth, and to say I had a lot going on would be an understatement. But my boyfriend had moving on the brain and he'd gone ahead and organized everything for me. He'd had my apartment in Chicago packed up and delivered to his home this morning, in lieu of us flying there after the party to move out. He didn't want to wait. It was insane how much you could organize from a distance these days. I'd moved out of an apartment hundreds of miles away without stepping foot in the state of Illinois.

"You have a package from Amazon," Harrison called out as he tore open another box.

"*Oh*, I know what this is," I said, hurrying to cut the boxes open and then asking him to grab one and follow me outside. We walked out, a box in each of our arms to the cement slab that he was going to have removed from his yard at some point. It used to be a basketball court, but he was redoing the whole space and had removed the hoops and poles. There was a cement wall on the back side bordering it and I set down the box and motioned for him to do the same.

"Baby, we've got a shit ton to do today. What is his?" He stood there with his hair disheveled, wearing navy joggers and a white fitted T-shirt. His muscles flexed against the cotton fabric, and I had to chew the inside of my lip to keep from jumping on him. He was too handsome for his own good.

I pushed up on my tiptoes and kissed his soft, plump lips. "Do you trust me?"

"Always." He pushed the hair back from my face. His gentle touch sent chill bumps down my spine.

"Okay then. Open yours." I handed him a butter knife after opening mine.

"Plates? Are these for the party?"

"Nope. These are for us." I turned to face him. "Remember when you said you wanted to hit something?"

He laughed. "Yeah?"

"I do too. So, we've each got a set of thirty-two cheap plates to smash against that wall. Let's get busy."

"You're serious? We're just going to break these dishes?"

"Yep." I picked up the first plate and closed my eyes, thinking about how long I'd carried the guilt and shame, and I leaned back and chucked the plate against the wall as hard as I could. It smashed against the bricks and shattered into a million little pieces. I looked up at Harrison. He stared down with mischief in his eyes and a wide grin.

"Damn. All right. I suppose this is cheaper than therapy, and equally productive." He picked up his first plate and stood, deep in thought, before wailing it at the cement wall. And damn, my boyfriend was a badass when he wanted to be.

My head fell back in laughter and I reached for another. We took turn after turn, letting all the bad memories shatter before us. It was therapeutic, and somehow Harrison made it sexy. The way he unleashed that inner rage he worked so hard to keep hidden from everyone but me.

"I think we should make this a monthly ritual any time something pisses us off." He chucked his last plate at the wall before pulling me against him and kissing me hard.

"Not a bad idea. But right now, we need to get changed and get to work." I tipped my head back to look at him.

"Shower first. Together."

"You dirty dog. We'll have to hurry," I said, reaching for his hand and leading him inside.

"No way. I plan on taking my time with you, Laney Landers."

I walked backwards toward the shower, his hands in mine. "Oh yeah? Don't make promises you can't keep, Montgomery."

"Never," he said, yanking his T-shirt over his head and tossing it on the floor. He leaned in the shower and turned on the water, before tugging my tank over my head.

I pushed down my shorts and panties as he kicked off his joggers and briefs and we stepped into the steaming shower. The water beat down over me, and I tipped my head back and closed my eyes. Harrison's hands were on me. He backed me up until I hit the shower wall, and he kissed me. Gently at first, as his hands roamed my body. His lips moved down my body, lavishing each hard peak as he grazed over my breasts. He dropped to his knees as he kissed his way down and pressed his palms against my inner thighs, pushing them apart. He buried his face between my legs and kissed me in my most sensitive area. I gasped with surprise, arching off the wall and tangling my fingers in his wet, thick hair. I closed my eyes and gave in to the sensation. Building and aching with such a need only this man could fill. He moaned against my heat and it was all I could take before I cried out my release. Water droplets rolled down his chiseled back, and he looked up at me with a wicked smile. Ridiculously sexy.

"Not a bad way to start the morning," I said over the rushing water. My raspy voice was hardly recognizable.

He pushed to his feet, towering over me as he licked his lips. "I can't think of a better way to start my morning."

My head fell back in laughter. Because he was right.

I dropped to my knees, eager to return the favor and he groaned when I looked up to meet his gaze. Water beat down on his handsome face, and I smiled up at him.

As long as Harrison was beside me, I'd always be happy.

And very satisfied.

twenty-two

· · ·

Laney

"THIS LOOKS PERFECT HERE," I said, taking in the space.

The tent was up. Three chandeliers hung from above to provide soft lighting for tonight. One hundred and three guests had RSVP'd to attend Monica's surprise party, and I couldn't wait. We'd been working on this event for the past six weeks. Planning parties was my favorite thing to do, and having an unlimited budget—well, that was hard to beat. We'd pulled out all the stops. Harrison and his brothers wanted this to be a forever memory.

I had a slideshow put together of her life and highlighted the special moments of her wedding and the birth of her three boys. Photofetti covered the white linen cloths on each table, with small circular photos of Monica throughout each decade of her life. It was fun to go through the pictures with Harrison and let him choose his favorites. One of the perks of dating the event planner, I guess. The white and blush arrangements were centered around her favorite flowers. Roses, hydrangeas, and peonies. There wasn't a detail missed. The décor was elegant and classic, just like the woman being honored.

We'd transformed Harrison's property. The tent was set up out on his acre of land, between several tall trees as grape fields sat in the distance. We'd cornered off one section of the yard for parking and hired several valet attendants to make sure things ran smoothly. Jack had pushed to have the food catered by Monica's favorite Italian restaurant that she and Ford Sr. ate at every year on their anniversary. Ford would give a speech after dinner. It impressed me that these three men, who were each strong and powerful in their own right, had been so determined to give their mother an evening she'd remember forever.

Not everyone knew how thoughtful the Montgomery boys were, but I had a front row seat to just how kind they were to the people they loved. I'd been overcome with nostalgia lately. Maybe it was going through all the pictures for the party. Maybe it was telling Harrison what happened to me all those years ago and letting go of the guilt and anger that I'd held onto for so long. Or maybe it was just being back home where I belonged with the only man who ever owned my heart. But I was feeling all of it lately. From the way he looked at me to the way he held me. But most importantly—the way he loved me.

"This looks insane," Harrison said, as he stepped out of his car and joined me. He'd been at the winery all day so his mom wouldn't be suspicious. He told her I was in the city working on the event for Montgomery Media.

"It's coming together, isn't it?"

"You're so talented, baby," he said, wrapping his arms around my middle and settling his chin on top of my head.

"Thank you," I said.

"Laney, do the outhouses go over here?" Craig, one of the many workers that was helping me set up, asked.

"Yes, let me show you," I said, kissing my boyfriend on the cheek and leading them both over to where it would go. "We have two sinks that I want in the center, and the five outhouses set up in a line here."

"Got it." He jogged off toward his truck.

I led Harrison into the tent and showed him where everything would go. "I can't even wait to see Harley's desserts. She's been sending me pictures of the cake she made. It's...indescribable. She's so talented."

"She is." He nodded.

"So, let's talk about how you're going to get your mom here and go over the plans for her entrance. She's arriving thirty minutes after our guests, so be sure to text me when you're on your way. I can make sure everyone is inside the tent and out of sight. She'll be dressed for dinner at our house so just bring her up the driveway when you get here, so she won't see all the cars on the other side of the tent. Then tell her that you want to show her something out back and the golf cart will be parked right off the patio for you. Jack and Ford will already be sitting on the cart waiting for you. And then just drive her down. I'll have lanterns lining the path for you all the way down to the tent."

He shook his head. "Damn, baby. You don't miss a beat."

"It's my job *not* to miss anything."

"No. It's all you, Laney." He wrapped an arm around my shoulder and kissed me. "Okay, I'm going to get back to the winery and then I'll head over here to change clothes before I pick her up."

"Okay. I'll see you later, handsome. I need to get back to work," I said, as three people stood off to the side waiting for me.

"Love you." We both said it at the same time and laughed.

I spent the rest of the day getting it all done. Parties were always more work than you anticipated, and the last few hours were crunch time when you threw events of this nature. There were a lot of moving parts. But this was going to be an amazing night, and I couldn't wait.

I'd had to hurry to get ready and scolded my boyfriend numerous times when he'd tried for a quickie in the bathroom as I hustled to slip on my dress and pull my long hair into a chignon. He had a one-track mind these days, and most of the time I was right there with him. But not when we had over one hundred guests on their way to the house.

"Go. I love you." I straightened his tie and pointed at the door. "Remember, when she asks why you're in a suit, you know what to say."

"*Laney is excited about having our first dinner party at the house and she made me wear it,*" he grumbled before leaning down and nibbling at my ear.

"Oh my god, Harrison Montgomery. Get out of here. You're killing me," I said through a fit of giggles as goose bumps covered my arms at his teasing.

He laughed and moved toward the door. "All right, baby. I'll see you in thirty minutes. It looked like the lot was filling up when I drove by on my way here. Ford, Harley, and Jack are down there now, so they'll get everyone assembled until you get there."

"Okay. Remember to hold her there until it's time. Send me a text when you're on your way."

"Got it. Love you."

"Love you," I said, giving him a chaste kiss.

I dabbed on some lip gloss before I jumped in the golf cart and made my way down to the party.

The drive to the tent was lit by candlelight tucked in over seventy-five wooden lanterns. The elegant décor tied into the outdoor scenery, which sat in the distance like a painting. The sun had gone down, the stars were twinkling, and the air was just cool enough to keep people comfortable. I parked the golf cart and found Harley slapping Jack on the hand.

"If you eat one more of those, I swear to all that's holy, I'll kick your ass," she said through her laughter.

"Damn, Harls. Your hormones have sure been funky since my brother put that baby in you. Tone it down, girl. It's a party."

"I told you, brother. Don't piss her off right now," Ford said, draping an arm over his wife's shoulder and kissing her neck.

I barked out a laugh at their banter. "Hey, how are we doing?"

"Laney, this looks incredible. Wow. She is going to absolutely love it." Harley pulled me in for a hug.

"You outdid yourself, girl," Jack said over a mouthful of something, and Harley punched him in the arm.

"Mom's going to love it. You did good, Laney Mae." Ford pulled me in next.

Harrison had opened up to his brothers about what happened to me when I'd returned to school, and I'd been okay with it. He needed to share his anger with someone he trusted and seeing as I trusted them as much as he did, I'd been fine with it. They never brought it up to me, as I'm sure my boyfriend made them promise they wouldn't, but they'd both looked at me with such empathy after they found out. It had brought me to tears on more than one occasion. They hugged me a little tighter these days and that was okay. I wasn't offended or self-conscious. They loved me as much as I loved them, and they hurt for what I went through. We were moving forward, and I was glad Harrison had them to lean on.

"Thanks, I'm happy you guys are pleased. I can't wait to see her face," I said.

Theresa walked over to show me the guest list and inform me that everyone had arrived. I shot a quick text to Harrison to let him know we were ready. I then put Ford and Jack in the golf cart and sent them up to the house to wait for Monica.

"Laney, this ice sculpture is incredible." Harley pointed at the large sculpture of the number fifty sitting on the bar top.

"Yes, I think it's gorgeous. But nothing compares to your pastries. And this cake. Harley, you outdid yourself," I said, taking in the four-tiered white and blush pink floral cake. It was the focal point of the dessert table. "This is incredible."

"Thank you. I really wanted to make it special for her. We're lucky. Marrying into a family like this. With so much love and all." Harley shrugged.

"I'm not married just yet." I chuckled. "But I agree. We are lucky to be part of such a special family. Even *Jack-ass* is irresistible."

"Don't get me started on that one. I lost my new employee because he, well, how do I say it without being crass? He hooked up with her, and of course, she fell head over heels, and he didn't want anything serious. So, there were tears. A few cupcakes thrown at his head. And she waltzed out the door." Harley closed her eyes and laughed. "He's ridiculous. He needs a woman that doesn't take his shit."

"He sure does. It'll happen one of these days, but it will take one heck of a special woman," I said.

We both chuckled at the thought as my parents walked up and I introduced them to Harley. And before I knew it, Harrison was texting me that they were at the house.

"It's game time," I said, gathering everyone into the center of the tent.

We all stood quietly until we heard the golf cart approaching. When Monica stepped out and the whole group erupted with birthday wishes, the party truly started. Music played through the speakers, people bustled around, visiting and waiting to hug the woman of the hour. Monica truly looked stunned, and when her gaze locked with mine over Harrison's shoulder, tears streamed down her face. She wore a lavender dress and she looked stunning.

"Laney, I don't even know what to say," her voice shook as she pulled me in her arms. "I love you, sweet girl. Thank you for this and for making my boy so happy again."

I tried to keep the emotion at bay, but a few tears escaped, and I quickly swiped them away. "Of course. Happy Birthday. Get ready to have some fun."

The night was a blur. There was dancing and chatting and lots of laughter. The slideshow was a hit, and Monica cried through the entire thing. Ford's speech brought the whole room to tears as he praised his mother's strength for keeping them all afloat these past few years. He raised his glass, and everyone cheered. Harrison hustled me onto the dance floor, and I lost feeling in my feet somewhere along the way, so I finally kicked off my heels. It was a night to remember. Even my mom danced the night away and seeing her smile and laugh as Dad twirled her around was something I'd never forget.

The party lasted late into the evening and ended just before midnight.

"Thank you for everything." Monica beamed.

"Glad you were surprised, Mom," Harrison said, as he wrapped his arms around her.

"Love you, Laney." She gave me one more hug and thanked me no less than a dozen times throughout the evening. It felt good to have pulled off such a grand surprise for a woman who'd always been like a second mother to me.

"Love you, too. I'll see you tomorrow."

Ford, Harley, and Jack took her home, and Harrison and I made our way back to the house. We both collapsed in bed within minutes.

It had been one heck of a day.

And I was thankful for all these moments with him.

"I don't understand why we're going up in the tree house," I whined as I climbed the ladder.

We'd spent the entire day in bed after the party, and I would have been just fine staying there for the rest of the night. I was exhausted. Harrison had gone out for a few hours to take care of a few things at the winery while I'd slept some more. But when he came home, he insisted I get dressed and come with him.

To sit in my childhood tree house.

Really?

We had a very comfortable bed back at home, so I didn't know why he insisted on coming here.

"My parents are going to want to come out and then they'll insist we go in and visit. I say we just go grab some takeout and eat it in bed," I grumbled on my way up the ladder.

"Stop your whining and get up there." He smacked my butt from behind me.

"It's dark as all heck," I said as I got to the top rung and looked down at him.

"Oh. Is it?" he whispered before clicking something in his hand and lighting up the entire tree house and the overgrown tree that held it.

I gasped, as twinkle lights lined the ceiling, and I climbed inside. There were white floor pillows, vases filled with white flowers, and champagne with two glasses. A little plate with chocolate-covered strawberries sat in the middle, and photos of the two of us were hung on a clothesline wire all the way around the space. I covered my mouth as I took it in. Pictures over the span of twenty years hung from the string. I turned around to say something, and Harrison was down on one knee, looking at me like I hung the moon.

"Laney Mae Landers, I have loved you my entire life. I loved you when you threw sand in my face. I loved you when you loved me too. I loved you when I pushed you away. And I love you today."

"Harrison," I said, the word breaking on a sob.

"There was never a doubt we were meant to spend our lives together. You're the only one for me."

"Say it," I said, swiping frantically at my tears and] e chuckled.

"Laney, will you marry me and make me the hap iest man in the world?"

"Yes," I shouted, lunging at him before I even look d at the ring he was holding.

Because none of that mattered. All that mattered w is that we were going to be together forever.

He laughed and leaned back to look at me. "I love y ou."

"I love you, too." He held out the ring and my jaw hit the ground. It was a princess-cut diamond, and it sparkled in the li ht coming from above.

A whistle came from below and I peeked out to nd both of our families. His brothers and Harley. My brother and Gi . Monica stood beside my parents. And I turned back to look at Har ison and shook my head with disbelief.

"You're not the only one who can pull off a surprise " he said.

"You're damn right about that." I leaned through t e door, waving at everyone below.

They all said they'd meet us inside, as apparently ny parents had set up a bunch of appetizers and cocktails to celebra e. But Harrison and I sat in the tree house reminiscing about our childhood and dreaming about our future together.

Always together.

twenty-three

. . .

Harrison

I HAD several meetings in the city and received a call from Big Joe, a college buddy I'd kept in touch with. He usually came out this way for business at least once a year and we'd get together.

"Har, my man. Sorry for the last-minute call. My company cut travel budgets this year and they were only sending the top two reps, but someone got sick last minute, so here I am."

"Well, if they knew what was good for them, they'd have sent you off the bat," I said with a chuckle. Big Joe was a good guy, and a top salesman for his company.

"No shit. And get this, I ran into Coop at the convention, haven't seen the dude for years, and we run into one another here. What are the chances?" He laughed. Coop was a fraternity brother who was a year older than us and a bit of a ball breaker, but he was an okay guy.

"Small world. How long are you guys here?"

"It's a short there and back for me. I fly out in the morning. Any chance you can grab dinner? Laney's welcome to come, too. I miss the shit out of that girl," he said, and I chuckled. He and Laney had been good friends back at Columbia.

I scrubbed a hand over my face as I thought about it. "I can't meet you in the city, but you're both welcome to fly back with us to Napa and join us for dinner. We're meeting my mom, Laney, and Ford's wife at the winery in an hour."

"All right. Sounds good. Count me in and I'll see i Coop wants to tag along. He kept asking me for your number so he could give you a call, so I'm guessing he'll want to join us."

"Okay. Meet me in the lobby in thirty," I said, a I walked into Ford's office to find him staring at his computer from b hind his desk.

"Got it. See you soon."

I ended the call. "We need to leave in half an hour. Are you almost done here?"

"Yep, that works. Thanks for crunching those numbers. I just took a look at everything and I think we're going to have a re ord year," Ford said, leaning back in his chair and stretching his arms over his head.

"Not a problem. You know I like that stuff."

"You always were a numbers nerd," Jack said with a laugh as he entered the office.

I rolled my eyes. "Big Joe's in town for the tech convention and he ran into Coop, so they're both going to meet us in the lobby and join us for dinner back at the winery."

"Big Joe's a cool dude, but I don't remember Coop." Jack dropped to sit in the chair beside me.

"Yeah, he was an older dude. I wasn't all that close with him. He was the one who locked us all out in the snow for hours in our underpants." I laughed.

"He sounds like a dick," Ford said with a shrug. My older brother was the skeptic, always suspicious of anyone he didn't know well.

"It's a good thing you didn't join a fraternity." Our younger brother glanced down at his watch and pushed to his feet.

"It's dinner. And you like Big Joe. You've met him several times," I said.

"Why does he insist on being called Big Joe? He's a fucking grown up," Ford huffed and made his way to the door and we all walked toward the elevators.

"It's a nickname. The dude is huge." Jack laughed.

"Anyway, they wanted me to meet up with them n the city, but I said we were having dinner at the winery tonight and they were welcome to join us. Harley's still there, right?"

"Yeah. After she, Mom, and Laney shopped for baby stuff she just hung out there with them and I said I'd meet her there for dinner."

"Do you mind if the guys ride back with you on the helicopter after?" I asked, as they'd need to get back to their hotel.

"I'm not a huge fan of the idea, but I guess I'll handle it. Who calls an hour before dinner? They should have called when they booked the trip."

"Ford. They're dudes. He didn't know he was coming, and he hasn't seen Coop in years. Don't make it a big deal. They'll come for dinner and they'll go back to their hotel."

"Har's right. I don't give people a heads-up when I'm in town. And everyone's always happy to see me," Jack said with a laugh.

"Doubtful." Our older brother hissed and stepped off the elevator.

"Montgomery," Big Joe called out and pulled me in for a hug. The guy was a teddy bear, and we'd hit it off from the start.

"What's up? Good to see you. Coop, you're looking good," I said, leaning in for a half dude hug.

"Thanks for making time for us," Coop said, his cheeks rosy. He smelled like booze.

"Yeah, no problem. Do you remember Ford and Jack?"

They both extended their hands to my brothers, and Ford barely cracked a smile. Jack made up for it with his animated chatter.

Big Joe filled us in on how he planned to propose to his longtime girlfriend, Tessa, the next weekend. They'd been together since college, and I was happy for him.

"Everyone's getting married these days," Jack shrugged. "How about you, Coop?"

"Nah. I've got a chick I bang whenever I want to, but who has time for that shit? I'm actually at this convention because I'm starting up my own tech company. Why work hard and give all that money to someone else, right?" His words slurred as he spoke, and Big Joe made a face at me and shrugged. He didn't know this dude any better than I did.

The guy was three sheets to the wind, and I was already regretting inviting him to dinner.

"I thought you were here with one of the companies hosting the event?" Big Joe narrowed his gaze at Coop.

"Nah. Fuck that. I'm starting up my own shit. That's why I wanted to talk to you. I'm gonna do you a solid, Montgomery, and let you invest early on. I'll make you a shit ton of cash, brother."

The comment made me uncomfortable, and I didn't miss the way Ford glared at him as he sat to his right. Jack's gaze locked with mine and I shrugged. I didn't know what to say. I hadn't seen the guy in years, and we weren't close.

Big Joe glared at Coop before turning his attention to me. "How's Laney doing? Congrats on the engagement, man. Always knew you two would end up together."

"Laney Landers? I thought you guys broke up years ago," Coop said.

"We did. Just reconnected after a few years apart."

"I'm looking forward to seeing her. I only ran into her a few times on campus after you left," Big Joe said with a shrug. "Congrats on your wedding, Ford. Harrison told me you recently tied the knot."

"Yes. Thank you." Ford loosened one button on his dress shirt and continued to watch Coop closely as he unbuckled his seat belt once we settled on the ground.

I shot Laney a text to give her a heads-up that they were joining us for dinner, and I let Mom know to add two chairs to the table. We got into the car and made our way to the winery.

"So, Harrison, I was hoping to actually talk to you about this business proposition. I'm only going to consider a few investors out the gate and immediately thought of you." Once we settled in the car, Coop reached into his suit pocket, pulled out a flask and tipped his head back, taking a long pull. Big Joe and I exchanged a look and he shook his head with disbelief.

"And coming to a family dinner plastered is the best you could do?" Ford hissed.

Coop laughed. The guy thought my brother was kidding.

He wasn't.

"I came here to catch up with a few old friends and I thought I'd give him first dibs on an investment opportunity in my company. There's some big names out there wanting to throw in. But I saved a spot for Montgomery, as we are brothers after all." Coop stared hard at Ford. He'd never win a staring contest with him. My brother didn't get intimidated, and it annoyed him when you thought that shit worked on him.

It didn't.

"Yeah, it's fine. I'll take a look at it later," I said, clapping Coop on the shoulder.

"Don't take too long, though. People are coming out of the woodwork for this, buddy. I'd hate for you to miss out." He tucked his flask back in his pocket when we pulled up to the winery.

Ford barked out a laugh. "Sure, they are. That's why you're here, right? To do my brother a favor?"

Coop flicked his thumb at Ford. "Is this guy always a buzzkill?"

"Listen. Let's just move on. No more shop talk. Let's enjoy dinner," I said, wanting to cut this visit short. If there was a way out of it at this point, I'd take it.

"Yeah, that's a good plan. I mean, we haven't seen or heard from you in years, Coop. Let's catch up, brother. What have you been up to?" Big Joe said, studying the man as if just realizing he didn't know who the hell this guy was either.

"Well, frankly, the only thing on my mind is my company. It's going to be big. Huge, actually," he slurred.

Jesus. This was painful and he was only making it worse.

The veins in Ford's neck pulsed, and his gaze locked with mine.

Who the fuck is this guy?

"Damn, Dude. This is your winery? Badass," Coop said, springing from the car.

"Slow your roll there, Ace. Pull yourself together before you go in there. We're having dinner with Ford's wife Harley, Laney, and our mother. Your frat bro attitude won't fly here," Jack said, gripping Coop by the shoulder and slowing him down.

"Shit. I thought you were the fun one. Don't be butt hurt, bro. I'll let you invest your money as well. I'm not exclusive to Harrison." Coop winked at Jack and I let out a long breath. This was a mistake.

"I'm not remotely concerned about missing out on anything. I do rather well, if I say so myself. But I am concerned about you disrespecting the women inside, and that shit won't fly with any of us. So, pull your sloppy ass together, put your flask away, and shut your mouth. We don't talk business at family dinners, and Harrison was nice enough to include you in ours. You can either join us for a business-free meal, or we can have someone take you back to the city." Jack stared hard at Coop, and Ford and I watched him with disbelief.

Where the hell did that come from?

Well said, brother.

"Fuck. No problem, dude. Let's go inside and have a good time," Coop said, making his way toward the entrance.

"Jesus, dude. I'm sorry. I haven't seen the guy in years, and he wasn't drunk earlier when we ran into one another." Big Joe leaned in so only I could hear as he looked at me in apology.

"Not your fault, man. The guy seems like a bit of a train wreck." I clapped Big Joe on the shoulder.

I led the way inside and smiled at the hostess before spotting my mother in the dining room. Good, she'd added two seats to the table. There was no sign of Laney and Harley, but Mom stood and greeted my friends.

"Boys, so nice that you could join us. It's been a long time." She hugged them and waved her hand at the table for them to take a seat.

"Where are Laney and Harley" I asked, and Ford crossed his arms over his chest waiting for an answer.

"They ran over to check on Laney's mom. Harley made her some pastries, so they went to drop them off. They should be back shortly. I just ordered us some wine and thought we could visit while we wait for them to return."

"That's odd. I texted Laney to let her know we were heading back but she hasn't responded." I dropped to sit beside my mother.

"Oh man, Harrison. You still a worrywart with this chick?" Coop's words were jumbled and slurred, and Mom turned to study him.

She picked up Laney's phone and handed it to me. Yes, she left her phone here. I texted Harley to let them know you were on your way back a little while ago."

"Okay, good." I said, swirling the wine in my glass when our server, Henry, poured me a bit to sample. "This is perfect. Thank you."

"Yes. Give me a hearty pour there, bro. I'm sure this is the good shit. Nothing but the finest for the Montgomerys, am I right?" Coop said, and Henry stared at him with disbelief.

Mom narrowed her gaze and looked at me, and I just shrugged. "How about we get some appetizers going? Surprise us. I think my friend could use some food about now."

"You got it, Harrison. I'll get some bread out here right away as well."

"Yeah, I haven't eaten since I landed this morning." Coop chugged his wine and then set down the empty glass.

Are you fucking kidding me? This was not a brewery, it was a winery. Luckily, the place was packed, and no one was paying us much attention.

"Well, maybe slow down on the wine, and let's get some food in you first," Big Joe hissed, and his face reddened.

"Yeah, yeah, yeah. You've all got to learn to loosen up a little," Coop said, leaning forward and resting his elbows on the table. "So, Mrs. Montgomery. I actually came to talk to your boy about an opportunity. But we don't discriminate. Hell, I'd never hold out on a fine ass woman such as yourself. So, be aware, your money works here too."

Ford, Jack, Big Joe, and I were on our feet. All four chairs screeched against the tile floor as we did so.

"I believe you were warned," Jack said, waving his hand in front of him to escort Coop out.

"Wait. Are you for real? From where I'm sitting, your mother's money is as green as yours," Coop said.

"Get the fuck up. *Now*," I hissed, surprising everyone.

"Harrison, Harrison, Harrison. You need to chill, brother."

"If you aren't up and moving in the next thirty seconds, I'll have you removed from this restaurant and thrown out on your ass. The choice is yours. If you want to leave peacefully, I have a car ready to

take you back to the city. This little reunion, or whate er the fuck this
is—is over."

Big Joe gripped Coop's shoulder. "Time for you to g), asshole."

"Not you too, Big Joe. I thought we were cool."

"You thought wrong, Coop. You need to leave. Nov ."

I paused to kiss my mother's cheek as she remaine I seated. "Sorry
about that, Mom."

She patted my hand and forced a smile.

"I'll call you tomorrow, Har. Seems like a pretty up ight group here
tonight. But I won't cut you out of the deal over th ;, so don't you
worry." Coop stumbled on his feet, and the hostess hel the door to the
lobby open, watching us with wide eyes.

We all followed him out and I called my driver o bring the car
around.

I couldn't get him out of here fast enough. My brot ers and Big Joe
were pissed, my mother was appalled, and this had t en an absolute
bust. He'd come for money. It wasn't my first rodeo vith people like
this. I just hadn't seen it coming, but why would I I hardly knew
the guy.

twenty-four

. . .

Laney

"GIRL, your family is so sweet. It's so refreshing," Harley said, rubbing her little belly as we walked back to the winery.

"What do you mean?" I laughed, and a smile spread clear across my face. But I got it. My parents were pretty amazing.

"They're so nice. The perfect parents. I hope Ford and I are like that with our kids. They just love you so much. It's so nice to see. It explains a lot, Laney."

"It does?"

"Yep. You're good peeps. Your parents are good peeps. The apple never falls far." She laughed.

I knew Harley had it rough growing up, and I hated that she went through so much. "Yeah. But sometimes the apple does fall far. You're pretty amazing yourself there, missy. And you and Ford are going to be incredible parents."

"Well, I hope so. It won't be for lack of effort. But let me tell you— I'm so freaking hungry these days. I'm ready for a whole lot of pasta." She chuckled as we walked up the path toward the winery.

"I'm hungry too, and I'm not carrying a human in here." I patted my belly and she barked out a laugh.

Our gazes moved to the entrance as we heard shouting in the distance.

"Get the fuck out of here," Ford shouted, and Harley and I started to run in that direction. Something was wrong. I saw Harrison dragging someone down the walkway toward us. I couldn't make them out.

"What the hell is going on?" Harley asked, as we got closer.

The guys paused under the overhead light, and I froze. Big Joe? He was a good friend of Harrison's and mine back in college. My gaze moved to where Harrison held someone by the collar. Coop. My legs were stuck. My breaths came short and fast. I bent forward and tried to catch my breath.

"Laney?" Harley stopped and turned back to place a hand on my back. "Are you okay?"

I dropped to the ground, as I couldn't stand any longer.

"Harrison," she shouted, but everything went still around me.

Every secret.

Every lie.

Every fear.

It was right here in front of me. I thought I could escape it. I thought I could make it less complicated. Protect Harrison.

"Baby, what is it?" He hurried over and bent down in front of me, trying to pull me to my feet. Jack and Ford called out to ask if I was okay.

Harrison held me up and tipped my chin, forcing me to meet his gaze. "What is it? Are you hurt?"

"Should we call 911?" Harley shouted, but everything blurred together as I stared into his dark gaze.

"Har. I'm sorry. I never thought we'd see him again," I croaked through my sobs.

Jack was yelling something in the distance and arguing with Coop to get in the car. Big Joe moved beside my boyfriend and asked what was going on.

"What are you talking about, Laney?" Harrison studied me, and then it was like a lightbulb switched on, and his gaze hardened. "Coop?"

"Yes."

That's all I had to say. He called out to Ford, "Take her and call the police."

And just like that, Harrison lunged at Coop, startling everyone. He took him down to the ground and pummeled him, blow after blow. The sound of bones cracking and fists flying filled the air. Jack tried to tear his brother off of Coop and shouted for Ford to help him.

Harley reached for me and held me against her as we watched the scene play out like something out of a movie. Ford and Jack held Harrison back as Big Joe stared with disbelief.

"Fuck you, Montgomery. Shit happens." Coop struggled to get to his feet and glared my way. "She's hardly worth it. She was a boring fucking lay, anyway."

Jack and Ford let go of their brother, allowing Harrison to charge Coop again. "You sick fucking rapist. You're a fucking piece of shit."

People came running out of the winery and sirens blared in the distance. "Good fucking luck proving anything. She didn't say no. That's all that matters."

Jack and Ford intervened, pulling their brother to his feet when the police cars pulled up. "You fucking drugged her. You sick fuck."

"Oh, come on. It's something people did back then. And good fucking luck proving anything all these years later. I did her a fucking favor. She was an uptight mopey bitch. I sat there listening to her sad ass all night. It's the least she could do. Come on, man. Don't let some chick come between brothers."

Harrison lunged at him again, as several police officers intervened. The lights from the squad car flashed red and white blurred patterns around the crowd gathering outside.

Ford and Jack asked their staff to escort the guests back inside before turning the attention to the police. Harrison was on his knees, Big Joe holding his shoulders as he stood behind him. Tears streaming down Harrison's face as he tried to process what was happening. My heart split in two. His gaze landed on mine and he just stared, before turning his attention back to the officer pulling him to his feet.

"Laney, let's go inside," Harley whispered.

"I need to make sure he's okay."

The police officers did their best to get through the information being offered. Coop was slurring and insisting Harrison attacked him. Big Joe moved over to stand beside Harley and me, asking repeatedly if I was okay.

This was no longer a secret I could keep to myself.

It was out there.

Coop was handcuffed. Obviously, the cops were biased. They knew the Montgomerys as longtime locals, and everyone that knew Harrison knew he never lost his cool. But right here, right now in front of my eyes—he'd unraveled.

Monica came running outside, and tears sprang from her eyes as she took in the scene.

I found my footing and rushed over to Harrison, trying to speak through my sobs. "Har, are you okay?"

He nodded. "I'm so sorry, Laney. I'm so fucking sorry."

The officer said he'd need to take him in for questioning. Ford and Jack were shouting and arguing with the police, and Harrison put a hand up. Silencing everyone. "It's okay. Let me take care of this. Keep Laney with you."

Ford was already on his phone calling their attorney. "Nelson will meet you at the station. We'll be there soon."

"I'm coming with you." I fought to break free of Jack's grip.

"Let me do this, Laney," Harrison said.

"What? No. You didn't do anything," I shouted.

He paused and looked over at the officer waiting for him. The older man nodded and turned to give him a minute. "Baby. I'm going to have to tell them everything and they may need to question you."

I nodded. "Okay. I don't care. Let me come now. I'll tell them everything."

"I don't want you around him. They understand that. I'm going to tell them what I know. I don't know that anything will come of it because there is a statute of limitations. But he can't get away with this, Laney. No fucking way."

I covered my face with my hands. This was what I'd feared. That my dark, ugly secret would infect everyone I loved, most especially Harrison. That it would come back to haunt me. And that's exactly what was happening right now. I broke out in sobs as the officer led Harrison toward the car. Jack wrapped me in his arms and whispered in my ear.

"Don't you worry, Laney Mae. That fucker won't get away with what he did to you. Not on my watch, and certainly not on Harrison's."

"It's going to be fine," Harley said, reaching for my hand and clasping it with her own. "Let's go get a nice cup of tea and the boys can head down to the station to wait for Harrison."

I nodded, but this was not something a cup of tea could fix. My heart shattered as I watched the police car drive away. Harrison and Coop were both gone.

We settled in Monica's office, and Ford, Jack, and Big Joe left to go help Harrison. Harley and I sat on the sofa in Monica's office and she entered with a tray of tea. The tears wouldn't stop coming. I'd opened the floodgates, and now there was no turning back. I didn't feel the panic to cover the secret I'd been keeping for so long the way I'd expected. I just wanted Harrison to be okay. I wanted to start our life together. I didn't want this dark cloud to force us to lose more time. More years.

"I've already heard from Nelson. Harrison is just there to answer questions. He's not being charged with anything, sweetheart. It's going to be okay."

I nodded. She and Harley didn't know the whole story. They were probably confused and unsure about what was going on. But neither pushed. Neither forced me to explain anything.

"I was drugged the night after I returned to school without Harrison. I'd gone out, and Coop had stayed with me the whole time listening to me cry about my broken heart. He'd been a friend of Harrison's, and I trusted him."

They each sat on one side of me and held my hands. Monica spoke first, as tears streamed down her face. "You don't need to tell us anything if you don't want to."

"It's okay. I've held it in for so long, and I've lost so much time running from it. I woke up the next day and had no recollection of the night before. But I was naked, and there was a used condom on the floor. I went to the hospital and found out I'd been drugged. But I was too ashamed to tell them what happened. I lied and said I just got sick and went home. But I changed that day. I was so ashamed that I'd allowed it to happen. That I'd put myself in that situation." The sobs racked my body as I relived the events of that night again.

Monica wrapped me in a hug. "There's nothing to be ashamed of, my sweet girl. You're so brave. I'm proud of you for telling Harrison what happened. For coming to terms with it. This is not your fault. Do you understand me, Laney?"

"No. But I will."

"Yes, you will, girl. You will not allow that piece of shit to take anything else from you," Harley said, swiping at the tears running down her face.

We sat there for an hour, while I talked, and they listened. I finally insisted Harley get something to eat. The poor girl was starving, and this had been a traumatic evening.

And we waited.

Waited to see what would happen to Harrison.

———

"Laney," Harrison's voice whispered in my ear and I pushed to sit up. I was still on the sofa in Monica's office. I must have dozed off.

"Hey. You're here." I reached up to hug him. "Where's your mom and Harley?"

"Relax, baby. Everything's okay. Ford just took Harley home, and Mom is out in the lobby talking to Jack."

"What happened?" I asked, as he dropped down to sit on the couch beside me and pulled me onto his lap.

"It's going to be difficult to prove because it happened over five years ago, and you have very little memory about the actual assault. Either way—rape by definition, is having sex with someone against their will. Without consent. And everyone is in agreement about that. But after doing some digging, it turns out the reason Coop went into business for himself is because he served six months in a New York jail. He's a convicted sex offender. Your anonymous tip did come up in his record, as the date matched the timeline, so you reporting him did get recorded, Laney."

"Oh my god. He did it again?"

"Not sure about that. The six months he served was for something different, but still alarming. He dated a sixteen-year-old when he first graduated from college."

"So, he was twenty-two? That's disgusting. She's a child."

"Well, the girl's father and the state of New York agree with you. Apparently, they're still together now. The girl's parents reported him, and he served his time. But she's now old enough to legally date the sick fucker. It's so fucking twisted. He has a slew of accusations against him, but he wasn't accused of drugging anyone again. I clearly didn't know this guy at all. He's a piece of shit. And he comes here asking for money? After what he did to you." He shook his head and I studied him. There was dried blood splattered across his white dress shirt. His knuckles were bloody, and he had a small bruise under his eye. I traced my finger gently over the purplish-black mark there.

"I'm sorry I didn't tell you who it was. I knew you'd do something, and I didn't want you to get in trouble."

He pulled me close. "I get why you didn't tell me. I want to kill him, Laney. I hate him so fucking much. But I'm going to let that demon take himself down. He can't get a fucking job. He's dating a teenager. You reap what you sow."

"Where is he now?"

"He's down at the station waiting for his attorney to get him out."

"What about Big Joe?"

"Jack took him to the helicopter to get him back to the city. He hadn't seen Coop in years either, so he was stunned by everything that happened. He apologized profusely for bringing him here. He'd just run into him at the convention. He sends his best and said he'd like to come back and see you under better circumstances."

I swiped at the tears streaming down my face. "Of course. I always liked him." I shook my head with disbelief. "Your mom and Harley know about what happened."

"How do you feel about that?"

"Surprisingly fine."

He feathered his fingers across my cheek. "Good. I'm proud of you."

"I'm going to tell my parents. I know it will hurt them, but I think they should know why I stayed away so long. What I was haunted by."

"I agree. And I'll be right there beside you the whole way."

"I'm sorry about tonight. I love you."

"The only thing I'm sorry about is that I can't hurt him more."

"Don't be. He's made his bed, Har. And we have so much to look forward to. I don't want to waste any more time on him. He's taken too much already."

He nodded. "Let me take you home, baby."

"Nowhere else I'd rather go. Home. With you."

He leaned down and kissed me, before pulling me to my feet and leading me out the door.

epilogue

. . .

Laney

WEEKS TURNED INTO MONTHS, and Christmas was right around the corner. I'd found my footing back home, and Harrison and I had flown to Chicago for a business trip that he had there. He'd been very understanding about my need to see Charlie while I was there.

Telling my parents about what happened to me all those years ago turned out to be a good decision. They hadn't been judgmental or disappointed in me, as I'd feared. They'd been empathetic and compassionate. Angry and upset, of course. But thankfully, they finally understood why I'd pulled away for so long. Why the light had left me.

But I was getting it back.

One day at a time.

And I felt a deep need to tell Charlie about my past as well. Maybe I wanted to help him understand why I'd never been able to emotionally connect. Why I'd held back so much. Why I'd hurt him the way I had. Because I was in love with someone else but too afraid to admit it. Because it would mean admitting everything. And getting it off my chest gave me a peace I hadn't felt in a long time.

Of course, Charlie had been beyond understanding and thankful that I'd told him. He cried with me as I shared what happened. He listened as I walked him through all the years of den al. Shame. And how it all came to a head. He told me that he was happ / I'd finally told Harrison. That I finally felt loved enough. Safe enough

And he was right.

Charlie told me about the woman he was dating, and we actually talked about it and laughed about old times. He was h ppy for me that I was finally engaged to a man that I wanted to spend ı ıy life with.

Were we going to be best friends? Probably not.

But had some of the pain subsided? Definitely.

I hoped that someday we would get to a place wh ·re we could be in one another's lives, but I was thankful that we'd had this closure.

In the meantime—I was busy planning a wedding f my own. And I was actually excited about it, because I was marı /ing the man I loved. I loved him in a way I'd never loved anyone bı t him. With my entire being. We just fit. Always had. Harrison and I were getting married in the barn at his family winery on Valentine': Day. It symbolized so many firsts for us. And it was where I wanted t seal the deal.

The Montgomerys had built a new barn out on the ıroperty as they needed a larger space, and they were going to get rid o the old one. I'd convinced Harrison to renovate it and use it as the venue for our special day. So, we'd turned it into a darling receptioı hall, and we'd have the actual ceremony outdoors at the winery. It ı /as more than I could have hoped for.

"How do you feel?" Harrison asked, as we pulled away from the post office. We'd just sent out our wedding invita ions. We were having a small intimate celebration, but every detail ᴠ as thought out. Each invitation would be delivered in a wine crate ᴠith a bottle of wine made just for our celebration.

The Harrison & Laney Montgomery Cabernet, with oı r wedding date written in script on the label.

Inside the box was a photo of us on our first day of indergarten.

The invitation was tucked inside the box with detai ; for those close to us to come and share in our special day.

It wasn't just a *day* for either of us.

It was a journey. And ours still had a long way to ;o, but we were going to do it together, moving forward.

"I feel great. I'm excited. There's still a lot of work to do out at the barn, but everything is coming together."

He reached for my hand. "It is. And it all feels right because I have you by my side."

I smiled and leaned back against the seat. "So, I wanted to talk to you about something."

"Okay, shoot."

"Well, you know how I spoke at that meeting Jenny set up at the high school?" Harrison and I continued to go to therapy, as we both still had anger about what had happened to me all those years ago. I'd spoken to a few small groups of seniors at our old high school about what had happened to me. Turns out I wasn't the only one, and several girls opened up to me about experiences that were similar and equally frightening. It felt good to allow this trauma to at least help others in some way.

"Yep. And I'm damn proud of you for that."

"Well, the local community college reached out and asked if I'd be willing to come share my story during orientation at the beginning of the semester. What happened to me is not all that uncommon, Har. But being educated, being aware—that could make the difference for someone."

He nodded. "I think that's great. I'm all for it."

"Good."

"Every time you talk about it, it seems to help you a little bit."

"I agree. I feel like I can finally move forward. I honestly didn't know if I'd ever be happy again. I didn't know if I deserved it, or if it were even possible. But it is."

"You deserve it all, Laney Mae Landers."

My chest squeezed. He'd said those words to me before, but they'd never resonated the way they did today. Because he was right. I'd been punishing myself for a crime I didn't commit.

I was finally coming out on the other side of hell.

And the light was shining bright on Harrison and me.

———

"Are you ready?" Mom asked, looking down at me as her glossy gaze locked with mine.

"I am."

We were at the house I shared with Harrison because he'd insisted on getting a horse and carriage to bring me over to the barn. It was unnecessary, but he was just bougie that way, and I was grateful for all of it.

"You look gorgeous," Harley said, rubbing her oversized baby bump. She and Ford were having twin girls in just a few weeks. We'd all fallen over laughing at the news because the idea of Ford Montgomery with one little girl was hard to wrap your head around.

But two?

Amazing.

Everyone was thrilled. Between the wedding and the babies, the Mongtomerys had found their way out of the dark. And I'd learned a valuable lesson about life. It wasn't always perfect. It didn't always go your way. But if you loved someone deeply enough, all of the risk was well worth it.

And today I was celebrating the love I'd had for this boy since I was five years old. Sure, it had started out as friendship. But it was a love that had never stopped growing. Tethering us together in a way that I couldn't explain.

"How are you feeling?" I put my hand on Harley's baby bump. We had grown very close, and I'd asked her to be my maid of honor. She refused to be called *matron* of honor because she said it made her feel old, which made us all laugh. Nat and two of my sorority sisters, my cousin, and my brother's girlfriend, Gia, were standing beside me as well.

Harrison's brothers, my brother, and three of his friends were his groomsmen. He'd been Ford's best man, so Jack was going to be his, and Ford would be Jack's someday—if that ever happened. I knew there was a girl out there that could hold her own with him, but he just hadn't met her yet. I couldn't wait until the day Jack Montgomery got knocked on his ass.

"I feel great. And you look amazing." Harley swiped at the tear falling down her face.

"Okay, let's do this. Is Dad at the barn already?" I asked my mother.

"Yes. He's waiting for you out at the edge of the road. Let's go."

We rode down the street in the carriage, and a few locals stood outside taking pictures. The sun was just going down, and the weather was absolutely perfect. I wore a long sleeve fitted dress with a low dip in the back. It was classic and elegant, and everything I'd dreamed of. My hair was in a loose low chignon, with a few waves framing my face. I had baby's breath tucked in all around. My bouquet was lush with white hydrangeas and light pink peonies. I let out a long breath as we pulled up to greet my father.

"Look at you, Laney Mae." His eyes were wet with emotion and his voice cracked. Mom started blubbering before covering her mouth, and Harley and I laughed.

"Thanks, Dad. Okay, you two take the carriage a bit further. I don't want Harley to walk more than she has to. We don't need those girls attending this wedding. It's a little too soon," I said.

Harley chuckled. "Are you sure? I don't want you to walk on your wedding day."

I nodded. This was the final leg of the journey for me, before I started a new one. I wanted to enjoy every single minute. I'd run out in these fields more times than I could count. Taking the final steps to tie the knot with the boy I'd loved my entire life—the man of my dreams—would be a bonus.

"I want to walk. I need to take it all in."

She nodded before leaning over and hugging me. I turned to hug my mother as well before Dad helped me out of the carriage.

"See you on the other side, Mrs. Montgomery," Harley said as they took off.

"You ready, kiddo?" Dad asked, holding his arm out to me.

"So ready," I said as we started down the path.

I heard the music in the distance and butterflies swarmed my belly. Not because I was nervous, but because I was happy.

We approached the chairs set up in the clearing out in the field and the sight took my breath away. The pink and orange sky looked like something straight out of a painting. Twinkle lights covered every tree surrounding the outdoor ceremony.

A ridiculous amount of flowers lined the aisle where Harrison stood at the end. I was a wedding planner—was there ever too many flowers? I didn't think so. Whites and pinks, ribbon and lace, everything had come together so beautifully. A little over fifty guests were in attendance, all there because they meant something to us. Harley stood waiting for me and insisted on shaking out my train so it would trail down the aisle behind me before she joined Ford up front.

The wedding march started to play, and I looked up at Dad and paused to kiss his cheek. "Let's do this."

He chuckled. "That's my girl. Here we go."

Harrison's gaze locked with mine. Dark and full of emotion. Honest and true. The eyes that had always grounded me. Guided me. Believed in me. I sucked in a long breath as the lump in my throat grew.

"Who gives this woman away?" Pastor Nate asked.

"Her mother and I do," Dad said, before shaking hands with Harrison and kissing my cheek. He jumped over my train to take his seat and everyone laughed.

But I was lost in Harrison. I'd always been lost in this boy. And now he was mine.

Forever.

Pastor Bob allowed us to read our vows.

"Laney Mae Landers, you are the single best thing that's ever happened to me. My heart is yours—it always has been. I promise to spend my life making you happy. I promise to give you everything you want and then some. I promise to love you until I take my last breath, because honestly, there's no other option. You complete me, baby. Always have. Always will."

Tears streamed down my face, and I gave up trying to swipe them away. I was in the moment. And all these feeling were a long time coming.

"Harrison Thomas Montgomery, you are the light that I thought I'd lost." My words broke on a sob. "You are the love that I thought I didn't deserve. You are the only promise I ever wanted to keep. You are my best friend and the other half of my soul. There is no me without you. And I can't wait for a lifetime of us. Together. I cherish the old memories and look forward to making new ones. I want to grow old with you. You and me. I promise to love you always."

Pastor Bob said his spiel, but I didn't listen. I just stared into my husband's dark gaze, feeling all the love in the world.

"You may kiss the bride," he finally said, and Harrison dipped me back and kissed me as the crowd cheered.

———

When the doors opened to the barn, I lost my breath. Yes, I'd planned every single detail, but seeing it all put together with everyone we loved inside...

Magical.

Several chandeliers hung from above, creating diamond shapes on the tables. Flowers and candles covered every surface. The sit-down dinner would be served on Harrison's great grandmother's china. Monica was thrilled to tie in a piece of family history to the ceremony.

Music played, the DJ announced the wedding party, and I was lost in the moment. Dad and I did the father-daughter dance, and my husband and I danced for the first time as a married couple. If I had to pinpoint the happiest moment of my life—it would be right now. I was overcome with emotion and cried more times than I could count.

All happy tears.

Finally.

Happy tears.

"Laney Mae Montgomery. Yeeeees. *My sister from another mister.* Fucking finally." Jack picked me up off the ground and spun me around.

The Montgomerys had been family to me long before today—but making it official just felt so...right.

"Put her down, asshole," Harrison said, trying to hide his smile as his brother pulled him in for a hug.

"I'm happy for you, brother. Happy for you both." Jack wrapped an arm around each of us.

"Thanks, Jack-ass," I teased.

"Have you guys seen Buck yet?" Jack asked, waving his best friend over. He was Jack's college roommate at SC and he and Harrison had grown close over the years.

"Hey Buck, thanks for being here today. Do you remember Laney?" Harrison said.

"Yes, of course. Happy to be here. Congratulations to both of you."

"Thank you," I said, after he hugged each of us and settled beside Jack.

"We finally got your sister to agree to an interview," my husband said.

"Yeah, CBS has pulled out all the stops. They extended her internship while she finished her masters, but she's ready to get out there and charge the tundra," Buck said with a laugh.

"Well, we're going to do whatever we can to get her to come work for us," Jack said. "Hopefully, she doesn't hate me anymore."

"Not sure about that one, bud. But she'll come around. And it's better if she hates you, because you know I'd kill you if you ever touched her." He laughed.

Jack held his hands up. "Not happening. I wouldn't cross that line. But seeing as she can't stand the sight of me, I don't think we need to worry about that."

We all chuckled over Jack's ridiculousness.

"Ford has a pretty strong package to offer to sway her our way," Harrison said, as he laced his fingers with mine.

"Well, I know she wants to stay in San Francisco, so I think it'll be a great fit. She's a damn hard worker too. You won't be disappointed." Buck paused to accept a glass of wine from the waiter, and Jack reached for a glass as well. I smiled as he spoke, because you couldn't miss the pride in his voice when he spoke about his baby sister.

"We'd be lucky to have her," Harrison said.

Jack and Buck left to dance with my two little cousins who were the flower girls, and our attention was pulled to the dance floor by the DJ. He called us over to cut the cake. Harrison and I settled around the elaborate four-tier wedding cake made by my sister in-law, and we each took a slice. We'd never been proper or followed the rules, and tonight would be no different.

I'd dreamed of the day I'd smash cake into this beautiful man's face.

And today was the day.

He held out a fork and allowed me to take a dainty bite, before I reached back and slammed my plate into his face. Before I knew what was happening, he had a handful of cake spread across my cheeks.

We laughed as we fought back and forth, and everyone cheered.

It was the perfect ending to the perfect day.

The perfect start to the perfect life.

And I relished in the moment.

In this man.

And in the future waiting for us.

THE END

Are you ready to see Jack Montgomery fall hard...

Read REBEL FREE in Kindle Unlimited HERE

https://geni.us/RebelLP

acknowledgments

Greg, Chase & Hannah, thank you for being my biggest supporters and always believing in me. I would be lost without you!! Love you so much!

Willow, there are not enough words to thank you properly. You are such a huge part of my writing process now! LOL! Thank you for pushing me, helping me strive to be better, and encouraging me every step of the way. Your friendship means the world to me. Thank you for all of the work that you did on this story. I cannot tell you what it means to me! You wore a lot of hats this time around, and I am so thankful. Thank you for working your magic and making Peacekeeper shine!! xo

Pathi, Natalie, Doo, Annette and Abi, thank you for being the BEST beta readers EVER! Your feedback means the world to me. I would be lost without you!

Thank you, Sarah Hansen (Okay Creations) for working your magic once again!

Sue Grimshaw (Edits by Sue), Thank you for your encouragement, your guidance and your support. This story took a bit more tweaking than usual, and I wouldn't have gotten there without you. Your input and support mean the world to me. xo

Tamara Cribley (The Deliberate Page), so thankful to get to work with you again. I love all of the little details that you add to the formatting and appreciate your patience and support so much!! Thank you my friend!

Jo and Kylie (Give Me Books Promotions), you know how much I adore you, and cannot wait to finally meet you at the Four Brits Book

Fest!! You keep me calm and handle every hurdle with absolute grace! So thankful for you!!

Ashlee (Ashes & Vellichor), what would I do without you? Thank you for bringing my characters to life with your amazing teasers!! You amaze me each and every time you send me something!! So grateful that I found you, and now you're stuck with me for life

To all the girls at Grey's Promotion, Mary, Amber and Josette! Thank you for taking a chance on me with this story!! I appreciate all of your support!!

Mom, thank you for your love and support. Love you!

Dad, you really are the reason that I keep chasing my dreams!! Thank you for teaching me to never give up. Love you!

Sandy, thank you for reading and supporting me throughout this journey. Love you!

Eric, there is no one that listens and supports me more than you!! Love you, E$!

Sissy, thank you for making me laugh when I need it most. Do you have to let it linger??? Love you!

Pathi, I am so thankful for you! You are the reason I even started this journey. Thank you for believing in me!! Love you!

Natalie (Head in the Clouds, Nose in a Book), Thank you for supporting me through it all! I appreciate all that you do for me from beta reading to the newsletter to buddy reading extra steamy books so I have someone to talk about it with!! LOL! Love you!

Nicole, Thank you for believing in me, snapping me daily, making me laugh and holding me to our streaks! Love you so much!

Steph, Thank you for always supporting me! Peas & Carrots! Urban & Doodles! Love you!

Sweet Sammi Sylvis, Thanks for making me laugh and helping me stay sane through these releases! Glad we have one another to lean on!!

To all the bloggers and bookstagrammers who have posted, shared and supported me—I can't begin to tell you how much it means to me. I love seeing the graphics that you make, and the gorgeous posts that you share. I am forever grateful for your support!

Lisa, Julie, Eric, Jen and Jim, I am very thankful to have such supportive and encouraging siblings in my life. Love you!

Nicole, Sue, Thompson, Pathi, Bell, Natalie, Annette, Carol, Margy, Steph, Mindy, Kristin, Laura, Anne, Abi, Kelly, Maggie, Leigh Anne, Julie, Nancy, Bev, Leslie, Florence, Tina, Renae, Cindy, Kelly & Kate, Darleen, Althea, Jess, Ariel, Heather, Shannon, Gabe, Brandon, Logan, Brock, Caroline, Hendershot, Liva, Kennedy, all the amazing ladies at d'annata boutique and Bloom boutique, and all of my friends who have supported me along this journey...thank you so much!!

other books by laura pavlov

Magnolia Falls Series

Loving Romeo

Wild River

Forbidden King

Beating Heart

Finding Hayes

Cottonwood Cove Series

Into the Tide

Under the Stars

On the Shore

Before the Sunset

After the Storm

Honey Mountain Series

Always Mine

Ever Mine

Make You Mine

Simply Mine

Only Mine

The Willow Springs Series

Frayed

Tangled

Charmed

Sealed

Claimed

Montgomery Brothers Series

Legacy

Peacekeeper

Rebel

A Love You More Rock Star Romance

More Jade

More of You

More of Us

The Shine Design Series

Beautifully Damaged

Beautifully Flawed

The G.D. Taylors Series with Willow Aster

Wanted Wed or Alive

The Bold and the Bullheaded

Another Motherfaker

Don't Cry Spilled MILF

Friends with Benefactors

keep up on new releases...

Linktree

Linktree Laurapavlovauthor
Newsletter laurapavlov.com

follow me...

Website laurapavlov.com
Goodreads @laurapavlov
Instagram @laurapavlovauthor
Facebook @laurapavlovauthor
Pav-Love's Readers @pav-love's readers
Amazon @laurapavlov
BookBub @laurapavlov
TikTok @laurapavlovauthor